Totally Spellbound

Kristine Grayson

D0035420

ZEBRA BOOKS
Kensington Publishing Corp.
www.kensingtonbooks.com

ZEBRA BOOKS are published by

Kensington Publishing Corp.
850 Third Avenue
New York, NY 10022

All Kensington titles, imprints, and distributed lines are
available at special quantity discounts for bulk purchases for
sales promotion, premiums, fund-raising, educational, or
institutional use.

Special book excerpts or customized printings can also be
created to fit specific needs. For details, write or phone the
office of the Kensington Special Sales Manager: Attn. Special
Sales Department. Kensington Publishing Corp., 850 Third
Avenue, New York, NY 10022. Phone: 1-800-221-2647.

Zebra and the Z logo Reg. U.S. Pat. & TM Off.

ISBN 0-8217-7598-7

First Printing: August 2005
10 9 8 7 6 5 4 3 2 1

Printed in the United States of America

For Pam Eckley,
who likes stories better than anyone I know

Acknowledgments

Many thanks to all the readers who've let me know how much they like these novels. Thanks also to John Scognamiglio for his willingness to give these books a chance. And thanks to my husband, Dean, for helping me brainstorm the silliest things.

I

Megan Kineally usually liked driving at night. The silence, the empty roads, the darkness surrounding her car made her feel like she was the only person on the planet. Driving in darkness calmed her—usually.

But she wasn't calm tonight.

She blamed the road. Interstate 15 between San Bernadine and Las Vegas had become a superhighway. Well-lit, congested, a gazillion lanes wide, it ruined the effect of night driving. Trucks zoomed by her Mini Cooper, shaking it. By the time she reached Barstow, her hands had formed new grooves in the steering wheel. Another hour later, she wished she had taken the back roads and risked breakdowns, desert heat, and the occasional wild-eyed loner.

Her best friend Conchita had tried to convince her to rent an SUV. *You're gonna be driving your nephew around Vegas. The last thing you want is a teeny tiny car.*

Rated best in its class for safety, Megan said.

In its class, Conchita said. *The class of David, not the class of Goliath. Not even David would survive getting smushed by really big tires.*

Megan was beginning to agree. Half the trucks that passed her—all of them doing at least twenty over the speed limit—could've crushed her tiny car with little more than a thought. Some careless trucker dozing at the wheel could drive over her and not even notice.

She blew an errant strand of red hair out of her face and shrugged her shoulders, trying to loosen them. She'd been unsettled ever since she had spoken to her brother a few hours ago. Travers the Unflappable had sounded flapped. She'd teased him about being in Sin City—Vegas, a place he hated—and he hadn't risen to the bait.

Instead, he swore and confessed that he was in trouble.

Travers the neat freak, Travers the accountant, Travers the exceptionally cautious was never ever in trouble. The trouble role in the family had gone to their oldest sister, Vivian, who had blackouts and strange psychic moments and crazy friends.

When Vivian had gotten married in Oregon a few weeks ago, the entire family had breathed a sigh of relief.

Then Travers, who had vowed he was heading straight home to L.A., had somehow ended up in Las Vegas, and now he needed his baby sister, not to help him out of whatever crisis he was in, but to baby-sit his precocious son, Kyle.

Megan loved Kyle more than anyone else in the world. They were both misfits—Kyle because of his big brain and his strange interests and Megan because—well, because she was Megan.

She sighed, straightened her spine, and heard her back crack. She flicked on the radio for company, spun through the dial, and heard talk, oldies, talk, rap, talk, hip-hop, talk, talk, and more talk. Finally she shut the thing off, preferring the sound of her own worries to the constant nattering of people who thought they were in great trouble.

She had enough of that at her job, which was why she was shutting down her practice. She was a child psychologist with a boatload of rich clients who all thought Little Johnny or Little Suzy needed a little talking-to to go with their Prozac.

She had become a psychologist to help people. Instead, she couldn't convince Johnny and Suzy's parents that when the kids had trouble, the troubles ran through the entire family. Usually, all Johnny and Suzy needed were some time and attention (and love would be nice too), but nothing Megan did could get that message through to the parents. So she tried to patch the holes where she could.

And she was getting tired of patching.

Three more trucks zoomed by, their horns blaring in the night. She squinted but couldn't see anything ahead.

In fact, the long stretch of interstate had cleared. Either everyone had vanished, or her speedometer was screwed up. She'd been keeping pace with the traffic before (not the trucks—she didn't want the ticket), but now there was no one ahead of her.

She glanced in her rearview mirror. No one was behind her either.

The road was empty, and even though it was what she'd wanted, she was a little freaked out.

Ahead, the street lights (unnatural looking things on a desert highway) winked out.

Darkness surrounded her. Darkness and silence and long, empty stretches of road.

The hair rose on the back of her neck.

She rolled down her window, hoping a little fresh air would calm her. Cool and dry, the air smelled of sage brush and sand.

Maybe she should pull over. Maybe she was asleep and dreaming. Maybe—

A creature ran into the road so fast she couldn't see what it was, only she knew it was in front of her. She slammed on the brakes, and the car skidded for a moment on the empty pavement before coming to a stop.

Ahead of her, the creature—a rabbit?—had frozen in her headlights, its round eyes staring at her as if she were the very image of death.

Then, out of nowhere, a falcon swooped down, caught—the rabbit??—in its talons and carried the thing, screaming, into the air, disappearing in the darkness.

Now Megan knew she was dreaming. There weren't rabbits in the Nevada desert. Nor were there falcons. And creatures being carted off to certain death didn't scream like that, did they? Not unless they were human creatures.

She glanced in her rearview mirror. Still no cars. She took a deep breath, and limped her vehicle to the shoulder. Then she got out, and slapped herself hard across the face.

Didn't work. Nothing had changed.

Except now her face hurt.

A man stepped onto the shoulder from the side of the road. He had a leather glove on his wrist, and he held a tiny hood in his hand. In the swirling dust illuminated by her headlights, he looked like a ghost.

"Did you see a bird?" he asked.

He was tall but slightly built. His hair was long and brown, tied into a ponytail with a leather cord. He seemed to like leather—not the shiny black leather that bikers wore but soft brown leather, maybe even some kind of suede. If she had to label his shirt, she'd call it a jerkin—it even looked handmade—and his tan pants seemed just as crude. Even his boots looked medieval—all fabric with soles too soft for the desert on a cold summer night.

He was looking at her like he expected something from her. Then she realized that he did—an answer. To his question. About a bird.

"Um, yeah," she said. "I think it ate a rabbit."

"Nonsense," he said.

"That's what I thought," she said. "But it took the rabbit in its claws and flew off—"

"You didn't see it eat the rabbit then, did you?"

"No." She couldn't believe she was having this conversation. "I saw it capture the poor rabbit and cart it away. I think the rabbit was screaming."

He nodded. "They do that."

As if it was the most normal thing in the world.

"Which way did they go?"

She pointed.

He stepped out of the headlights and into the darkness of the road. By reflex, she looked over her shoulder. Still no trucks or cars or SUVs. No sign of anything but her, the mighty hunter, and his bird.

Only she hadn't seen the bird for nearly five minutes now, and the screaming had ended long ago (except in her memory) and even though she squinted, she no longer saw the man on the road.

The streetlights flicked on one by one, and then a truck whizzed past, the wind in its wake so strong that she nearly toppled into her car.

Standing on the shoulder was not the brightest thing she could do.

She got back into her car as more trucks, and SUVs, and sedans went by—all the things she had thought she missed. Her breathing was hard, and she wasn't quite sure what had happened.

She'd have said she had fallen asleep at the wheel, but she had felt the wind and smelled the truck exhaust. She knew she hadn't taken any drugs, so she wasn't hallucinating. And she wasn't prone to wild flights of fancy—those were reserved for Vivian and their late Great-Aunt Eugenia.

And Kyle, of course.

Kyle, who saw superheroes and monsters behind every tree. Kyle, who kept saying that Vivian's new husband looked just like Superman.

Megan could not see the resemblance. But then, she rarely read comic books. Relaxation wasn't her forte.

Maybe it should be. Maybe this was some kind of psychotic episode.

Because it certainly hadn't felt like a dream. Her cheek still stung from her self-administered blow, she was a little chilled from the night air, and her eyes had taken a minute to adjust to the increased light.

And somehow, she had gotten to the side of the road.

Somehow.

She couldn't quite believe she had driven there in her sleep, without hitting anyone, without being hit.

That was as much of a miracle as seeing a medieval hunter in the darkness, following the trail of his falcon into the desert.

She glanced at her watch. Somehow, she'd lost about fifteen minutes.

If she were being logical and practical, she would find a place to turn off and get some sleep before going any farther. But she only had an hour to drive, less if she kept up with the trucks, and the way her heart was pounding, she wouldn't get any sleep anyway.

She'd known the stress was getting bad, but she'd had no idea it was this bad.

Maybe she should call Travers and flake out on Vegas. She wasn't in the best shape to deal with trouble.

But Kyle needed her. And just as a baby-sitter, Travers had said.

She could baby-sit her only nephew. That couldn't be stressful, not compared to life in L.A.

She'd be all right.

At least for the time being.

2

How had she gotten into his bubble?

Rob Chapeau stood beside the interstate for a good minute, watching the Mini Cooper slam on its brakes and then limp to the side of the road. When the pretty woman had gotten out of the driver's side and slapped herself, he knew that she saw his magical little world.

And she wasn't supposed to.

No one was supposed to.

He brought Felix out to hunt at least five times a week—a falcon got restless in the big city—and he did it as far away from anything as he could get. Of course, he didn't go too far because there were sorcerers nearby, ones who would take advantage of regularly scheduled magic.

He tried to vary his locations, using the interstate only when he felt he had no other choice.

Like tonight. He'd gone to his favorite spot only to find that someone was holding a rave there. He probably could have created a bubble in that spot—bubbles warped time just enough so that most normal folks felt a shiver as they passed through or saw a heat shimmer—and no one would have noticed.

But he hadn't wanted to risk it.

And then this: No one had ever driven into one of his bubbles before, skidded to a stop, and slapped herself.

He knew he had to do something—and quickly— but he wasn't sure what. He couldn't just dissolve the bubble: There was Felix to think about, first of all, and he didn't want the falcon to know that his night's catch wasn't real. Besides, the woman might get into trouble if she stepped into the road at the wrong moment.

So he walked out onto the road, pretended a nonchalance he didn't feel, and said, "Have you seen a bird?"

Which he had been kicking himself about ever since. *Have you seen a bird?* Of course, she had seen a bird. She had slammed on her brakes (nice woman, that) and she had pulled over to the side of the road. She'd probably seen the rabbit too, and then she saw him, in his hunting garb.

He liked to wear the clothes he'd grown up in on these nights, even though they were more suited to an English forest than to a Nevada desert. Just a little touch of his past.

But he saw her lovely green eyes assess his clothing as if he were dressed like Bozo the Clown, and he noted something like weary resignation on her face. Either this woman expected strange things to happen to her, or something had been going wrong in her life long before he'd asked his inane question.

She answered him, of course. She had a deep, throaty voice that sent a tingle through him. He hadn't heard a voice that beautiful in centuries.

But he tried to ignore it. He didn't even smile at her, he did nothing to put her at ease, and then he hurried off the road, only to crouch on the other side of the interstate and watch her gather herself and get back into the car.

He felt bad; he really did. He had added to her difficulties without intending to, and she looked like she hadn't needed that. So he decided to be especially gentle in easing her out of the bubble.

Instead of simply dissolving the bubble over the interstate, he dismantled it piece by piece, sending her little warnings such as the lights coming back on, a few trucks going by, a whole host of small things before he let her out of the magical protection and back into her ordinary life.

If, indeed, she had an ordinary life. Not many people could see magic if the mage didn't want them to. Unless, of course, those people had magic themselves. And she was too young. No one had skin that creamy in middle-age, not even women who had fortunes to spend on reinventing themselves with plastic surgeries and too many cold creams.

He remained crouched by the side of the road long after she had driven away. He restored the bubble over the interstate, and no one else entered it, so he knew that his magic hadn't gone awry.

Just that woman—that young, pretty woman— had managed to get through his defenses.

No one had been able to do that for more than

eight centuries. He felt a pang of loss, mixed with a sharp thread of loneliness.

Eight centuries.

And he had let her drive away.

3

Megan arrived in Las Vegas at one in the morning. The streets were filled with cars, the neon stabbed her eyes, and she had never felt so relieved in her life.

She was beginning to think she had seen a mirage in the desert—and it wasn't a hotel designed by Steve Wynn. That hunter got handsomer and handsomer the more she thought about him, a dream lover appearing in the foggy mist of her lonely headlights.

Lonely. That probably was the cause of her mirage, her hallucination, her dream–vision. She hadn't spent quality time with anyone—her family, her friends, let alone a man—in a very, very long time.

The hotel that Travers had picked was a no-name thing off the Strip. That didn't surprise her. What surprised her was how nice the hotel was. Travers, once the poorest of the siblings, had become the richest (at least, Megan thought so, although Vivian inherited all of Great-Aunt

Eugenia's estate). Travers claimed he had made his fortune by staying at the lowest priced hotels, refusing to splurge on the latest fad, paying cash for his house.

He called it "being frugal." Megan called it "unnecessarily cheap."

This place looked like a splurge from Travers's perspective. From Megan's, it seemed like a godsend. It actually had a front lobby instead of some dweeb living on-site, and rooms inside the main building instead of cabins down a long sidewalk. Elevators, a fitness room, and a restaurant inside—all the necessary amenities from Megan's point of view.

It took only a few minutes to check in (competent desk clerks! What a concept!) and take the elevator up to Travers' floor. A bellman, on duty in the middle of the night (such luxury!), hefted her single bag all the way to her room for her.

According to the numbers that greeted her when she got off the elevator, her room was at the end of the hall. She walked past door after door, wondering how Travers had found this place. The farther she got into it, the more unlike him it seemed.

Then she used her keycard to open the door to her room and stopped in amazement. He hadn't gotten her a room. He had gotten her a suite, complete with living room, small kitchen, and a single bedroom.

Three large rooms behind one locked door, and quite obviously hers, because the bellman had placed her overweight bag on the luggage rack inside the nearest coat closet.

Nearest coat closet. There were others.

A shiver ran through her. This was confirmation that Travers was in trouble. He would never voluntarily take a place like this—and he would never pay for one like it for her.

Maybe she should check to see if hell had frozen over.

Instead, she pocketed her keycard, spun on one toe, and walked out of the room. She stopped at the only room beside it, the one with the same number she'd been using when she called him back, and knocked. (There actually was a doorbell beside the door, but she was too scared to use it.)

For a moment, she was afraid that she had the wrong room or that no one had heard her. She raised her fist to knock again when the door swept open.

A tall, willowy blonde answered. She was stunningly beautiful, with delicate little features that formed the most perfect face. She wore a pink negligee and a matching robe with feathers trimming the sleeves and hem.

She was everything that Megan was not—slender, gorgeous, perfect, tall—the kind of woman guaranteed to make Megan even more nervous than she already was.

"I must have the wrong room," Megan said.

"Nonsense." Even the woman's voice was feminine—light and floaty with just a hint of dumb blonde. "You're Travers's sister, aren't you? Come on in."

The woman stepped aside. Her negligee flowed around her as if she were onstage. Megan walked in, peering around the corner for Kyle.

She didn't see him, but she did see a pristine

comic book on one of the end tables. He was here somewhere.

This room was a suite too, only it was filthy. Two other women sat on the couch—a brunette with a petite skinniness that made her look athletic and breakable at the same time, and a redhead who was as heavy as Megan. Only that redhead—whose hair really was flaming Vegas red, not the auburn that Megan was blessed with—had her curves in all the right places.

She wore a green negligee, while the brunette wore a white one. They were eating popcorn and staring at the big screen TV, their mule-covered feet resting on the coffee table.

At that moment, Megan realized she had seen them before. The three women had been at Vivian's wedding less than a month ago. Megan hadn't had a chance to talk to them, though, because every time she glanced at them, they seemed to be talking to one another.

The blonde walked over and shut the television off. The redhead looked up grumpily. "It's the best part."

"We have to know if the nassty shadowy creaturesss are going to get the hobbitsses," the brunette said.

"We've seen it already." The blond sounded grumpy. "Besides, Travers's sister is here."

The redhead stood and extended her hand. She was tall, too. No wonder her curves worked. "You're Megan? I'm Lachesis."

"I'm Atropos," said the brunette.

"And I'm Clotho," said the blonde.

"Sure you are," Megan said. "It's late, but it's

not that late. And if you ladies are the Fates of Greek Mythology, I'm going to eat my shorts."

"Please don't," said the redhead.

"You're not wearing shorts, are you?" asked the brunette.

"I think she means underwear," the blonde said.

Megan wanted to slap herself again. This was worse than a falconer in the desert.

"And we are the Fates, I'm afraid," the redhead said. "Or at least—"

"We used to be," the brunette said.

"We're trying to get our job back," said the blonde.

At the mention of a job, Megan felt a little calmer. They were some kind of Las Vegas lounge act, and they'd hired Travers to help them.

"Travers is good with money and accounting," Megan said. "I'm sure with his business savvy, he'll get the casino to rehire you."

"We're not looking for a casino hire," the redhead—Lachesis?—said.

"But close enough for the moment." The brunette—Atropos?—glanced at the other two. "Right?"

The blonde, Clotho, nodded. "Because that's where he is right now. Getting our—ahem—job back."

Megan's head ached. She rubbed her nose with her thumb and forefinger, getting a sense that she wouldn't understand what was going on if she tried.

"Where's Kyle?" she asked.

All three women smiled. Lachesis nodded toward

the nearest bedroom, Atropos pointed, and Clotho indicated it with her hand.

"In there," they said in unison.

This day was getting stranger by the minute. Megan excused herself and walked to the door. She put her hand on the knob, then held a finger to her lips, indicating that the three strange women remain quiet.

She opened the door. The familiar scents of Gatorade, peanut butter, and little boy reached her. She smiled in spite of herself and closed the door behind her.

A night-light gave the room a faint illumination. Bottles, a Spider-Man thermos, and some wrappers littered a bedside table. Kyle was sprawled on the bed, his bare feet sticking out of the covers, his round little face looking naked without his glasses.

Kyle looked just like Travers had at that age, or like Travers would have if he had preferred computers to basketball and comic books to track. Kyle was pudgy where Travers had been thin and nearsighted where Travers had had 20/20 vision, but they shared a heart-shaped face and blond hair with the same cowlick right in the center of the forehead.

Travers had gotten the classic good looks in the family—not that the family had been doling out looks. All three children had been adopted. Vivian was slight and dark with the curliest hair any woman had ever had; Travers was tall and blond—the male equivalent of Clotho, if truth be told; and Megan was small and round, "round" being the operative word.

Her parents had never said anything about it, preferring to love their children as they were. If Megan commented on her weight, her mother would smile and say that Megan would grow out of it.

At twenty-five, she was still waiting for that miracle to happen.

She approached the bed. Her nephew looked so vulnerable there, his hand curled beneath his chin. She was reaching for the sheet to pull it over his shoulders when something growled at her.

She leapt backwards in complete fright, her heart pounding. She hadn't seen anything, but she had heard it. She knew she had.

A growl.

Wasn't it?

Or maybe it was some weird noise that Kyle had made in his sleep.

She walked back to the bed and heard it again. A huge growl. She was shaking. She had been attacked by a dog when she was little—a German Shepherd that had knocked her to the ground and bit her and growled when her father pulled it off, wrestled it off, really—and she hadn't liked dogs ever since.

But she didn't see a dog.

Was she losing her mind? First the falconer on the highway (and the lights going out. What was that?), then the Fates (had they really said that? Or had she imagined it?), and now this imaginary dog.

She steeled herself and reached for the sheet again, only to hear a half-bark and feel the snap of teeth as they closed near her hand.

She yanked it back so quickly that she nearly hurt herself. The side of her palm was wet. Drool? Slobber? She couldn't tell.

"Aunt Megan?" Kyle was looking up at her, his adorable face mashed together in a squint. "You're here."

"Indeed I am, boyo," she said and went to ruffle his hair, then thought better of it. "Everything's gonna be okay now."

He smiled, snuggled deeper into the pillow, and sighed. Something moved across his shoulder. That something was black and long and never-ending.

Megan squealed.

Kyle raised his head. "It's just Fang, Aunt Megan."

"Fang?"

He reached over and snapped on the light beside the bed. An obese dachshund guarded the space between Kyle's chest and Megan, its black eyes glittery and fierce.

"Fang," Kyle said. "He's my dad's familiar, but really, he's my dog."

She hadn't heard that right. "He's a what?"

"Oh, yeah." Kyle rubbed his eyes. "Nobody told you."

"Told me what?"

"About the magic."

She'd wandered into a *Twilight Zone* episode, only life hadn't become black and white. Maybe it was an episode of *Punk'd*, and Ashton Kutcher would reveal himself at any moment.

That wouldn't be so bad, right?

The dog was still staring at her.

"Does it bite?" Megan asked, nodding toward the dog.

Kyle put his hand on the dog's back and pressed it toward the sheets. "That's my Aunt Megan," he said as if the dog could understand him. "She's one of the good guys."

The dog laid down and then sighed as if a huge burden had been lifted off it.

"You still didn't answer me," she said. "Does it bite?"

"No, *he* doesn't," Kyle said, "unless you're like totally evil. Or incompetent."

She blinked, trying to make sense out of all this. The women in the next room had been watching one of the *Lord of the Rings* movies. Maybe they'd let Kyle watch it before he went to sleep. Maybe he was still half asleep, which was why he was talking so oddly.

"If he doesn't bite," she said, being careful with the pronoun, "why did you name him Fang?"

"Because he told me that was his name. His previous owner called him Bartholomew, which Fang thinks is stupid, but he doesn't mind it when Zoe calls him Bartholomew Fang."

"Zoe? Is she one of the women outside?"

"Nope. She's a detective. She thinks my dad doesn't like her because she's too old, but he doesn't care. And she doesn't look that old anyway."

Megan had to be in a *Twilight Zone* episode. This conversation was too complicated for *Punk'd*.

"A detective?" Megan pushed her hair away from her face. "What's going on? Is your dad in trouble?"

"No." Kyle shoved his pillow against the back of

the bed, picked up the obese dog, and moved it—him—to one side. Then he patted the space where the dog had been, like he thought Megan should sit in it, doggy smell and all.

She gave the blanket a sideways look, squared her shoulders, and then sat down. It was still warm from that dog body. The dog watched her, but didn't growl any more.

"It's okay, Fang, really," Kyle said to the dog. "She's just cautious because some big old dog tried to kill her once."

That was as blunt as anyone had ever put it. She'd never told a soul about her fears. Even her father had said the dog wasn't trying to hurt her all the way to the hospital, where they'd given her rabies shots and five stitches in the bite on her shoulder.

"Fang says that other dog was stupid, and he'd only have hurt you if you'd have hurt me." Kyle still had his hand on the dog's neck.

The dog was looking at Megan as if indeed it—he—had said those words. In fact, it—he—had that expression people got when they expected an answer.

Kyle's expression mirrored it.

"Thanks, Fang," Megan said as sincerely as she could. "I'll work on the trust issues."

The dog nodded—or it seemed to nod—then it (he, dang it!) circled three times and laid down beside Kyle.

"You're cool, Aunt Megan," Kyle said. "I didn't know how much dogs scared you till just then."

Uncanny. She always forgot how uncanny this kid was, how supernaturally intuitive. Just like

Vivian when she was little. Everyone was convinced Viv was psychic. Megan had learned in all her psych courses and her subsequent work that there was no such thing as psychic. But there were amazingly in tune people who could read signals better than most. Vivian had that skill, and somehow, Kyle had acquired it too.

Kyle's cheeks were red as if what he had just said had embarrassed him. He plucked at the blanket.

Megan tried to get the conversation back on track. "If your dad isn't in trouble, what's he doing with a detective?"

"Besides kissing her?" Kyle asked.

It was Megan's turn to blush. She hadn't seen Travers with a woman since Cheryl had left him and baby Kyle over nine years ago.

"Yeah, I guess," Megan said.

"They're trying to rescue some spinning wheel for the Fates," Kyle said.

"Excuse me?" Megan asked.

Kyle hit his forehead with the heel of his hand. "I keep forgetting that you haven't been here the whole time. You always know what's going on and this time it's been kinda weird."

"Just tell me," Megan said.

And so he did.

Even if Megan believed in magic and fate and all that mumbo jumbo, she still wasn't sure his story could be true. It sounded like Kyle had recounted a dream. Still, her profession had taught her the importance of dreams—in them lurked the subconscious, with its wants, desires, and knowledge—so she struggled to pay attention.

What she finally understood was this: the women in the living room of the suite truly believed they were the Greek Fates who had ruled over mankind for centuries. They had been all powerful until Zeus had initiated a coup and instituted his daughters as new Fates.

This, however, was a problem as the Fates administered more than life and death. They kept alive all the rules that created true love.

Zeus, for grown-up reasons that Kyle didn't really want to understand, wanted to destroy true love. In order to destroy true love, Zeus had had to get rid of the Fates, which he had done, even tricking them into giving up their magical powers.

The Fates needed to get their magic back. To do that, they needed their old spinning wheel. It could restore their powers ten thousand times over.

The problem was that the spinning wheel had been stolen by the Faerie Kings, who had needed the magic to start their rival magical kingdom. They had hidden the wheel, and now the Fates had to find it.

Which was why they needed a detective. That was Zoe.

So Travers was helping Zoe find a magic spinning wheel. And, oh, by the way, the reason Travers had always been so good with money was because he was magical too. Just like Zoe, who was over a hundred years old.

Megan wasn't sure she had gotten it all, but she

clung to this: the Fates had magic once, but they didn't any longer. Her stolid brother, who didn't even like fiction about magic, was really a magician, and he had fallen in love with a woman who was at least seventy years older than he was—a woman who was both detective and magician.

It was, if Megan did say so herself, one of the most inventive stories a kid had ever told her. And she had heard some doozies over the years.

"And I should probably say one more thing." Kyle was watching her as she absorbed the information.

"What's that, hon?" she asked.

"The reason I'm so 'intuitive' all the time is that I can read minds."

She stared at him. He actually believed that part of it. Was it a defense mechanism? Some way to cope with being off-the-charts brilliant and so incredibly precocious as a result? Not many ten-year-olds had the vocabulary he did, the maturity he did, and the sensitivity he did.

His shoulders wilted in the face of her silence.

"It's okay," he said quietly. "You don't have to believe me."

She took his warm little hand in hers. "I do, Kyle," she said, telling herself she wasn't really lying. She believed that he believed all of this.

"You'll see," he said, slipping grumpily under his blankets. "This is all true. You won't be able to explain it away, Aunt Meg. If Dad can come around, you can too."

She bent over, kissed his forehead, and tucked the sheet around him. Then she shut off the light.

"I'm sure I can, kiddo," she said quietly. "I'm sure I can."

4

The Fate women were crowded around the bedroom door, apparently attempting to eavesdrop. Megan nearly knocked two of them over as she pushed the door outward. They scrambled backward and didn't even try to apologize.

Megan had learned over the years that rudeness was something she couldn't abide. It was, according to her own counselor (all therapists had to have a therapist during their educational phase. It was a requirement for the advanced degree), part of being the youngest child in a chaotic household.

The Fate women watched her as if they could divine her reaction.

She wasn't going to let them know how much her conversation with Kyle had disturbed her.

"You want to tell me where my brother is?" she asked.

The women looked at each other, obviously surprised. That pleased her. Keeping others off balance was always good. It kept everyone from concentrating on her.

"Well?" she asked, a little too loudly, to drown her own thoughts.

"He's probably in Faerie by now," Clotho said.

"Although he might not be," Lachesis said.

"He might be out," Atropos said.

"If we still had magic, we could find out for you," Clotho said.

"Alas, we do not," Lachesis said.

The "alas" was the last straw.

"You women are the ones who are screwing up my nephew, aren't you?" Megan snapped. Part of her was startled at herself. She never snapped at people. She always took a reasonable tone of voice, always counted to ten before she spoke, always made sure she had thought through everything she had to say.

But the last twelve hours had strained her. She had rearranged her schedule, worried about her brother, driven here much too late, seen that falconer (he was cute), and watched the lights go out on the interstate; then she came here to three weird women, a dog, and a nephew who was convinced he was psychic.

"Screwing up?" Atropos asked. "Young Kyle is the sanest person we know."

"Which doesn't say much for the people you know," Megan said. "Why did my brother leave Kyle in your custody?"

"Custody," Clotho whispered to Lachesis. "She uses police talk."

"You didn't tell us you were a police officer," Lachesis said to Megan.

"I'm not," Megan said, wondering how they could think such a thing and why it mattered. "I'm a child psychologist, and I'm now convinced you people are poisoning my nephew's mind."

"Ooooooh," Atropos said. "You're a *scientist.*"

As if that were a bad thing.

"Yeah," Megan said. "So mumbo-jumbo and I don't get along. Now, tell me where my brother is."

"Well." Clotho looked at the other two women. "We're not exactly sure."

"Thank you," Megan said. "A little honesty is much more like it."

Lachesis bit her lower lip.

"So why did he leave my nephew alone?"

"Because," Lachesis said, "someone had to rescue Zoe."

Megan's eyebrows shot up. "Travers is not the kind of man who rescues a detective."

If, indeed, this Zoe was a detective. All Megan had was Kyle's rather jumbled word on that.

"Of course he is, dear," Atropos said.

Megan bristled at the "dear." Atropos wasn't much older than she was. She hated it when people who were her age called her dear.

Of course, she hated it when people who weren't her age called her dear.

"You may see my scrawny brother as some kind of superhero, but he's not—"

"No, dear, that's Dex," Clotho said.

Dexter was Vivian's new husband. Megan admittedly didn't know him very well, but she knew for certain he wasn't some kind of flying-through-the-air, rescuing damsels in distress superhero.

"*But,*" Megan said even louder, even though she knew that loudness wasn't the best way to take over a conversation, "I grew up with Travers, and I know he doesn't have magical powers—except that he's a math whiz—"

"Precisely!" Lachesis said.

"*And,*" Megan said, determined not to get sidetracked, "he doesn't know how to fight or use a gun, so he'd be useless in the rescue business. So—"

"A gun?" Atropos asked. "Who said anything about a gun?"

"I believe she got caught up in 'rescue' and 'detective,'" Clotho whispered. "After all, she has a penchant for police language—"

"I do not!" Megan said. "I'm trying to make a point here."

"Which is?" Lachesis asked.

"That there's no way Travers could be off rescuing someone, so please, just tell me where he is, and then I'll shut up."

The women looked at each other with perfectly coordinated movements, as if they'd stepped out of a Marx Brothers comedy.

"We don't know where he is." Atropos bowed her head and sounded very subdued.

Clotho said, "He went with Gaylord to find Zoe. That's all we know."

"Gaylord?" Megan asked.

"He's a faerie thug," Lachesis said. "Um, that is, a thug who's rather nice, but—"

"He's gay?" Megan asked.

"Well, no." Atropos looked confused. "Not that I've seen. But he does laugh a lot."

Megan resisted the urge to hit her forehead with the heel of her hand just like Kyle had. "Gaylord. He works for the mob?"

"No, he . . ." Clotho sighed and shook her head. "I don't know how to tell you this."

"She doesn't want to hear the truth," Lachesis said.

"Then how are we supposed to do our job?" Atropos asked.

"What's your job?" Megan asked, feeling left out.

Clotho took a deep breath. "Look. Here's what we know."

"Travers left with Gaylord to find Zoe. We think she's in trouble," Lachesis said.

"But we don't know for sure," Atropos said.

"And since you weren't here yet," Clotho said.

"Your brother asked us to babysit Kyle," Lachesis said.

"But since you're here now," Atropos said.

"We can go to bed." Clotho headed toward the door. The other two followed. Lachesis pulled the door open, and as they stepped into the hallway, Atropos waggled her fingers at Megan.

"We're six doors down if you need us," Lachesis said.

"Ta-ta," Atropos said.

And then they left, gently closing the door behind them.

"Ta-ta?" Megan whispered. "Who says that any more?"

But this time, no one answered her. Thank heavens. She rubbed her eyes and walked into the living room. *The Two Towers* still played, albeit silently, on the large screen.

She shut off the television and sank down on the couch. It smelled faintly of lavender perfume. She was exhausted. And confused. And not about to return to her nearby room because Kyle wouldn't know where she was.

So she needed a plan. It had to be a simple one because she wasn't up for complex.

She would sleep on the couch until Kyle got up or Travers got home, whichever happened first. Then she'd make breakfast for the three of them and get the real story. Maybe by then these flights of fancy would be over, and she could find out why everyone was making up such elaborate stories.

A bed on the couch. How very polite she was. She could just take Travers' room. But she didn't feel right doing that. So she'd just take his blankets instead, and maybe a pillow or two. He could sacrifice a pillow to her after all this strangeness.

Strangeness—and a dog. Why hadn't anyone told her about the dog? Were they afraid she wouldn't come if she knew there was a dog? (Of course, she would have thought twice about it, but Kyle in need always trumped a dog.)

Maybe when she woke up, she'd see the absurdity in all of this. She knew it lurked—a dachshund named Fang proved it—but her sense of humor was sleep-impaired.

She yawned. Morning was already here, and she was wasting valuable sleeptime trying to figure out the unfathomable. She always told her patients everything looked better after sleep.

It was time to take her own advice.

5

Rob arrived at the office about six in the morning ready to work. Exercise and a few hours sleep always rejuvenated him, but they reminded him how different his life was these days. It had been a lot easier to take care of the poor and oppressed in a small village—even before he realized he had magical powers—than it was to care for them now.

Of course, over the past several centuries, his perspective had changed. He no longer believed that the imposter King of England, John, and his henchman, the Sheriff of Nottingham, had created poverty all by themselves.

In fact, over the years, Rob had come to realize that the Bible was right: the poor would always be with us.

That didn't mean a man had to stop trying to help them.

He still robbed from the rich to give to the poor, but now he did it legally, through charitable corporate entities that he'd set up over the space of decades. And now the rich pretended to enjoy the privilege, believing they would get a return on their dollar.

They rarely did.

He pushed the papers aside on the Lucite desk that some designer had thought would be a pleasure to work on, and pulled his plush chair away from the window.

Outside, the Vegas strip winked at him, its bizarre architecture ruining the view of the mountains that he'd had when this office was built sixty-five years ago. The desert had its own stark beauty: the browns of the sand, the greens of the cacti, and the subtle whites and grays of the mountains in the distance.

He used to love the clear air, the way that the land met the horizon so softly that they seemed to blend into each other. But over time, the air had become the most polluted in the nation, the buildings had destroyed the view of the horizon, and the city had sprawled so far across his lovely desert that he couldn't find a comfortable place to fly his falcon any more.

Rob sighed and adjusted the window tint to dark before he sat down. Now he tried to avoid the Vegas office as much as possible. He worked out of New York and London whenever he could. The cities were what they had always been: centers of commerce, places where humans congregated, places where he would never consider setting his falcon free for a hunt.

The office itself looked stark and foreboding in the shaded morning light. The plants, all some form of desert succulent, seemed faded; the furniture was that horrible see-through stuff that he'd been meaning to replace for some time.

Even the rug's geometric design—a black triangle bisecting a gray square—irritated him. He just couldn't justify a remodel on a office that he used only three times a year.

And unfortunately, this was one of those times. Vegas cooled to 102 degrees at night—if 102 degrees could be called "cool" (and he supposed it could, considering the temperatures were 115 during the day)—and was the warmest place on the planet this side of hell.

Even though he hadn't lived in England full-time since the nineteenth century, he still considered himself an Englishman at heart, and Englishmen preferred their cool nights to have a bit of ground fog, a touch of rain, and temperatures below 55. Anything else was a complete and utter abomination.

He sighed again. Perhaps the exercise and sleep hadn't improved his mood. It was still as foul as it had been yesterday evening when John had kicked him out of the office and told him to take care of himself.

As if on cue, the door opened, and John Little poked his head in. The man was hideously misnamed. He was six-seven and two-seventy-five when he was trim, and he wasn't always trim. He'd gone on the Atkins Diet a few years ago, saying it reminded him of the Good Old Days, and had lost about fifty pounds, making him seem less like a treehouse and more like a tree.

The name John worked—although over the centuries, he had sometimes called himself the

Irish version, Sean, and occasionally (always under duress) the French Jean. He'd use different variations on Little too—sometimes opting for Petit and sometimes for Pequeño.

He'd had fun with his name in ways that Rob couldn't. Even though John Little had lived on through the mythology as Little John, the name wasn't nearly as recognizable as Robin Hood.

"You don't look happy," John said as he stepped inside. He crouched as he did so. While the other doors in the building had been redone to accommodate John, this one hadn't.

Rob liked to keep his office tailored to his own size—which wasn't exactly small, except in comparison to his best friend.

"Happiness is overrated," Rob said.

John shook his head. "You never used to say that."

"Overrated is a relatively new term." Rob tapped the computer on the far side of his desk out of sleep mode. The day's stock reports were already updating themselves.

"Relatively is a relatively new term," John said, "but you know what I mean."

Rob glanced at the Dow, watching the lines move, knowing that the money lost with each downturn could feed a thousand families for a year. Sometimes he lost faith, that was all. Sometimes he felt like everything he did—everything he had always done—was completely futile.

"You're ignoring me," John said. "The midnight falconry didn't work, huh?"

"It was the woman." The words left Rob's mouth

before he even thought about them. He raised his head.

John's bushy eyebrows hit the edge of his curly brown hair. "Woman?"

Rob grabbed the mouse and clicked open his NASDAQ window. The lines were moving on that thing too. Making and breaking fortunes all over the world.

Pretend money.

He missed gold pieces.

"What woman?"

Rob shook his head. "A pretty thing. She drove her car right into my bubble."

"That's not possible."

"That's what I thought, but it happened."

"And it made you unhappy?"

"Threw me off my rhythm." He had thought about her for the rest of the night, not about falconry and magic and the lovely, albeit desolate, scenery.

"A woman did that?" John's gray eyes glinted.

"We hardly spoke to each other. I was just a bit startled that she had appeared, that's all." Rob tried to focus on those lines for what they meant to him—a double check to see if he had talked with the right CEOs about the right investments, so that they would make the right amount of money, so that they could funnel an even righter amount of money into his nonprofits.

"She was magic, then," John said.

"No."

"She's going to be magic, then," John said.

"I have no idea."

"She's attractive, then," John said.

"Well, of course," Rob muttered.

"Aha!"

The "aha" startled him and made him realize he'd answered the questions out loud. He really was off his game this morning.

"You haven't found a woman attractive since Marian died," John said.

Rob crossed his arms. "Have to."

"Have not."

"That's eight hundred years ago. A man would have to be dead not to find another woman attractive."

"If the shoe fits," John said.

"I wasn't dead," Rob said. Even though he had wanted to be.

For a very, very long time, he had wanted to be.

In fact, sometimes, when he saw an elderly couple holding hands, enjoying their last few years together, he felt cheated. He wanted a normal life with his lady love. He wanted a belief that even though the life ended, the love endured—and not just in story and song.

He wanted to feel his mortality, not her mortality.

"Was she pretty?" John asked.

"Of course she was pretty," Rob said. "You knew her. She was the most beautiful woman on earth."

"No." John's voice was soft. "The woman who burst your bubble."

Rob hit the sleep button and stared at the darkening screen, seeing not it but the woman. She lacked a modern beauty. She had curves where modern women had angles. Her face was full, not bony, and her eyes were the most spectacular green he had ever seen. She had perfect auburn hair—the color of a Sherwood sunset in the fall—and a generous, kissable mouth.

Her face was too lush for DaVinci, too pleasant for Rembrandt. There was nothing classic about her. Nothing expected, not even that deep, rich voice.

"Pretty?" Rob repeated. It seemed like a small word for that woman. She wasn't beautiful, not like Marian, who had been a true English rose with pale skin and dark hair and even darker eyes. "She was too amazing to be pretty."

"Amazing." John smiled approvingly. "So you chatted her up, used the old Hood charisma, and wrapped her around your little finger, right?"

"Of course not," Rob said.

"But you at least got her number, right?"

"Number?"

"As in telephone number?" John said. "You know, the way people in the new millennium do it?"

"I liked the old millennium," Rob said.

"Then I take it you didn't get her number," John said.

"Why would I?"

"Because she's the first woman that's interested you in eight hundred years."

"That's not true. There was Charise."

"Two dinners, a goodnight, and a thank you? Four hundred years ago?"

"Her parents scared me away."

"They just wanted to meet you."

"They wanted me to marry her."

"Dating wasn't a common thing in the early six-teenth century."

"I know." Rob wanted out of this conversation. "I lived through it, remember?"

"That's what we were discussing," John said. "You didn't live through it. You floated through it."

"Says the man who has never made a commitment in his entire life."

"I'm committed to causes, not women."

"Well, so am I," Rob snapped, hoping his tone would close the door on the conversation.

"What happened to the man who said you couldn't have a cause without a woman to support it?"

Rob glared at him. Even after all these years, he hated discussing Marian. And John was wrong. Rob had been involved with other women, and not just Charise (whom he always brought up to irritate John). He'd known several widows who had wanted nothing more than he had—some companionship, some shared times, and a warm bed.

Then there was that dancer in Paris in the 1920s—the only woman he'd lived with since Marian. She'd been interesting, and the entire fling had felt daring.

But he wasn't a fling sort of man. He was monogamous. In fact, he was a one woman kind of man.

The only problem was that his one woman had shown up—and died—at the beginning of his very, very, very long life.

The conversation had to end. It was making his sour mood even darker. He was going to change the subject.

But John got there first. "Were you afraid of her?"

"Go to work, John," Rob said. "Get out of my office."

"Because it seems like you were if you didn't get her number. Tell me you at least got her name."

"Out. Now."

Judging by John's expression, it was good he no longer carried a staff, or he would have thwacked Rob on the head with it. "You should've at least gotten her name."

"I could fire you."

"It hasn't worked before."

"I can still whup you," Rob said.

"Right," John said. "With the help of security."

Rob smiled for the first time that morning. "Whatever it takes."

John smiled back and eased out the door, closing it gently behind him. Rob stared at it.

John knew him well. Rob was afraid. He wasn't afraid of dating or seeing a new woman or even spending time with a companion.

He didn't mind meeting someone new.

He was afraid of something old.

He wasn't going to give his heart to a mortal again.

He wasn't going to go through that kind of grief ever again.

6

Someone stood beside her. She could hear him breathing. And he smelled of waffles and scrambled eggs. Bacon, too. And coffee. Oh, how she wanted coffee.

Megan opened her eyes. A man in uniform stared down at her. He had lovely blue eyes, fringed with long black lashes, a zit on his right cheek, and stubble beside it. His cap was a little too big, settling on the back of his head as if it were glued there.

He held a tray in one hand.

"I'm sorry," he said as if he'd repeated it more than once. "But the kid has disappeared."

Kid? What was a man, wearing a uniform and holding a tray, doing in her bedroom? And what did he mean by kid?

Megan blinked again, started to roll over, and realized she wasn't in her room at all. She was in a hotel room, in a suite to be exact, a suite Travers had voluntarily and shockingly paid for to be even more exact, and she was sleeping on the couch.

Her neck ached, her shirt had bunched up

over her stomach (which the kid with the tray was trying hard not to look at), and the waistband of her jeans dug into her left side.

Travers should have come back by now. He should have awakened her much earlier.

And who was this man with the patience of Job?

"Ma'am, I'm really sorry. But the tray? And I need you to sign for this."

Sign for. Tray. Bacon, eggs, waffles, coffee. Room service. Boy, her mind was working slowly.

"Um." Her mouth tasted like it was full of wet cotton. "On the table?"

The man nodded, gave her a polite smile, and executed a military turn. He walked into the dining area and set the tray on the table. Then he took the dishes off as if he were a real waiter.

Megan stood, pulled down her shirt, ran her fingers through her hair (not that it would do any good), and then stuck a thumb between her waistband and her side, trying to get the fabric out of her skin. It sort of worked, enough that she was no longer in pain.

The man finished removing the dishes, then he brought a computer slip to her, along with a pen.

"How did you get in here, exactly?" Megan asked, feeling as if he had seen her naked.

She never let anyone watch her sleep, and this guy could've been standing there for days.

"The kid let me in," he said.

"Kyle?"

"I dunno. He opened the door, pointed to the living room, and said you'd handle it."

Because he couldn't sign for the food. Megan scrawled her name, checked to see if there was a tip, then added one anyway, and handed the paper back to the room service guy.

"Thanks," he said with a little too much sarcasm. How long had he been trying to wake her up?

He grabbed his tray and left, slamming the door behind him.

Apparently he had wanted out of the room badly.

Megan sighed and scouted the area for Kyle. She didn't see him, but she heard a shower running somewhere nearby. She headed toward his room.

No boy, no dog.

No kid in the shower.

A shiver ran through her. How could she have lost Kyle?

At that moment, the front door opened.

"Hey, you're awake!" Kyle said. He had the dog on a leash. The dog lifted its long snout and sniffed the air, then pointed directly at the food.

Megan had no idea that dachshunds were pointers.

"They're not," Kyle said. "They just really like sausage."

She also had no idea she had spoken out loud.

"You're not," Kyle said, "but you're broadcasting."

This time, she did speak out loud. "Broadcasting?"

"Thinking really loud. Some people do that when they just wake up. It only happens to people who wake up really slow."

Like she did. Staring at a man in uniform— every woman's dream, Conchita would say. A good-looking (albeit much too young) man, bearing food.

"Can you think about something else?" Kyle's cheeks were red.

Megan blushed. If he could hear that, what else had he heard over the years? Was that why he was so precocious? Because he knew about—

"Aunt Megan, please. Stop."

Apparently he did.

"Oh my God," she said. "Kyle, why didn't you tell me before last night?"

"I did," he said miserably. "I told you and Dad and Gramma, and none of you believed me."

But he had never told Vivian, who had always claimed she had visions. Vivian would have at least understood. Or pretended she did.

"I tried to tell Aunt Viv too. She just thought I was making stuff up."

Megan looked at her nephew with a combination of horror and sympathy. Sympathy because she hated being misunderstood, and horror because he had heard things no child should hear.

"Kyle, baby, how long has this been going on?"

He shrugged.

"How long, really?"

He shrugged again. The dog tugged on the leash so hard that it nearly pulled him forward. He crouched and released it. The dog made a beeline for the table, looking like a heat-seeking missile with a tail.

"Crap," Megan said, and launched herself after the heat-seeking missile, hoping she'd arrive before all the sausages were gone.

She wrapped an arm around the dog's stomach—

which, despite its size, was surprisingly solid—and held the creature against her as she turned toward Kyle.

"What do we do with it now?" she asked.

He was watching with an expression of bemusement on his face. And then she realized that he had probably let the dog loose on purpose, just so that he could avoid her question.

"Kyle," she said as softly as she could. "How long have you been able to hear other people's thoughts?"

He shrugged for a third time.

The dog kicked her in the back, its sharp claws digging through her shirt. Still, she hung on to the creature, not willing to sacrifice her breakfast to something that resembled a sausage itself.

"Tell me what to do with the dog," she said.

"Put him down," Kyle said. "He knows better."

She bent over, set the dog down, and the creature took off again, only this time, it ran to Kyle. Kyle crouched, hands out, and let the dog lick his face.

Kyle looked like he needed the comfort.

Had the dog known that?

Kyle nodded, just a little, and Megan wondered if he was answering her thoughts or if he was just enjoying the dog.

"Kyle," she said, not believing she was asking the question. "How do I stop broadcasting?"

He shrugged one shoulder. "Stop concentrating, I guess. I dunno."

She took a deep breath, followed by another, focusing on her breathing. She had been trained to do this as a therapist. *Calm your thoughts. Calm your mind. Relax.*

And her thoughts did quiet.

Except for one really tiny, niggly idea.

Kyle had been hearing other people's thoughts since he was born. That's why he couldn't tell her how long he'd been psychic. He always had been.

Kyle had his face buried in the dog's fur. His eyes were squeezed shut, and he looked really sad.

Megan walked toward him and put a hand on his arm, helping him up. He stared at her— clearly expecting rejection, because she had done it so many times before (how could she believe in mind-reading? She'd been taught it didn't exist. Even though it had been so damn obvious. He always knew what people were going to say a half second before they said it, and she always said he was the most intuitive kid [maybe the most intuitive person] she had ever known).

"C'mere," she said, and enveloped him in a hug.

For a moment, he didn't respond, then he wrapped his arms around her as if she were a lifeline. She wrapped her arms around him too. God, she loved this kid, and she hoped she was broadcasting that.

"You were," he whispered into her side.

"I do love you, kiddo. You're the most important person in my life."

"I know," Kyle said. "I'm really lucky. I got you and Dad and Aunt Viv, and Gramma and Grandpa and Bartholomew Fang, and the Fates. And you all think I'm okay."

But he didn't name any friends from school.

No one outside his family, except the three strangest women Megan had ever met in her life.

"They're not strange," Kyle said. "I mean, they *are* strange, but they're not really strange if you know what they've been through. Like they gave up magic to learn what life is really like, and they've had magic since forever, and they even bossed the gods around, although that didn't pay off for them, not really and—"

"We talked about some of this last night." Megan's stomach growled. "How about talking some more over breakfast before it gets cold?"

"Okay." Kyle eased out of her hug. He looked toward the table and blanched. "Fang!"

The dog was in the center of the table, munching at one of the plates as if it had been placed there for him.

Megan looked at Kyle, who looked back at her. It felt like a Laurel and Hardy moment—if either of them moved, something would go wrong: the dog would run into the other plates, or it would pull the tablecloth off the table, or it would throw up all over the waffles.

"Dad would get mad and throw everything out," Kyle said.

"Your dad's right," Megan said, "but I'm hungry."

She led Kyle to the table. The dog kept eating, his stubby tail wagging. He had started with the sausages, and they were mostly gone now, but the bacon remained, along with the waffles and the eggs and some lovely looking pastries.

Kyle picked up the dog just like Megan had, wrapping his arm around the dog's stomach, and then grabbed the plate. He set dog and plate on the floor and then sat at the table.

Megan joined him and grinned.

Kyle giggled.

Megan giggled too, and then they laughed as if this were the funniest thing that had ever happened to them. It wasn't, but it certainly showed Megan how tense she had been durng the last twenty-four hours.

"Imagine if your Dad had walked in on that," Megan said.

"He'd've been really mad," Kyle said.

"He'd've made some comment about how nonparents don't understand the needs of children—"

"And he would have been right."

Megan jumped at the new voice. It belonged to Travers. He was standing at the door, a beautiful raven-haired woman at his side.

Megan felt a surge of anger. It wasn't Travers's comment so much as the fact that he had abandoned his child for an entire night to three obviously incompetent women, not knowing for sure when Megan would arrive.

And it was clear what he had been doing. Her tall, slender, handsome brother looked like he'd been kissed. Many times. His mouth was swollen, his eyes a bit glassy, his blond hair mussed.

He looked . . . ruffled. She'd never seen him look ruffled, not even with Kyle's mother, way back when Travers was a teenager.

"I know about kids, Travers," Megan snapped. "I specialize in kids."

"You specialize in kid theory. You should know better than to eat food that a dog has touched."

The raven-haired woman put a manicured hand on his arm. *She* looked well kissed too, and Megan didn't even know her. The woman was petite and stylish—black clothes that would've been too tight on anyone with an ounce of fat, a wedge cut hairdo that would have ruined any face except one with wonderful angles, and boots, high heeled boots that looked like they had come off a movie set.

Megan hated women like that.

"Give her a chance," Kyle whispered, which told Megan she'd been broadcasting again.

She hated the broadcasting thing too.

"You should know better than to leave your son alone with three insane women," she said.

"Oh," Travers said, shutting the front door and coming into the suite. "You've met the Fates."

"You call them the Fates too?"

He nodded. He had lipstick on his chin. She hadn't noticed that before. And some mud—at least she hoped it was mud—on the front of his shirt.

She had never seen Travers look like this.

"They are the Fates," Travers said. "They deserve the name."

"What is this all about?" Megan said. "Is this an elaborate practical joke? Let's see how thoroughly we can humiliate Megan? Is that what we're doing?"

"No." The woman spoke. She had a faint accent—French?—and her voice was as sophisticated as the rest of her.

She came all the way into the dining room and extended that manicured hand toward Megan.

"I'm Zoe," she said. "I'm very pleased to meet you."

Megan felt a momentary sullenness. She didn't want to take this woman's hand. But that would be rude, and Megan was never (well, not never as she had recently learned, but rarely) rude.

Megan took her hand. It was smooth and warm. "Megan."

"Travers says nice things about you," Zoe said. "He's a bit off balance right now."

"He's been off balance for days," Kyle said.

"I have not," Travers said.

"Have too," Kyle said.

"Have not," Travers said.

"Have too." Kyle crossed his arms.

"Have not."

Megan stared at her brother. He always told her that adults who interacted childishly with their children hurt their children. She had never heard this kind of interchange between Travers and Kyle.

"Have too," Kyle said.

Megan was feeling off balance as well.

"This," Zoe said loudly, obviously to stop the fight, "is not a practical joke. There are just things about the world that your family didn't know. And now you're learning them, which can be hard."

Hard. That was the understatement of the year. If magic existed and Zoe was a witch (magician?) and Kyle had psychic powers and the Fates had once been in charge of everyone's lives, then hard was nearly impossible.

Because it meant everything Megan had learned was wrong.

Zoe was watching her sympathetically, as if she understood what Megan was going through.

Megan felt a shiver of fear run through her, and it startled her. She had expected upset and discomfort, but not fear.

"You can't read my mind too, can you?" she asked Zoe. Suddenly, the reason for her fear became clear.

If magic existed, and everyone who had it was psychic, then Megan's privacy had been invaded all of her life—it had been anyway, if Kyle was to be believed, first by her sister Vivian and now by her nephew—but that didn't feel as invasive as having some woman she just met, some woman who claimed to love her brother, be able to know everything about her with just a single thought.

"No," Zoe said gently, "I can't read minds. Kyle is a special boy."

She gave him a fond look.

Megan glanced at her brother, who was staring at this woman with something like love. Megan had seen a similar expression on her brother's face before—that adoration had been in his eyes when he had looked at his newborn son—but this was something else, something passionate, something not Travers.

Or not the Travers she had grown up with.

Travers and passion weren't two words she had ever put together before.

"You know," Kyle was saying to Zoe, "I hate being called special. It makes me sound like there's something wrong with me."

"I meant it as a compliment," she said.

"I know that," Kyle said, but he still looked grumpy.

And that was when the knot in Megan's stomach loosened ever so slightly. Because if Zoe had really been psychic, she would have known that Kyle hated being called special. He also hated "weird" and "unusual" and "interesting."

The dog climbed into Kyle's lap and inspected the table, his nose twitching. Megan looked at the food. The eggs had congealed, the waffles looked soggy, and the coffee was cold.

She sighed and reached for the orange juice. Then she stopped, hand out, and contemplated something.

"If you're really magic," she said to Zoe, "prove it. Revive my breakfast."

"Aunt Meg!" Kyle put a hand in front of the dog's snout to prevent him from eating a strip of cold bacon off his plate. "You said you'd give her a chance."

"I am giving her a chance," Megan said.

"Revive it?" Travers said. "What are you asking, Meg?"

Megan blinked at him. Then her stomach rumbled. The smell of fresh bacon always did that to her, even if she wasn't hungry. Fresh bacon and fresh coffee—

She looked down. The scrambled eggs were fluffy, with steam rising from them. The bacon wasn't just hot; it was also crisp, which was exactly how she liked it. A new plate held sausages, cooked until they were shriveled and perfect. And the waffles looked like they had just come out of the waffle iron, little puffs of steam rising from their checkerboard surfaces.

Megan raised her eyes slowly from the food to Zoe.

Zoe smiled. "That's what she meant, Trav."

He came to the table, put his arm around Zoe, and then glared at Megan. "Magic has a cost, you know. You just made her waste some on something trivial."

"Da-ad." Kyle was clutching the dog, who was straining to reach the new plate of sausages. "Stop being mean to Aunt Megan."

"I didn't know magic had costs," Megan said. "I didn't even know it existed until a few hours ago."

She took a bite of the eggs. They were extremely delicious, light and soft and warm, just the way she liked them.

"This is really good," she said. "How much do I owe you for this magic?"

"That's not the kind of cost I mean," Travers snapped, just as Zoe said, "You don't owe me anything."

"So what's the cost?" Megan kept her gaze on Zoe, deciding to pretend that Travers didn't exist. She used to do this when they were kids, and it always irritated him.

"People who use too much magic age quicker than those who use it sparingly," Zoe said. "I don't even think you cost me an age spot. I wouldn't worry about it."

"Age quicker? I thought you lived forever. Kyle said you were a hundred or more and that the Fates were thousands of years old."

"They are," Zoe said, "and I don't know if they age. But mages age. Just very, very slowly. Once we hit our magic, that is. Until then we age like mortals."

"Mortals." The term sounded so derisive. "If you age—and presumably die—then how come you call us mortals?"

"I didn't call you a mortal," Zoe said, and Travers gave her a sharp look. She ignored it. "It's just a custom. I think mages used to believe they were immortal. But we're not. Several thousand years is the longest I've heard of anyone making it. Most only go for about three or so, max. It's tough to control your usage. I mean it's really tempting to do things—"

"Like fix breakfast." Megan was beginning to understand. And it bothered her. She was also beginning to feel embarrassed about how rude she'd been. "How about having some?"

"Don't mind if I do," Travers said.

"I was asking Zoe," Megan said. "Not you."

"Stop fighting," Kyle said. "Please."

Megan looked at her nephew. His nose was red, which had always been the first sign of tears. He looked miserable.

Now she remembered why she had given up sparring with her brother. It upset her nephew. It had upset him from the moment he was born.

"I'm sorry, Kyle," Megan said. "I didn't mean to upset you."

He nodded, grabbed a slice of bacon off his plate, and slipped it to the dog. Everyone saw the movement, and no one complained about it.

"Have some breakfast, Trav," Megan said. "After all, you're paying for it."

"I have a hunch I'm going to pay for a lot of things today," he said and slipped into a chair.

But he didn't look unhappy. He looked like a man with a plan.

A plan that would probably make Megan unhappy.

"Tell her, Dad," Kyle said, still feeding bacon to the dog.

"Huh?" Travers frowned at his son.

"What you and Zoe just did." Kyle still wasn't looking at him.

"I really don't want to know that," Megan said. Besides, she could guess, considering how well kissed each of them looked.

"You mean in Faerie?" Travers asked.

Whatever he wanted to call it, Megan thought but didn't say.

"No." Kyle finally looked up, his frown matching his father's.

"He knows," Zoe said to Travers.

"Oh." Travers's eyes widened. "I'm never going to get used to the psychic thing. Sometimes, I think it was better when I didn't know."

Kyle's cheeks reddened. He had clearly taken that badly. "I can't shut it off."

"I know," Travers said, and sighed.

"We should really discuss that," Megan said. "If Kyle has truly been able to read adult thoughts since he was preverbal, then he might have some issues—"

"I don't have issues," Kyle said. He grabbed another piece of bacon, and this time, he ate it.

Fang put his paws on Kyle's lap, his nose pointing upward, his little tail pinwheeling. "Dad, just tell her what's going on."

Travers glanced at Megan, then at Kyle. Then back at Megan. "You're right," he said. "I've been meaning to deal with it since I found out about it. It's just been so crazy here."

"In a good way, I hope," Zoe said with a smile.

Megan frowned. What she had seen in the last few hours hadn't been all that good.

"I'm sure you can help him during the next few days," Travers said.

Megan stiffened. She had a hunch she wasn't going to like what was coming next. "The next few days?"

"Zoe and I are getting married, and then we'd like a few days to ourselves. Can you stay? We'd really like to get this over with—"

"Such a romantic," Zoe said with a smile.

"You're the one who said Elvis chapel and black roses," Travers said.

She shrugged. "And I meant it too."

"Mom and Dad won't like that," Megan said.

"They didn't like it when I got married the first time," Travers said.

"And they were right," Megan said.

"What I mean is that they had the big wedding with me and Cheryl, and look what good it got us."

Kyle's cheeks got even redder.

"I think it got you a lot of good," Megan said, looking pointedly at Kyle.

Travers reached over and put a hand on his son's shoulder. "I just meant me and your mom,

Kyle. You know you're the most important person in my life."

Kyle nodded, but his gaze didn't meet his father's. "I would much rather have Zoe for a mom anyway," Kyle said bravely.

Of course he would. Cheryl hadn't been a mother at all. She had had dreams of home and family, but when the realities had hit her—the tiny apartment, the lack of money, the fussy baby—she had fled, leaving Travers to raise Kyle alone. Over time, she had lost touch with them, always claiming it was Travers's fault, although he had been conscientious about letting her know when he moved or about any changes in Kyle's life.

Megan had disliked Cheryl even before Travers had married her. Cheryl had seemed shallow to her, almost emotionless. Megan had somehow known from the moment she had seen her how much Cheryl would hurt her brother.

Megan looked at Zoe. She liked Zoe, even though she wasn't sure she wanted to.

And her brother was clearly head over heels in love with her.

"Kyle," Zoe said, "I'm not sure it's right that we cut you out of the honeymoon. I mean, you're going to be a big part of this relationship, and maybe—"

"Go along on a trip where you're supposed to just have sex and junk?" Kyle wrinkled his nose. "I don't think so."

"I didn't mean that you'd be around for the private parts," Zoe said, digging herself in deeper. "I just meant maybe we should rethink the honeymoon part and take a family trip. It'd be fairer. After all, this is a surprise for you too."

"No, it's not," Kyle said.

"We didn't know until a few minutes ago," Travers said.

"You knew from the minute you met," Kyle said. "You were just scared, that's all."

He sounded contemptuous and oh so much older than he really was. He also sounded like a little boy who was trying to be strong for the adults around him.

Megan's heart went out to him. "Of course I'll stay with Kyle while you two go off and have sex and junk."

Travers glared at her, but Zoe gave her a fond smile.

"And I think I understand why you want to avoid the big wedding. But wouldn't it be nice to wait a few days so that the whole family can come? I think Mom and Dad would like it, and I'm sure Zoe has family who would want to be here."

"No," Zoe said softly, "I don't. But there are a few friends that I wouldn't mind asking."

Travers looked at her with surprise. "I'm sorry. I just assumed that we'd do this fast. You said Elvis chapel."

Zoe smiled at him, and the smile was still fond. Megan would have been ripping his eyes out. Of course, that could be because he was her brother and not the guy she wanted to spend happily ever after with.

"I think fast is good," Zoe said. "But it wouldn't hurt to give family and friends a day or two to get here. Then maybe we could find someone to care for Kyle if Megan can't. I mean, you didn't really ask her. You sort of demanded, and she has a job, right, Megan?"

"Actually." Megan poured herself a cup of coffee. "Not exactly. Not anymore."

"You finally shut down the practice?" Travers asked.

She nodded. She didn't even feel sad about it, even though she should have. She just had a few loose ends to wrap up, and those wouldn't take much effort.

"Good," he said. "Those rich kids weren't your style anyway."

"Those rich kids need good old-fashioned discipline and parents who are home most of the time," Megan said. "They are overindulged and underloved."

Then she realized how harsh she sounded. Everyone stared at her with surprise. Except Travers, who was smiling at her. Fondly.

Where was all this fondness coming from?

"Guess you could say I'm burned out," Megan said.

"I'm a rich kid," Kyle said, "and I'm not overindulged."

"Or underloved," Travers said.

"And you're not taking Ritalin or Prozac or a host of other psychotropic medications for conditions that have nothing to do with medicine and everything to do with convenience," Megan said. "You should have heard some parents when I suggested taking their kid off antidepressants, and figuring out what was really going on. It was like I'd suggested shooting them or something."

"Sounds like they need you," Zoe said softly.

Megan shook her head. "I didn't make a difference. They'd just take the poor child elsewhere."

"That's what you want?" Zoe asked. "To make a difference?"

"Isn't that what we all want?" Megan asked.

"Not in the same way, Aunt Meg," Kyle said. "You want to save the world."

"One child at a time," Travers added. "Mind starting with mine? He's gonna need company for a week, maybe more. How's a week, Zoe?"

She grinned at him. "I think it'll do."

7

"Do you know how impossible it will be to find this woman?" John Little asked over lunch.

Rob sat across from him, two plates loaded with meats and breads and salads spread before him. He had loved buffets since learning about them in Vegas in the 1940s. He'd been one of the first and best customers of Beldon Katleman Midnight Chuckwagon Buffet at the original El Rancho Las Vegas Hotel. Now, of course, buffets cost more than a dollar, they were open for 24 hours instead of the few hours after the last entertainment show, and they had a wide variety of cuisines—not just steak and mashed potatoes and the occasional carrot.

But the food made him nostalgic for the Vegas he had lost, a place of clear skies and such corruption that no one realized honest businessmen could thrive here too.

This buffet, in one of the downtown hotels, looked nothing like that old one. There were plants everywhere that blocked the patrons from each other. The only time you saw someone else was when you got up to stand in line.

"I'm not talking about the woman anymore." Rob had two different kinds of mashed potatoes on his plate: regular (with lumps) and garlic. Maybe he hadn't changed as much as he thought.

John had three plates, all of them covered with various meats—steak, brisket, roast beef, chicken, ham, and several things that Rob couldn't immediately identify.

He wondered if the Atkins Diet meant you could eat as much meat as you wanted all the time or if John was ignoring some of the more important precepts.

"Listen, my friend," John said. "You've been getting more and more morose as the years have gone on, and you were never a happy-go-lucky guy in the first place."

"My friends were called merry." Rob ate a cherry tomato, surprised at its freshness.

"In marked contrast to you. If you'd have had your way, you'd have talked about poverty and Good King John and the evils of government until the wee hours. The only reason we laughed back then was because of Friar Tuck, young Will, and yours truly."

Rob sighed. "I suppose all our success in those days came from that lack of seriousness as well."

"No need to be snide." John ripped the flesh off a chicken leg. In that moment, with that movement, he looked like an old king—the kind Rob had always opposed—not King John the Pretender, however; more like King Henry the Eighth, a gluttonous, ruinous king if there had ever been one.

"Look," Rob said, "we have a lot more important things to do than think about some woman I'm never going to see again."

"I think we need to think about her." John picked up a second chicken leg. The first one, reduced to bone, had gone onto a plate John used only for discards. "If we don't think about her, you'll miss the first chance you've had in decades, maybe centuries. And I, as a good friend and boon companion, can't allow that to happen."

"Why?" Rob asked, not sure if he cared about the answer.

"Why?" John waved the chicken leg as if it were a pointer and he was a professor giving a lecture. "Why? Because I'm the person who spends the most time with you. And it's been a long, long time since someone has challenged you."

"How do you know this woman would challenge me?" Rob found more cherry tomatoes buried on his plate. He set them aside. They all looked as fresh and good as the first one.

"Because," John said, "she already has."

Rob looked up. John's mouth was smeared with barbecue sauce, and the chicken leg was half gone. John grinned at him like a little boy who'd just won a long argument.

"Being in that bubble was not a challenge," Rob said. "It was an accident, I'm sure. I'm sure I built the thing wrong—"

"After doing it for hundreds of years? Not likely." John gnawed the last of the flesh off the chicken bone, then set it on top of the other. If he remained true to form, he would make a small sculpture out of the remains of his food before the meal was done.

"Let it go," Rob said.

John shook his head. "I've been puzzling over this all morning."

"I don't pay you to think about women on company time," Rob said.

"You don't pay me," John said. "We're partners, and I can do whatever I damn well please. I probably should be in Ethiopia right now overseeing the new vaccination program, but I'm tired of watching children get stuck with needles. I need a new focus, and I've decided that's you."

"Lucky me," Rob muttered.

"Look, we have lackeys to oversee all the various giveaways and training programs and medical camps. I've done some of this stuff for nearly five hundred years. A man needs a break now and then."

"So you're focusing on my love life because you're bored," Rob said.

"Your love life?" John's eyebrows went up. "Now that's a phrase I don't think I've ever heard you use. And, oddly enough, I hadn't used that phrase in this context either."

Rob finished the cherry tomatoes. The rest of the lunch looked like overkill. What had he been thinking, getting this much food?

He always felt a little discouraged when he was done with a buffet. So much went to waste when so many people went hungry.

He shook his head.

"And thinking about the poor unfortunates isn't going to get you off the hook either."

Rob raised his head, feeling slightly surprised that John had read him that well.

"Sometimes people need to spread out, do something new, get a different perspective. You're running on fumes, Rob." John grabbed a napkin and wiped off his mouth. "So the woman's a distraction, but she's a good one."

"Who's impossible to find, according to you."

John shrugged. "If we keep our vow and use our magic only for work-related things."

"That's an important rule," Rob said. "If we start behaving like every other mage and use our magic only to help ourselves, then we become no better than—"

"—the kings we used to fight," John finished. "Blah-de-blah-de-blah. When was the last time you used magic for yourself? Hmmm?"

Then he blanched as he remembered the answer. Rob had used his magic to try to save Marian's life, only to get reprimanded by the Fates.

He had been summoned in front of the Fates after working a successful spell to reverse the aging that had caused Marian's organs to fail. The Fates had a temple near Mount Olympus, but the place wasn't real. The sky was too blue, the grass too green, and the temple itself too white.

The women had had an otherworldly beauty as well, but at the time, he had seen it more as an abomination than as a blessing. How could they be so lovely—forever lovely—when his Marian had to wither and decay and die like a summer flower on a fall day?

Each life has a termination point, Mr. Hood, Clotho had said to him that day.

You have no right to violate the workings of destiny, Lachesis had added.

He stood before them, a rough-hewn man who hadn't even known about the Greek gods until he had come back from the Crusades—a campaign that had soured him on following the lead of other men.

He had gained respect for other cultures while away from his own. The other soldiers hadn't. They had tried to destroy them.

We should imprison you, Atropos said.

He felt alarmed at that. They were going to take away Marian's magical good health and then imprison him so that he couldn't spend the last few days of her too short life with her.

If it were not for your history of good works, Clotho said, *and for your love of the unfortunate Marian.*

We are sympathetic to love, Lachesis said.

He let out a small breath, his hands folded in front of him. He felt so tiny, standing there. A single man warring against time and fate and rules he didn't entirely understand.

However, Atropos said, *we cannot allow love to violate the rules of existence.*

Of course they couldn't. Because every beloved of every mage would live forever then. As if that were wrong.

He wasn't sure how that was wrong.

Much as we would like to, Clotho said with more gentleness than was necessary.

They hadn't wooed him, exactly, but he felt a little better. At least he would be with Marian at the end.

Besides, Lachesis said, *you have yet to find your soulmate.*

What? he snapped. *Marian is my soulmate. You know that. All of England knows that. I love her more than life itself.*

And therein lies your problem, Atropos said. *You have given too much too early.*

No, I haven't, he said.

You have a long life ahead of you, Clotho said.

One that will be lonely if you are not careful, Lachesis said.

Of course it will be lonely, he said. *You won't let Marian live.*

She cannot. She has lived her life, Atropos said.

You knew she was mortal when you met her, Clotho said.

I thought I was mortal when I met her, Rob cried.

Then you should not have left her to fight in those silly wars, Lachesis said.

Those silly wars were where I discovered that I couldn't die, Rob said. He had learned, just outside Jerusalem, exactly what his powers were and how deadly they could be. He had turned away from them then; he'd never been a man to use his abilities to harm others.

War had been the exact wrong thing for him— the greatest mistake of his life.

He hadn't needed these Fates to remind him of that, and all the lost years, the years away from his beloved.

You might miss your love altogether if you do not open your eyes, Atropos said.

It was hard for him to focus on them. The sadness that he thought he had put aside when he had tried to save Marian's life was beginning to overwhelm him.

If you do not see how like follows like, Clotho said.

If you do not listen to the prophecy, Lachesis said.

You have never asked us your birth prophecy. It's time you hear it. Atropos looked mysterious and strong, standing against the pillar.

You shall regain your true self, Clotho said.

And save the world for true love, Lachesis said.

If only you recognize that true love has many lives, Atropos said.

You denied me that life, Rob snapped. He could take no more. He clapped his hands together, casting a powerful spell that flung him away from the Fates and their so-called justice.

Later, he found out through Little John that the Fates had nearly imprisoned him after that insolence. Only John's argument, and Rob's obvious grief, prevented it.

"I didn't mean that," John was saying. "I didn't mean to bring up Marian again. Really. I meant besides then. You know, in the past 800 years."

Rob must have had an expression then, something that told his best friend he had been reliving the prelude to the worst moment of his life.

Even now, he could barely think of that day, holding the frail shell of the woman he'd loved as she died in his arms and knowing that he had the power to save her—and everything he would do, everything he would try—would be reversed by those evil Fates.

"It's all right," Rob said, shoving his plate away. The food no longer seemed appealing. "I know what you meant."

The good humor was gone from John's face. He finally seemed to understand why Rob wasn't going to use his magic for something as trivial as finding an attractive woman.

If he hadn't been able to use that magic for something crucial, he wasn't going to waste it on a whim.

"I just think it's important, you know?" John said. "I think you had a sign last night, and I think you need to act on it."

"A sign from the Fates?" Rob asked with more than a touch of bitterness.

John shrugged.

"I did what they wanted one too many times," Rob said. "I don't care about their signs."

John sighed. "Maybe you should," he said, almost to himself. "Maybe you should."

8

Megan spent most of the morning on the phone, making sure that she truly had tied up all of her loose ends. She used the phone in her suite—which Travers swore she deserved (what had Zoe done to him, anyway? Whatever it was, Megan was starting to like it)—and then she returned to Travers's for lunch with Kyle.

She and Kyle finished first and went to the couch while Zoe and Travers discussed wedding dates.

"Dad's gonna leave soon," Kyle whispered to her. "You wanna do something fun?"

"Like what?" she asked, not questioning Kyle's knowledge of his father's future plans.

"*Star Trek Experience,* maybe?"

"You've already seen that," his father said from across the room.

"With the Fates. It wasn't the same. They really weren't into *Star Trek.*" Kyle looked at his dad as he said this last. "Aunt Meg loves *Star Trek.*"

"Classic," Megan said. She had a thing for the

young William Shatner that none of her friends ever understood.

"I'm saying no on a repeat of the *Star Trek Experience,*" Travers said. "How about something wholesome? There's got to be some museums around here."

"In Vegas?" Megan asked.

"There's a neon place," Kyle said.

"Not to mention the Elvis-A-Rama and the Liberace Museum." Zoe came in from the kitchen, munching on a candy bar.

Megan suppressed a sigh. How did women like that stay so slim when they ate so poorly?

"I don't think either of those are for Kyle either," Zoe continued. "But there's a children's museum that's across the street from the Natural History Museum."

Kyle blatted a bronx cheer. Megan had to work to suppress a smile. She'd had the same reaction——mentally, at least.

"We can find something to do, can't we, boyo?" she said. "If nothing else, we can go to the water park I saw."

"No," Travers said. "The last time Kyle went there, he got a hideous sunburn."

Megan looked at the boy. His skin was fine, so it couldn't have been on this trip. "The last time? You've brought Kyle to Vegas before?"

Zoe and Travers exchanged a look. "Long story," Travers said after a minute.

"And it wasn't my fault," Kyle said. "The Fates didn't have any sunscreen."

"You've spent a lot of time with those women,"

Megan said, trying to keep the disapproval from her voice.

Kyle shrugged. "I like them, even if they don't know much about *Star Trek.*"

"They shouldn't bother you too much," Travers said. "They have some business of their own to take care of."

"With the Faeries," Megan said, keeping her tone flat.

"Yeah." Zoe finished the last of the candy bar. "Now that we found the wheel for them."

Zoe and Travers were serious. Megan resisted the urge to shake her head. She had accepted the psychic part—she was aware of the studies conducted in the 1970s that showed psychic powers existed (even if all her professors had debunked those studies)—and she had been around Kyle for ten years. She liked the psychic explanation a lot better than the intuitive one. If the kid had been as intuitive as she had given him credit for, then he would have to have been almost superhuman.

She smiled to herself. For some reason, she didn't think that psychics were superhuman but that intuitive people were. That was one for her own shrink to figure out.

"Megan," Travers said, putting a hand on her shoulder. She started. She hadn't heard him approach. "We're going to get a marriage license. It shouldn't take long, but I'm leaving Kyle with you, if you don't mind."

"That's what I'm here for," she said a little too brightly. "And you can take as much time as you need. Maybe a little . . . alone time . . . would be appropriate?"

Travers grinned at Zoe, who grinned back.

"We've been so busy saving the world that we really haven't had time for ourselves," Zoe said, and once again, there was no real irony in her voice.

"We might take you up on that," Travers said.

"Just not here, please." Kyle put his hands over his ears. He was blushing furiously. "I don't want to think about that stuff."

Travers laughed. "Promise, kiddo. I don't want you thinking about that stuff ever, although I suppose I won't be able to stop you some day."

"Stop now!" Kyle said, his eyes squinched shut.

Megan shook her head.

Travers kissed Kyle on the crown of his head, then smoothed the hair over the kiss. "See you soon, kid."

Kyle nodded.

Zoe waved at them both, and then she and Travers almost skipped out the door.

"You can put your hands down now," Megan said.

"Not yet," Kyle said tightly. He brought his knees up to his chest and wrapped himself into a ball. "They're broadcasting from the hallway."

Megan put her arm around her nephew and pulled him close. "I'm so sorry I never realized what was going on."

He relaxed against her. "It's okay," he said after a moment. "You know now."

"Yeah." And it baffled her. How had Kyle grown up to be so normal with everyone else's thoughts in his head? How had he been able to tell the difference between himself and other people?

"Great-Aunt Eugenia taught me," Kyle said.

"What?"

He brought his arms down and slid his legs to one side, leaning hard on Megan.

"Great-Aunt Eugenia. She came to visit when I was really little, and she showed me how to keep private inside my own head if I had to."

Megan blinked. Something about this sounded familiar. She'd talked with Great-Aunt Eugenia too about privacy. Great-Aunt Eugenia had been such an outrageous woman, with her flowing clothes, her booming voice, and her strong opinions, that Megan had never been sure whether the conversation had happened or if she had only imagined it.

At that moment, the door to the suite banged open.

The three women who called themselves Fates poured into the room.

"We need a driver," Clotho said. She was wearing tight blue jeans, a pink blouse, and high-heeled sandals. Her make-up was perfect, just light enough to kiss her skin, and her hair seemed even blonder than it had the day before. She resembled nothing more than a life-sized Barbie doll.

"Quickly!" Lachesis said. The cream-colored blouse she wore untucked over a pair of stone-washed jeans gave her voluptuousness a studied air.

"We can't miss this opportunity!" Atropos said. Her tight black capri pants, white blouse, and slippers made her seem like an exotic version of Mary Tyler Moore from the *Dick Van Dyke* show.

"The front desk will get you a cab," Megan said. She wasn't going to get sucked into the vortex these women created. They'd had enough influence on her family.

"Aunt Megan, you got a car," Kyle said.

"And we wouldn't all fit in it," Megan said. "It's a Mini Cooper."

"We can squeeze," Clotho said. "We've done such things before."

"Please," Lachesis said. "We only have an hour."

"They'll get lost," Kyle said.

"No one gets lost in a cab," Megan said. "The driver always knows where he is."

That wasn't exactly true; she'd had a driver in New York when she had been there for a conference who hadn't known where Brooklyn was. But that was different. Vegas wasn't that hard to learn.

"We'll only be a phone call away if you need help," Megan added.

"We need help now," Atropos said.

"John Little says he'll fit us in," Clotho said.

"He's doing us a favor," Lachesis said.

"John Little." They spoke the name as if Megan should know it. "And I should care about this why?"

"Because true love is at stake," Atropos said. "You should always care when love is at stake."

Kyle looked up at her. "Aunt Meg, they're not kidding."

"I know," Megan said. "But I don't have to share the delusion."

"Please, they will get lost. They're pretty naïve about some things." Kyle batted those baby blues. Someday, some woman was going to get lost in those eyes. "For me?"

Megan was already lost. She'd been lost since she'd held him as a newborn, all red and wrinkly and warm.

She sighed. "Is this how your dad got roped in?"

Kyle grinned. "He didn't mind."

"I remember him at Viv's wedding," Megan said. "He minded."

"Oh, thank you." Clotho clapped her hands together. "We really do need an escort at times."

"Kyle tries, but he's still a tad young," Lachesis said.

Megan stood. She smoothed her hair, feeling very out of place next to these beautiful women. All her insecurities were back, every last one of them. Was it part of the stress she'd been feeling? Or the fact that she was leaving her practice without knowing what she was going to do next?

"Anyone want to tell me where we're going?" she asked.

Atropos smiled widely. "To hire Robin Hood," she said brightly. "We need him to steal our wheel."

9

John Little skulked outside the main doors of the building, trying to be as inconspicuous as possible. It was hard for a man of his bulk to be inconspicuous—people looked at him as they walked by almost as if they expected him to mug them.

One of Rob's many corporations had owned the building—or the lot it stood on—since the 1930s. Hotels had grown up around it, as had casinos, but most were shabby now. A number of them had been rebuilt, remodeled, or torn down, then replaced with other hotels and casinos.

The transformation of this neighborhood had been nothing short of miraculous. Of course, John thought most of Vegas was miraculous. He was still used to England where some of the buildings he had visited in his youth (over 800 years ago) were still standing.

Vegas hadn't been around much more than a hundred years, and in that time, it had gone through more transformation than London had in all of its centuries.

He never told Rob that he preferred Vegas. Rob liked London and the past. John still liked the fast-moving future, and he hoped he would never stop liking it.

Except he could do without the heat. Sweat ran down his face the moment he left the air-conditioning. If he'd have known the women would be late, he would have brought out a bottle of water.

He was waiting for the Fates, and for the life of him, he couldn't understand why they hadn't just popped in. He had been a bit stunned that they had called him—who knew that those three women understood how to operate a phone, let alone put it on conference call so that they could continue their wacky one-two-three way of speaking?

He had been a bit freaked out when he had taken the call in his office, and he would have thought it was all a hoax, except that no one could mimic those voices or that bizarre way they talked.

They had asked him for help, and he felt that he owed them. He had bargained with them for Rob all those years ago, and they had given in. They had never asked for anything else in return.

Until now.

All they wanted, they had said, was a meeting with Rob. They knew feelings were still sore (their words), so they had come to John to have him set up the meeting.

He hadn't set up anything. He had just told them to get here pronto. Then he'd take them to Rob.

But they hadn't gotten here pronto. Now it was half-past pronto, and they still hadn't arrived.

And he was getting really nervous. Had they

moved him aside so that they would have some kind of weird access to Rob without John around? And if that were the case, why hadn't they simply popped Rob out of his office and taken him to their rather stately abode near Mount Olympus?

John wiped the sweat off his forehead and shifted his folded lightweight suitcoat to the other arm. He was about to go back inside to page Rob and make sure he was still in his office when a Mini Cooper pulled up to the curb.

A beautiful redhead leaned out and asked if this was the address of Chapeau Enterprises.

"Yeah," John said, wondering if this was part of the trick.

"Great. Can I park here?" she asked.

He pointed to the parking garage beneath a nearby building, and she waved merrily at him, thanking him as she drove away. He squinted at the car. It was filled to brimming, like a clown car. He saw too many heads for that tiny interior.

Then the car disappeared into the parking garage, and he focused his attention back on the street.

Rob would want to know where he had been and what he had been doing. John wasn't sure he wanted to fess up to talking to the Fates, let alone setting up an appointment with them. He'd been Rob's best friend, confidant, and occasional head-knocker for centuries now, ever since they had met near Sherwood Forest.

Those years had been defining ones: they had lived an adventure, not realizing they had magical powers, and they had lived by their principles, something they lost briefly during the Crusades and something Rob had struggled to maintain ever since.

John liked the life they were living now—they were operating on a grand scale compared with the Forest—but he also knew that his friend was desperately unhappy. The unhappiness had gotten worse over time as Rob had realized how alone he was.

He had always believed that no one could substitute for Marian, and John agreed. Marian had been an original, just like all the other women John had met had been. But Marian had been suited to Robin, and he hadn't given any other woman a chance.

Not in 800 years. Every hundred or so, John tried to change Rob's attitude.

So far, he hadn't been successful, but that didn't make him stop trying.

The redhead came out of the stairwell, her arm around the shoulders of a pudgy young boy. The boy had intelligent eyes and an air of magic around him that was so strong, John felt it like a slap.

Kids shouldn't have that much power. It was wrong. It wasn't the way the world worked—or at least the world that John understood.

He was so focused on the kid that for a moment, he didn't see the three women trailing behind them.

A blond, a brunette, and a redhead. They looked so ordinary that at first, he didn't recognize them. Then they grinned at each other, in unison, and he knew who they were.

The Fates.

Only they looked like half of themselves—all the power and energy that they'd always carried had disappeared. They seemed almost . . . normal.

He shook that thought out of his head as the other redhead—the one with the kid—came up to him. She was built the way women should be built: sturdy, buxom, and broad, a good handful for a man who was tired of the scrawny things that passed themselves off as modern women.

The redhead said, "Sorry to bother you again. Chapeau Enterprises is inside?"

Her voice was rich and beautiful. This one had an incredible life force, and what was most charming about her was that she didn't know it.

"Yeah," he said. "It's—"

And then the Fates surrounded him, yammering all at once. The redhead stood back, looking amused. The boy stayed in the middle of it all, and it wasn't until the Fates finished speaking (they were greeting John, which he was trying to ignore), that the boy actually spoke.

"You know Robin Hood?"

He sounded like a star-struck fan. John looked at the Fates in great surprise. Didn't they know better than to talk like that? No one was supposed to know mages's real identities. Even though Robin Hood was not Rob's real name, it was close enough to get everyone in trouble.

"What's going on here?" John asked.

Clotho slipped her arm through his. It startled him. He had never been touched by a Fate before.

"We need Robin to do us a small favor," she said.

"A teensy-tiny favor," Lachesis said, moving a little too close.

"An itty-bitty favor," Atropos said, flanking him on the other side.

John was surrounded, and he didn't want to be. He was too polite—damn his chivalric upbringing—to shove women aside, much as he wanted too.

Besides, these three terrified him more than almost anyone else he had ever met.

"I don't think Rob is in a favorable mood," John said.

"Nonetheless," Clotho said.

"We do need to see him," Lachesis said.

"Then why not pop in and visit him yourselves?" John asked.

Atropos sighed. "It's so very complicated."

"Take us to him, would you, John?" Clotho asked, and now he wanted to sigh. But he didn't.

Instead, he did what they asked—and hoped he would survive the consequences.

10

The Mini Cooper caught his attention.

Rob stood at the window with his hands clasped behind his back. He had felt the weird little car before he had seen it, drawn to the window as if he were going to see a party.

And then the car had slowed and disappeared under an awning as it pulled up to the curb. For a brief moment—an hallucinatory moment—Rob thought he had seen that gorgeous woman from the night before, but of course, he hadn't.

That was the effect of thinking about her all night and talking to John about her all day.

Rob moved away from the window and sat in his chair, unable to look at the stock prices continually changing on his computer screen or to think about anything that had to do with work. Even after eight hundred years, thinking about another woman felt like he was betraying Marian.

Maybe John was right. Maybe Rob was clinging too hard to the past. He certainly couldn't change it.

Imagine what the Fates would do to him if he tried.

At that moment, his door burst open. John hurried in and tried to shove the door closed behind him. A slender female arm flailed against the wall as if its owner were trying to force the door open.

"Um, Rob," John said, his face turning red from the effort of holding the door closed. "It's not my fault."

Rob frowned. He hadn't seen John like this in decades. His face was flushed and sweat covered, his eyes wild, and his shirt drenched. He'd lost his suitcoat somewhere, and he looked almost feral.

"Should I call security?" Rob asked.

"No!" John sounded panicked. "I just want you to assure me that you won't blame me when—"

The door was shoved open the rest of the way, and women piled into Rob's office. But Rob wasn't looking at them. In the middle of the reception area, a small boy stood, and next to him was that woman.

The beauty.

He stood and started toward her. She hadn't noticed him. Instead, she was holding the boy's shoulders as if she was keeping him from something, and she was watching the scene before her with something like horror.

Then the door slammed closed.

"Really," John said again, "I'm sorry."

And with that, he pulled the door open, let himself out, and slammed the door shut again.

Rob blinked twice, trying to figure out what had happened. He had been looking at the beauty (was she real?) and then the door slammed, John left, and three women stood before him.

Three very familiar women.

Three very powerful women.

The Fates.

Rob had vowed he would never see them again.

"Get the hell out of my office!" he snapped.

"Robin," Clotho said, "just hear us out."

She did seem unusually tiny—he remembered these women as being larger than the mountains themselves—and she looked a little too ordinary in her pink blouse and tight blue jeans.

"The circumstances of our visit are quite unusual," Lachesis said.

She was a redhead. He had known that, but he hadn't focused on it, not really. And she was a well-proportioned redhead who knew how to dress. That cream-colored blouse did wonders for her figure.

But she wasn't the redhead he was looking for. That redhead had been outside the office.

Hadn't she?

"We want you to listen before you jump to any conclusions," Atropos said.

She seemed tiny too, and a lot more exotic than he remembered, with the heavy, dark eyebrows and black-black hair that was rare in this part of America.

"I don't want any of you in here," he said. "I want you out this minute. I don't care what you do to me. You can imprison me for the rest of my life, just get the hell out of my face."

"We know you're angry," Clotho said. "But—"

"Anger doesn't begin to cover it." He couldn't

remain in the same room with these women. He pushed past them, afraid he was going to be turned into a toad as he did, and grabbed the door.

Someone was holding it closed.

Damn Little John.

"We asked him to spell the door," Lachesis said.

"We knew you'd be difficult," Atropos said.

"We know you've never understood our position on the mortality of mortals," Clotho said.

"Or on the necessity of death," Lachesis said.

"But we believe we can overcome that little difference," Atropos said.

"And make an agreement that suits us all," Clotho said.

Rob focused on them again, mostly because he had no choice. "Little difference?" he asked. *"Little* difference? You let the only woman I've ever loved die."

"We didn't let anything," Lachesis said. "We just had to stop you from making a horrible mistake."

"Horrible mistake." His hands clenched. "I've seen so much death over the years, and I've never understood it. We have the power to reverse it, and you always get in the way."

"If we still had magic, then we'd show you why this is necessary," Atropos said. "We've learned a lot in the past few months."

"Months?" he repeated.

"Yes. We have learned how difficult it is to understand things you've never experienced," Clotho said.

"I've experienced more death than I ever wanted to," Rob said.

"That's not what we mean," Lachesis said. "We

mean a lack of death. It's happened before. Everything gets out of whack."

"In fact," Atropos said, "if I remember right, you lived through one of the back-in-whack moments. That plague?"

"The Black Plague?" His head was spinning. He was so angry. He hadn't been this angry in centuries.

"Yes. Too many mortals were surreptitiously saved by mages, and then what did we have? Necrotic tissue that had to escape somewhere, creating pustules . . ."

He didn't need this discussion. He didn't need these three creepy, controlling women in his office, ruining his day. And no matter what John said, it was his fault.

John knew how Rob felt about these three.

". . . hideous boils," Lachesis was saying, ". . . which wasn't as bad as the first time. The first time, an entire city was destroyed just to maintain the balance."

"That wasn't the first time," Atropos said. "The first time was before our time."

Rob focused back into the conversation. Really focused. And frowned.

The Fates were disagreeing with each other. They never did that. They always finished each other's sentences.

What had Atropos said earlier? *If we still had magic . . .*

"You don't have magic any more?" he asked, interrupting an argument of Biblical proportions.

"That's why we're here," Clotho said.

"We need your help," Lachesis said.

"Everything we care about is at stake," Atropos said.

"How very ironic," Rob said. "I remember having the same discussion with you eight hundred years ago."

The women bit their lower lips in unison. Their eyes grew wide.

"And let me tell you what you told me. I'm not going to help you. I don't care what's at stake."

Then he clapped his hands together and used his magic to get out of the room.

II

Robin Hood. A big, bulky man with a classically English face named John Little. In the middle of downtown Las Vegas. With the Greek Fates and one psychic child.

Megan wrapped her arms around Kyle's chest and held him against her. They stood in the reception area of Chapeau Enterprises, whatever that was, and watched as the Fates made fools of themselves trying to get into the door that Little John or John Little or whatever he was called was trying to keep closed.

She was becoming more and more convinced that the Fates belonged to some very bad Vegas lounge act and that John Little or Little John or whoever he was fronted for some other organization, one that hired entertainers.

Although for the life of her, she couldn't figure out how the Robin Hood of medieval legend and the Greek Fates had hooked up in the first place.

The Fates managed to shove the door open and get inside.

She held Kyle tighter. She could feel him strain against her. He wanted to go in there too, almost as if this concerned him.

It did not. None of it did.

He was a good boy, and she really believed the psychic child bit, she really did.

But the existence of the real Robin Hood and the Greek Fates was too much for her.

Besides, what was Robin Hood doing in a nice office building in Vegas? Planning to rob every casino in sight? They were what passed for the rich these days.

More likely, some wag had decided to use the legend of Robin Hood to get the important parts exactly backward. He was probably opening a casino that would rob from the poor to give to the rich.

After all, the slots were called one-armed bandits. She let out a small growl just as John Little slipped outside the door. He rubbed his hands over the edges of the door, and a light glowed around the frame.

Then he pulled away, put his face in his hands, and muttered, "May God forgive me."

"For what?" Megan asked.

He looked up as if he had forgotten all about her. He blinked once, then sighed. "Rob really doesn't like those women."

"I don't blame him," Megan said.

"They're nice." Kyle sounded defensive.

"I'm sure they are, kid," John Little said, "but they've been hellacious on Rob over the years."

Megan wasn't sure Travers would approve of the word "hellacious." She wasn't sure he would approve of them being here.

She wasn't sure if he would approve of this place with its myriad secretaries, blond wood, and air of wealth.

"You want to tell me what's going on here?" she asked.

"You want to tell me how you got tied up with the Fates?" The door shuddered slightly. John Little glanced at it, then put his hands on his hips, and looked at her. "Is it because the kid—what is your name, son?"

"Kyle," Kyle said about as sullenly as a boy could say his own name.

"Young Kyle there has enough magic for you, me, and the entire building combined, or he will when he comes into it. What're you now, youngling? Psychic?"

"Yeah." Kyle leaned against Megan.

She frowned. Was everyone in this city crazy? Or had she gone into an alternate world when she saw that man with the falcon last night?

Maybe she was dreaming and still driving. Maybe she was dreaming about being psychic and hoping she would wake up before she crashed into anything. Maybe she was about to die—

"You're awake, Aunt Megan." Kyle sounded tired. "And everybody knows about the magic because everybody we've seen has a little bit. It's because of the Fates. If you just went to one of the casinos, no one'd be talking about magic at all."

Megan wasn't sure she could get used to Kyle repeating her thoughts out loud.

John Little frowned at Kyle, his mouth slightly open. Then he looked up at Megan. "You're new to all this?"

She nodded wearily.

"And you're ferrying the Fates around?"

She was about to ask why that was a problem when the air around John Little shimmered. For a moment, it looked like a heat mirage in the desert or like a pool of particularly leaden water. And then the image coalesced into her falconer.

Only he wasn't wearing medieval hunting clothes. He wore a bespoke suit that fit him so perfectly it looked like he'd been sewn into it. The brown material matched the brown of his eyes. Only his hair, which was still tied back with a strip of leather, looked the same.

He was even more handsome up close—or he would have been if he weren't scowling worse than she'd ever seen anyone scowl. He didn't seem to see her at all. He whirled slightly and pointed at John Little.

"You let them into my office."

"I had no choice."

"They say they don't have magic anymore."

"I had no choice."

"I don't want them around me."

Kyle cleared his throat.

The man turned, his cheeks slightly ruddy—maybe from yelling at John Little—and his brown eyes widened. He stared at Megan as if he'd seen her before.

As if he'd seen her before and remembered her vividly.

As if she were the only woman on the entire planet.

The only person on the entire planet.

"You," he whispered.

"They really have lost their magic," Kyle said. "Honest. And that's my Aunt Megan. She *is* real."

Megan felt her cheeks flare so that their redness probably matched her hair. His cheeks had gone pale in the few seconds he had stared at her.

"You really are real," he said.

"I just told you she was," Kyle said.

But the man didn't seem to hear Kyle. He took half a step toward her and stopped.

"This is the bubble woman?" John Little asked. "She's perfect."

Megan felt her cheeks heat even more. Bubble woman? What were they talking about?

Behind them, the door banged against its frame but didn't open. The man blinked, frowned, looked at her, looked at the door, and then tilted his head.

"You know the Fates?" he asked.

"She brought them here," John Little said.

"Really?" the man said.

"I asked her too." Kyle sounded nervous. What was with this guy? How come he was upsetting her nephew?

"You did?" the man asked. "Are you her son?"

"Nephew," Kyle said. "I *told* you that. You have to start paying attention."

He sounded so much like a miniature Travers that Megan let out a small laugh. Which seemed to break the spell she was under.

"What is this all about?" she asked the man, just like she had asked John Little.

"Betrayal," the man said, "and the fulfillment of a debt."

12

Rob regretted those words the moment he said them. He didn't know this woman. It didn't matter that she was the most beautiful creature he had ever seen (and then he felt a momentary pang of guilt: *Sorry, Marian*). It didn't matter that she left him feeling only 250 years old.

All that mattered was getting the Fates out of his office and getting his life back in order.

"They want you to settle a debt?" asked the World's Most Beautiful Woman—whose name was, apparently, Megan. (A good old-fashioned name for a woman of a type that should never have gone out of fashion.)

"No," he said. "They apparently didn't realize I had a debt to settle with them."

"Because they betrayed you."

"Because they betrayed my wife!"

Megan took a slight step backward, pulling the young boy with her. The boy looked like the movement choked him slightly, then she loosened her grip on him as if she had known that too.

"You can't lust after my Aunt Megan if you have a wife." The boy looked like a fierce warrior himself, albeit of the modern kind—most of his battles probably happened on a computer rather than on the battlefield.

"I don't lust after . . ." Rob let his voice trail off when he saw Megan's face. She had the kind of face that carried every emotion she felt, and at the moment, she felt disappointment. "I mean, I don't have a wife. Anymore. She died."

"Oh," the boy said, and bowed his head. "I didn't know."

The last three words he said with surprise. Apparently, he had never met anyone who could block a psychic, even though it was easy, particularly with a young one.

Although maybe not as easy as it seemed. The boy had, after all, caught Rob's attraction to that woman from across the room.

"They betrayed your wife?" Megan asked with that sexy, throaty voice of hers.

His gaze met hers. She had such stunning green eyes—the color was as deep as a perfect emerald—but more than that, he could see so deep inside her that it was as if he could see her very soul.

He wanted to break eye contact but couldn't. He also couldn't lie to her. He wanted her to know.

So he settled on, "It's a long story."

She gave him a small smile as if she had heard that before and knew it for the evasion it was.

The door rattled again.

"We have to do something about them," John said. "You can't just leave them in there, Rob."

"Have security escort them off the premises."

"Rob!" John's entire face became the picture of shock. "Do you know what's going on?"

"No," he said, "and I don't particularly care to."

"Zeus is making a power play."

"So?" Rob asked, then mentally kicked himself. He really didn't want to know.

"He's trying to get rid of true love."

"So they say, right? Those lying Fates?"

"They're not lying." The boy shook off his aunt. "My dad's been fighting for them all along. My Dad and my Aunt Viv and my Uncle Dex. And now the Fates say they need you. So you should help them."

"I should, huh?" Rob asked. He'd never been comfortable around children, especially precocious ones.

"Yeah, you should."

Megan reached for her nephew, but he slipped away from her, walked up to Robin, and mimicked his posture, putting his hands on his hips and standing with his legs slightly apart.

"I never took Robin Hood for a coward," the boy said.

John gasped.

"Kyle!" Megan said, apparently in an attempt to admonish the boy.

But Rob just narrowed his eyes, feeling the anger flare. The boy wanted him to get angry. The boy was psychic, and knew how to make him angry, so Rob's shields weren't working as well as he thought.

Still, he loathed it when someone called him a

coward, particularly someone who didn't know his history.

Although this little boy had just called him Robin Hood. So the boy *did* know, and the boy still used the word.

"I'm not a coward," Rob said.

"You are too," the boy said.

"Because I won't help three women who let my wife die? You have a lot of living to do, boy, before you understand that." Rob crossed his arms and rocked back on his heels. "In fact, I hope you never do understand it."

"They were just following the rules!" the boy said.

"Yeah, I've followed rules," Rob said. "Just because the rules exist doesn't make them right."

"The Fates hurt your wife?" Megan asked.

"Eight hundred years ago, Aunt Meg," the boy said with deep sarcasm.

The anger Rob had only barely controlled flared again. What did that child know about pain, anyway?

"So you've told everyone that you're Robin Hood?" Megan asked.

"I haven't told anyone," Rob said. "You people have been calling me that."

"Please." Megan shook her head slightly. "Give me a little respect. This is Chapeau Enterprises, and 'chapeau' means hood or hat in French. Your friend is named Little John. I wouldn't be surprised if you called your secretary Maid Marian—"

"That's enough!" Rob was shouting before he realized he had opened his mouth. He couldn't take this lack of respect anymore. "Get them out of here, John, or I will."

"They came with the Fates," John said, unfazed by Rob's anger. John had seen it too many times before. "If you let the Fates out of your office, I'm sure everyone will leave happily."

They wouldn't, of course. The Fates wanted something from him, and the woman, with her blazing green eyes, hadn't stepped back at all. She seemed as angry as he felt.

"You have no right to yell at me or Kyle," she said. "You don't know us. We're not here to bother you. I drove the Fates here to discuss their contract dispute with you. I was only doing it as a favor to Kyle. I hadn't expected to walk into a place filled with angry people and a lot of blame. Had that been the case, I wouldn't have brought along a sensitive ten-year-old—"

"Aunt Meg!" The boy, Kyle, rolled his eyes in obvious embarrassment.

"—and I wouldn't have brought the Fates. They're unusual women, and I'm not sure if I like them, but they don't need this abuse."

She was beautiful when she was mad. She spoke softly, which people rarely did when they were angry, and the emotion flooded her creamy skin with color that accented the auburn of her hair. Those green eyes flared and held him like he hadn't been held in a long time.

Normally, this kind of anger calmed him down— he liked being the reasonable one in the room— but he wasn't feeling reasonable.

"Abuse?" he said softly.

"Abuse." She crossed her arms. "You shout and

bluster as if you control the very world. When, in fact, all you've done is lock three helpless, naïve women in your office and somehow got out on your own and then shouted at a little boy you've never met before. If that's not abuse, then you're bordering on it."

He stared at her. She was young, younger than she seemed at first glance. Clearly a product of this country and the last thirty years.

"Lady," he said as gently as he could, considering how angry he still was. "When I was a boy, beatings were common, women were little more than property, and if one of your betters killed your brother, you had no recourse at all. I've been a soldier in one of the bloodiest, most senseless conflicts in all of history. I've seen more abuse than you can even imagine."

She raised her chin at him, that fine face filled with skepticism. John had moved away so that he clearly wasn't part of the discussion. Kyle had moved to the other side of the room, almost as if he couldn't stand to be between Rob and Megan.

"Locking three—in your words—helpless and naïve women in my office isn't abuse. It's reasonable, considering how badly I'd like to slap all three of them. And raising my voice isn't abuse either. It's justified when my best friend lets in the three women who hurt me the most because they want a favor!"

Her eyebrows had risen so high in her forehead that she looked comical. But her expression told him she found nothing funny about the moment.

"I don't care how you were raised," she said in

that horrible reasonable tone. "Your parents were obviously wrong, and whatever country you were in was barbaric. But that doesn't mean you can treat people here like this. I demand that you unlock the door and let those women out."

"Or?" Rob asked.

"Or what?" Megan said.

"What will you do?"

"I'll call the police," she said.

He laughed. "What will they do? Arrest me for locking women in my office?"

"I'll tell them that you threatened those women, which you did, and that you raised your voice at my nephew and that I was worried for his safety."

"Then why not get him out of here?" Rob asked.

"Because I brought those women," Megan said. "I'm responsible for them. Let them out!"

"All right," he said. "On one condition."

She was breathing hard. He tried not to look at her breasts. They were as perfect as she was, moving up and down with each deep, angry breath.

He hadn't been this attracted to any woman in a long, long time.

"What condition?" she snapped.

"Have dinner with me." The words came out before he realized what he was going to say. That was the second time he'd done that in this conversation. Whatever had he been thinking?

Of course, he hadn't been thinking. That was the problem.

"You think you can manipulate me into having dinner with you? You're delusional."

"You want those women, don't you?" Rob asked.

Her mouth opened slightly. Then it closed. She looked at young Kyle, whose eyes seemed extra wide behind his thick glasses.

"I don't even like those women," she said.

"You don't like me either," he said. "So it seems like an even trade to me."

"That's not entirely true," Kyle said. "I mean—"

"Kyle!" Her voice was harsh, although she hadn't raised it.

The boy closed his mouth too and leaned against the wall. But Rob didn't need to hear any more. The boy was psychic, and she was undefended. She might not like Rob, but she was intrigued by him.

"I'm not sure you're nice," Kyle said to him.

Rob looked at the boy.

"I always thought Robin Hood was nice."

Rob chuckled. "I fought a sheriff and killed his men, all in the name of a cause. I was a soldier after that. They called me a man's man. And you thought I was nice? Who cleaned up the legends you've been reading?"

The boy dropped his chin. "Zoe says you're nice."

"Zoe?" Rob only knew one Zoe—at least, only one Zoe who was still alive. "You know Zoe Sinclair?"

"She's marrying my dad."

"Zoe's getting married?" Rob couldn't believe it. He hadn't thought of Zoe as the marrying type.

"To my dad," the boy said again. "She thinks you're nice too. In fact, she thought it was a good idea for the Fates to see you."

"*Zoe* sent them?"

"She found their spinning wheel," the boy said. "They want you to steal it."

Rob looked at John, who shrugged sheepishly. "The famous wheel? The one on which they spun life and death? The one they told me about but never showed me?"

"They said it was stolen three thousand years ago," John said. "But they're not very good with time."

"This fantasy is convincing you to help these women?" Megan asked. "What has my brother stumbled into here?"

Rob looked at her. She really didn't know.

"Let me show you," he said and snapped his fingers.

13

She wasn't standing in the reception area of an office building anymore. Instead, she wobbled slightly on stone-covered grass. The air smelled of the sea. Before her, cliffs rose, their walls blindingly white in the hot sun.

The sky was as blue as Kyle's eyes, and the ocean matched it. But Kyle wasn't anywhere around, and neither was John Little or Little John or whatever he was called.

Instead, Robin Hood stood beside her, watching her with a bemused expression on his face.

He looked out of place here, in that beautiful suit, with his brown hair and his pale, pale skin. His eyes twinkled, though. She'd never seen his eyes twinkle. That made him seem almost human.

The first time she'd met him, he'd looked like a fantasy man. This afternoon, he'd been a nightmare.

And now, his eyes were twinkling—on this rock-strewn hillside, with an ocean pounding hundreds of feet below.

"What's going on?" she asked. She'd been asking that too much in the last few days.

"Do you like ozo?" he asked.

"What?"

"Or don't you drink?"

She shook her head.

He nodded toward a white building she hadn't seen until now. It was hidden against the upper part of the cliff face. "They serve a mean ozo. But we can go somewhere else if you like."

Somewhere else? Where were they now? She made herself take a deep breath. She'd never breathed air quite like this, filled with the sea and such sunshine and scents she'd never smelled before.

The sun in Vegas wasn't this bright, and the sky wasn't this clear. This looked as unreal as the highway had last night, when she'd seen the rabbit and the falcon and this very strange man dressed like a hunter.

"Take me back to Kyle," she said, not sure if she was away from Kyle or just having some sort of bizarre hallucination.

"Not yet," Robin said. "You wanted to know what was going on, and you were wedded to your perception of reality, even though it's not an accurate one."

She had spoken those words to patients over and over again. But her patients hadn't understood how the real world worked. The world she had grown up in. The world with Mini Coopers and Las Vegas office buildings and little boys who read too many comic books.

Not a world with psychics and people who talked about the Fates as if they were real.

"I don't know what you're talking about," she said.

He gave her a soft smile. It made his face seem—less harsh? Warmer? And yet somehow even more masculine and mysterious—then he pointed in front of him.

Her gaze followed his finger. Ahead stood a mountain shrouded in fog. The fog looked fake, especially in this bright sunlit world with the clear, clear edges.

"Mount Olympus," he said. "You've probably read about it."

She hadn't just read about it. She'd been there during her junior year in college. She'd managed to travel all over Europe that spring semester and get college credit for it. At the end, she had gone to Greece all on her own, seen the Parthenon, and looked at Mount Olympus.

It hadn't looked like this.

Which wasn't exactly true. It had looked like this in a broken down, real world sort of way. The mountain before her looked like the Hollywood version of Mount Olympus. It certainly was not the version she had seen on her trip.

"Uh-huh," she said. "Where's the trapdoor? Is this like Disneyland where we find some sideways exit and return to the world of neon, gamblers, and the Blue Man Group?"

He studied her for a moment, the soft smile gone. "There's no trapdoor."

"Then how did we get here?"

"Like this." He snapped his fingers again.

And suddenly, she was standing in the living room of her condo. Newspapers were scattered across the floor. The three novels she'd been reading simultaneously were all facedown on her coffee table, along with two open cans of Diet Coke.

The dirty dishes she had left for later were still sitting in her sink, and the suit she'd worn to the office two days ago littered the hardwood floor of her hallway.

Her life really was a mess. She never used to be this sloppy.

"Is this better?"

She jumped. Robin stood beside her. She hadn't realized he was still there.

He studied the portraits on her wall, all photographs of her family taken with her black-and-white camera. She'd been quite the photographer once, but she'd given it up to concentrate on her career.

"Why would this be better?" she asked.

"You were obviously having trouble seeing Mount Olympus as the real world. I thought maybe your home would be real to you."

She walked to the window and looked out. Condos, strip malls, and freeways. Yes, she was in Los Angeles. The mountains were lost in a polluted haze, and even though the sun was out, the sky looked a vague gray-green.

"What's going on?" she asked again. Only this time, she really wasn't asking him, she was asking herself.

He took her hand. His fingers were warm and dry and callused, which surprised her. She thought an arrogant businessman like him would have soft fingers. Then she remembered the falcon.

He led her to her couch, pushed some magazines aside, and sat her down. He sat beside her, not letting her fingers go.

"There really is magic in the world," he said gently.

She looked at him. This man had gone from furious to tender in the space of a few minutes. Of course, if he were to be believed, they both had gone from Vegas to Greece to LA in those same few minutes.

"Why would you put it on yourself to tell me this?" she asked.

He shrugged. She had a sense that he wasn't going to tell her the whole truth.

"Somehow you've gotten mixed up with the Fates," he said. "They're dangerous women. You have a psychic nephew who knows Zoe Sinclair, who is also magic. You're surrounded by people who have a power you haven't been aware of until just recently, and even so, they haven't helped you see that power. I don't think that's fair."

"To whom?" she asked.

"To you." His voice was still gentle.

"Why would you care about me?"

His eyes were a rich brown, the color of mahogany wood, and inside them, she saw layers of emotions, so many she couldn't identify them all.

"That's the question, isn't it?" he asked. "Logically, I should have thrown you all out of my office today and gone on with my life."

He didn't say any more. After a few seconds, she prompted, "But?"

He shrugged. "I feel responsible for you some-how."

She dropped his hand and stood up. No one was responsible for her except herself. *She* had always been responsible for herself. She didn't need anyone else's help.

"Take me back to Kyle," she said.

Robin frowned, looking confused. "What did I say?"

"You don't have to take care of me," she said. "No one takes care of me."

"That's pretty clear." He was staring at his hands, but he was probably referring to her condo. It was in a state because she had left in a hurry, she wanted to say. But she didn't. Because it had been like this for months. One of the classic signs of depression—letting herself, her home, her world fall apart.

"You brought us here uninvited," she said and then stopped. How had he done that? This wasn't a planned set like the fake Olympus. (Had that really been fake?) This was her condo, right down to the slightly vanilla odor that had lingered ever since she had knocked over a mostly melted scented candle behind her kitchen counter.

He looked up at her. "I wasn't referring to your place. I haven't been in my home long enough to make it this comfortable. I envy places that are lived in like this."

He sounded sincere and a bit baffled at her emotion. She sank back onto the couch. "Then what did you mean?"

"No one around you has been kind enough to explain the magic that clearly exists in your life."

His words made her heart twist. Kyle had always tried. Travers hadn't known until recently. And then there was that thing Zoe had done with the eggs this morning.

"It's more complicated than that," Megan said.

"It seems pretty straightforward to me," Robin said. "Sometimes when people learn about magic, they learn about it slowly. It takes a while for their new reality to filter in. But you don't have time for a slow dawning. You're driving the Fates around as if you're their personal chauffeur. You have to know how dangerous that is."

"You've used the word dangerous twice now about them," Megan said. "What do you mean?"

He shook his head and sighed. "Where to begin?"

She was familiar with this. It almost felt like a therapy session, only she didn't want to analyze this man. Still, she took those callused fingers in her own.

"Begin wherever you like," she said.

14

Suddenly he was back there, the place he had never really wanted to be ever again.

The day that Marian had died.

Only he wasn't really there. He was standing outside it, like an observer of his own life, and this other woman was beside him, holding his hand.

They stood in the cooking area, but they could see through the doorway into the bedroom. He had forgotten how small and mean the rooms were. The cottage was made of thatch and smelled like old hay mixed with sickness and spoiling meat. Two wooden bowls sat on the table, both filled with an oily stew that no one had touched.

He remembered making it, just like he remembered trying to choke it down even when Marian hadn't been able to eat any at all. She had wrinkled her nose and turned away.

She looked so tiny on their bed, her white hair strewn across the blanket he had folded up to form a kind of pillow. The mattress was stuffed with hay as well, and it had been very uncomfortable. To this day, he remembered how it felt to roll over at night, only to have a sharp straw poke him in the side.

Her breath was weak and rattly, her eyes rheumy, her hand clinging to his. He stared at himself, looking only a few years younger than he did now and so devastated. Had he really looked that broken? She wasn't even dead yet, but he had known she was going to die.

The Fates had already ruled that he could do nothing about it. They had reversed the spell he had cast, the spell which had brought her back to her younger, healthier self. And they had erased her memory of those few days. As far as she had known, she had been in that bed for weeks, dying by inches, her young-looking husband still at her side.

She had liked his magic. She had found his forever youth intriguing. Unlike the woman who currently clung to his hand, Marian had always believed the world had a touch of magic. She had been happy to learn that Robin held a piece of it, even at the end, when it couldn't save her.

"Your mother?" Megan asked him.

Rob glanced at her. Her eyes were lined with tears. She understood the scene before her without him even explaining it—all except one piece.

"My wife," he said. "My mortal wife."

How he hated that word "mortal." Technically, he was mortal too, but not in the same fragile way that Marian had been.

Megan said nothing else. She just observed as his younger self bathed Marian's face.

Marian had reached up and touched his younger

self's face. He still remembered how her hand had felt—like the finest crystal, about to break with a single touch—and cold, oh so very cold.

"You did what you could," she whispered. "Take comfort in that."

Instead of watching, Rob turned away. He didn't need to see this again. It was burned into his brain.

His younger self had shaken his head, and she had smiled at him. Her smile had never changed. It was always fond and warm and so full of love.

"I'll love you forever," she whispered.

And then she died.

He made a small sound, tried to step away from the old memory, and nearly tripped over a newspaper. Somehow, he had spelled himself and Megan back to her condo.

His magic hadn't been this out of control since he had first discovered he had it, in the middle of that damn Crusade, in a land that everyone seemed to call Holy.

"My God," Megan said softly. "You never got over her."

He raised his gaze to hers. Her eyes were filled with the most amazing compassion. She understood. No one he had ever told had understood.

People had always told him that a man should have gotten over losing a loved one after so many years. It was only natural, right?

He couldn't say anything. There was nothing to say, really.

Megan kept a hold on his hand. "But I don't understand how the Fates were involved in this."

"They wouldn't let me save her." His voice was

husky. He swallowed, cleared it. "They said it was wrong."

Their words still echoed, even now: *We cannot allow love to violate the rules of existence.*

"Why?" Megan obviously had heard that echo. She had heard it, just like she had entered his bubble.

What was this connection between them?

"They said it took the world out of balance, and the world would find hideous ways to come back into balance. They said a few mages had tried this before, and the world *had* found hideous ways to come back, and they didn't want that to happen again." He didn't look at her as he said that. His voice shook.

"As if that mattered to you," Megan said.

"Precisely." He spoke with a little too much force.

"So they let her die," Megan said.

He shook his head. "They reversed my spell. It was a deliberate act. They killed her. They didn't let her die. They took an action that made her die."

"Changing what you had done," Megan said.

"Because they said it was wrong."

She closed her eyes for a moment as if she were absorbing his words. Then she shook her head, frowned, and opened her eyes.

"Have you seen them since?" she asked.

"No," he said. "Of course not."

"Until today."

"Yeah." He whispered because he no longer trusted his voice. He was afraid it would break. If it broke, he might lose what little grip he had on himself.

"When they came, asking for a favor."

"Yeah."

Megan's lips thinned. "That is so wrong."

His gaze met hers, and then, despite himself, he smiled. It *was* wrong. But she had expressed her objection in such a thoroughly modern manner that her words had brought him back to the present.

"No wonder you locked them in a room," she said. "I might have killed them with my own bare hands."

"Do that to the Fates," he said, "and you'd be imprisoned forever."

Megan sighed. "I really don't understand this new world, do I?"

His smile grew fond. "But you're beginning to."

She smiled back at him. She had no idea how beautiful she was, and he loved that. Too much, these days, women knew exactly how attractive they were.

Then Megan broke the eye contact. Her cheeks were slightly flushed. "My nephew says they've lost their magic. Would they still be dangerous without it?"

"Lost their magic." Rob shook his head. Both the Fates and John had mentioned that, but he hadn't believed it. "It could be some sort of test."

"Why would they test you?"

He shrugged. "I've never responded to any of their summonses in the past. Maybe they decided to come to me."

"To ask a favor," Megan said as if she was thinking about it.

Now it was his turn to sigh. He didn't owe them anything. And the idea of a test didn't really ring true to him. The Fates were devious, and they lacked a sense of time, but they usually played with emotional things, not spinning wheels.

If they were messing with him, they'd be doing something with true love and death, not spinning wheels and little children.

"How long have you known the Fates?" he asked.

Megan gathered the last of the newspapers and clutched them to her chest. "About twelve hours."

"About twelve . . . ?" he let his voice trail off. "My heavens. And you're here?"

"My brother is getting a marriage license. He's not in the mood to help the Fates anymore. Technically, all I'm supposed to be doing is babysitting Kyle." Then her mouth opened slightly. "Kyle! I left him there. We have to go back!"

"He'll be fine," Rob said.

She shook her head. "I don't know your friend John, and the Fates are locked up, and Kyle might just take matters into his own hands."

Rob wanted to tell her that John was very capable. In fact, he had an innate understanding of children that Rob had always relied on.

But he didn't say anything. Instead, he snapped his fingers again, taking the two of them back to the office.

As they shifted, he felt an acute sense of disappointment. He wanted to be alone with her.

Maybe this was Fate-caused. Maybe this woman was his test, not the silly spinning wheel.

And then he was back in the reception area, Megan beside him. The young boy, Kyle, sprinted across the room and wrapped his arms around her, shooting Rob an angry glance.

John had a bemused expression on his face. He was looking at Rob and Megan fondly, as if he couldn't quite believe Rob had taken her away.

The door to Rob's office rattled, and muted female voices cried out, their words muffled by the door's thickness.

"You're not upset," Kyle said to his aunt as he stepped back slightly from the hug.

Her gaze met Rob's. He felt a shared moment in that look, as if what he had told her had made her value him. His heart fluttered, and he wished it would remain still.

He didn't want to find any other woman attractive.

He didn't want to feel that heady, almost giddy feeling of someone in the first stages of courtship.

"Mr—Hood?—was trying to help me understand this magic you're all talking about," Megan said.

"Chapeau," Rob said. "I'm Rob Chapeau."

Her eyes widened slightly, and that flush she'd had became a full-blown blush.

She obviously recognized the name. She hadn't put two and two together before, but she had now.

He cursed that media image John had insisted on creating for him. The billionaire playboy, the one who hadn't cared about anything.

It was so far from the truth, but it enabled him to walk in circles that he wouldn't get into otherwise.

"Chapeau Enterprises." Her voice was cold. "Forgive me. I had somehow missed that you were *the* Chapeau."

The way she said it made him feel ridiculous. The chapeau. As if he were nothing more than a hat to her.

"It's not like it seems," he said.

"Well, you've proven to me that nothing is." She kept her hand on her nephew's shoulder, but she pulled all the way out of the hug. "You and Kyle and those three women and my goofy brother. Are you all trying some kind of upscale David Copperfield thing? Am I the preferred guinea pig? Is that why Travers has been calling me for the last few days? Did he give you pictures of my condo? Is that how it worked?"

The boy was frowning. John's smile had grown, just a little, and he crossed his massive arms. The door rattling had become door banging.

"I don't know any Travers," Rob said.

"He doesn't, Aunt Meg," Kyle said. "He really isn't trying to trick you either."

She looked at her nephew, then back at Rob. "Rob Chapeau, according to the press—"

"Is a manipulative man who doesn't care how he makes his money," Rob said. "Does that sound like Robin Hood to you?"

"Maybe you've given up on the nobler parts of the legend," she said. "Maybe it's the party side that continued to appeal to you. Or did you just think you'd rather be on the side of the winners?"

He winced when she said that. It echoed words he'd used throughout the centuries—how he hated that the cheaters, liars, and destroyers were often the ones on the top of the heap in wealth or power or both.

"Rob has never been what he seemed," John

said, moving forward to insert himself into the conversation physically. "He's always been something other. Even back in Sherwood, he maintained a dual identity. He was born into privilege, and could have lived that way despite what the sheriff and King John were doing. Or didn't you know that part of the legend?"

Her face didn't soften, but her eyes did. Those compassionate eyes.

Rob frowned. She had almost disappeared in those moments when he'd been telling her about Marian (and what was that about? He never told any other woman he'd been near—let alone the ones he'd been involved with—about Marian. These days, only John knew. John and those horrible women still locked in Rob's office). Megan had become the perfect listener in those moments, almost as if she could absorb his pain into herself.

It was when the attention was focused on her that she became unsettled. When she thought someone was deliberately making a fool of her.

She had been hurt too, and no one had ever noticed.

"I'm not making fun of you," he said gently. "This isn't a scam that anyone planned with me. Those are the Fates in my office, and I'm not some billionaire playboy testing a new entertainment system."

Although he was richer than he liked. It was necessary for the work he did. Most of the money he made, however, went into the various corporations that he ran, which then distributed it to worthy causes around the globe.

"I think you should let the Fates out of your

office," she said quietly. "I'll take them back to the hotel."

The door truly was banging now. Eventually, those three women would get it open from sheer force of will.

"It won't be that easy." John cast a wary eye on the door.

It actually might be since it was becoming clearer and clearer that the Fates had no magic. And with no magic, they were truly vulnerable to those who hated them. Rob could control them if he wanted, with just the flick of a finger.

He wouldn't, of course. It wasn't his way.

But he knew a lot of mages who didn't have those qualms.

He caught a movement in the corner of his eye. Young Kyle was nodding. When Kyle saw Rob looking at him, Kyle said, "I've seen mages try to hurt them. Zoe protected them. My Uncle Dex did before."

Rob didn't have to be psychic to understand the implications of that sentence. Now, for some reason, the Fates expected him to help them.

"You help other people," Kyle said as if he and Rob had been having an out-loud discussion.

"Needy people," Rob said.

Megan was watching him. Her right hand still rested securely on Kyle's shoulder. She clearly wasn't following all of the conversation, but she was paying attention.

"The Fates are needy," Kyle said.

"The Fates are bossy, and they don't understand anything, and they hurt people, young man. The sooner you learn that—"

"They're here to learn how to be better Fates." The boy's voice rose. "That's why they gave up their magic, so they could learn diplomacy and how to be helpless and a whole bunch of other stuff. Then they found out that it was all a scam, and they'd been made fools of so that Zeus could put his daughters in as Fates—"

"Which daughters?" Rob asked. "Athena wouldn't be bad at it."

Megan's eyebrows rose. That was the second time he'd seen her do that, and he was beginning to like it. It gave her face even more warmth.

"I don't know," Kyle said. "You'd have to ask the Fates."

"I'm not talking with them," Rob said.

"Rob, you have to." John extended his meaty hands. "If they get back into power—"

"I'll worry about it then." He was about to spell the Fates somewhere else when he caught Megan's eye.

That amusing eyebrow-raised expression was gone, replaced by one of concern.

"What?" he asked, trying not to snap at her. He liked her too much to snap at her. And she was sensitive about things aimed at her. He didn't want to hurt her in any way.

She took a deep breath. Kyle grinned up at her as if he already knew what she was going to say. And, of course, he did.

"Your . . . intervention," she said, obviously choosing her word with great caution, ". . . leads me to believe that there is magic in the world. And if there is—"

"There is," John growled.

She ignored him. Rob understood her caution. She was still feeling her way in this new world.

"If there is," she repeated, "then it sounds to me like something major is going on in your government. The Fates are part of your government, right?"

"Right." Rob didn't like them or what they stood for, but they were part of the ruling class.

Of course, he'd always had his issues with the ruling class.

"Then," she said just as slowly, just as gently, "you might want to talk to them and intervene. Not to help them, but to help your people."

"My people." His gaze met John's. John closed his eyes and shook his head. Megan didn't know—she couldn't know—how that phrase had backfired on him over the years.

First, his people had been the peasants in Nottingham, and he had done his best to save them. His men, they too were his people, and it had taken all his cunning to keep them alive.

When it had become clear that he couldn't, he joined Richard the Lionhearted in his crusade against the infidels, only to learn that there weren't infidels, only different systems of belief, and that the people he'd always thought of as his people were really very different from him.

They had no magic, and he did.

He was part of a special class after all.

And, as he had always done, he eventually rejected that class and used his powers to help those less fortunate without resorting to ruling them, directing them, or controlling them.

His people.

He had no people. He wanted no people. He only wanted to live his life his way.

"Good argument, Aunt Megan," Kyle whispered. "But it probably wasn't the most effective."

She shrugged and smiled at the boy. Her love for him was so obvious that it made Rob's heart twist. So many children didn't have that kind of love.

"Then what would be effective?" she whispered back, even though she glanced sideways at Rob, and clearly knew he was listening.

The boy squared his shoulders and turned to Rob. "The Fates say that true love is at stake. For some people, love is all they get. They don't get money, they don't get superpowers, they just get love. You want to make that go away? Because the Fates say that's what'll happen if you don't help them."

Rob felt that heat rise in his face again.

"I'd hear them out, boss," John said, putting the sarcastic emphasis on "boss" that he'd been using for the last century or so.

"You hear them out," Rob said, "and then send them back home, wherever home is."

"What're you gonna do?" John asked.

"A little research of my own," Rob said. He extended a hand to Megan. "You want to help me?"

He wasn't exactly sure why he had offered, except that he didn't want to leave her presence. Maybe that was enough.

"I guess," she said. "So long as I can bring Kyle."

"No," Kyle said. "I want to stay with the Fates and Mr. Little."

Megan looked at the boy with surprise. "We don't know Mr. Little."

"I do. He's really nice. C'mon, Aunt Meg. You can tell that. Besides, the Fates'll be here."

"I'm not sure that's a good thing," she said, glancing at Rob.

"John can handle them," Rob said to her softly, knowing that her fears were more about the Fates now that he'd scared her with them.

"I know." She bit a cuticle. The movement was clearly a nervous habit. "It's just that Travers left Kyle in my charge . . ."

"I got to get back to let Fang out anyway," Kyle said. "I don't want to go on a mission."

Rob started. He hadn't realized that he had been thinking that word, but he had, deep down. He felt like he had a mission.

"Besides," Kyle said. "Mr. Little thinks the two of you need time alone. He thinks you're the best thing—"

"Kid!" John snapped. "Enough already."

Megan glanced at her nephew, then at John. She was obviously intrigued.

So was Rob.

"Why don't you tell us what you think, Mr. Little?" Megan asked.

John looked trapped. Rob would have laughed if he hadn't recognized the expression. John always had this look when he was afraid he'd offend someone.

John shook his head. "I can't."

"It's okay," Rob said, wondering if he wasn't making a mistake. "Tell her what you think, Little John."

15

Megan's stomach clenched. Something in Rob's tone told her that she might not like what John was going to say.

She looked at John, mostly so that she wouldn't have to look at Rob. She could get lost in Rob's eyes, forget where she was, forget what she was doing.

She couldn't afford that at the moment. She was slow on the uptake, but she was beginning to realize that she had stumbled into something momentous, and she would have to act accordingly.

Kyle took her hand and squeezed it. The door kept banging against the wall. Those poor women, locked in there, unable to get out. They must be panicked.

Even if they did deserve that imprisonment, at least from Rob's point of view.

John looked at Megan sideways, his expression sheepish. He was such a large man. She finally understood all the jokes that had filtered down through history; John Little was anything but.

Although he was a gentle giant. She had probably hurt his feelings by implying that Kyle couldn't stay with him because she didn't know him.

"I think, Miss," John Little said to Megan, his tone oddly courtly, "that you're the best thing that's ever happened to Robin."

Meg's stomach clenched worse than it had a moment ago. How could she be the best thing for him? She'd only just met the man.

Then she caught a glimpse of him out of the corner of her eye. He had stiffened, his body posture so formal that it looked as if he might break if she touched him.

There was a shadow of the expression she had seen on his face in that old memory which he had played for her like a movie when they'd been in her condo. He had looked so shattered. She had never seen a man so shattered.

And the remnants of that emotion were with him still.

"I can't be." She made sure she was facing John Little instead of Rob. "I haven't happened to him at all."

John Little bowed slightly. "But you have, Miss. You've already seen his magic, and he's taken care of you."

There that phrase was again. She didn't like it, but this time, she didn't say anything.

"He doesn't take care of just anyone, Miss."

If he was Robin Hood—the real Robin Hood—

didn't that mean he took care of everyone? Or that he had at one time?

Didn't that mean she was just one of many?

She bit her lower lip, then started to chew it. The moment she tasted blood, she stopped.

Old habits. Why in the world were old habits coming up now?

"I'll be okay, Aunt Meg," Kyle said again. "It's okay. We need to help the Fates."

As if the Fates had heard him, the door that imprisoned them banged so hard that the entire wall shook.

"Magic's fading," John Little said to Rob.

Rob still had that expression. This couldn't be easy for him, poor man. Especially not if those three women had deliberately destroyed his life.

If Kyle was right—and why would he be wrong?—then there *was* a lot at stake here. Megan wasn't even sure she believed in true love. Friendship, passion, long-term companionship, and yes, love, but not *true* love, not the Hollywood variety, not the stuff legends were made of.

Although she had seen Rob's devastated face. That love affair was part of a legend. An old, old legend. His love for a woman whom Megan had originally mistaken for his mother had been so powerful it had resounded through all of time.

And now he needed *her*? She didn't believe it.

"Believe it, Aunt Meg," Kyle whispered.

His round face was upturned toward her. He seemed so vulnerable. She was trusting the judgement of a ten-year-old. A precocious, psychic one, but a ten-year-old nonetheless.

"Aunt Meg . . ."

Rob wasn't saying anything. He wasn't even looking at her. It was as if John's words had frozen him.

Maybe he didn't want to influence her decision.

AUNT MEG!!!!!!!!!!!!

Kyle yelled at her so loudly that she stumbled backward and nearly hit the wall. She covered her ears with both hands. Her eyes watered.

She blinked at him, trying to catch her breath. A single tear ran down her face, but it wasn't a tear of sadness.

It was a tear of pain.

"What was that?" she asked.

"Me." Kyle straightened his shoulders. "The Fates taught me to do that when I'm in trouble."

"Do what?" Rob had lost that rigidity. He had moved toward her as if he were going to help her, but she raised a single hand, keeping him back.

"Children aren't supposed to yell like that," she said.

"He didn't yell." Rob glanced at John for confirmation.

John shrugged. "I didn't hear anything."

"It's broadcasting," Kyle said, obviously pleased with himself. "Remember? I told you. You were doing it this morning, only not so loud. And I aimed mine. Yours was just out there, kinda general."

Aimed it? He had made her ears ring, her eyes tear up, and her head ache with a single thought?

She wiped her cheek with the back of her hand.

"Don't do that again," she said. Her tone was a little harsh.

Kyle grinned. "Unless I'm in trouble."

"Unless you're in trouble." But she wasn't even sure about then.

"So, see? It's okay to leave me here with Mr. Little and the Fates. I can ask for help if I need it. And if you don't come, I can do the same thing to Dad."

"I'm sure he'd appreciate that," Meg mumbled.

"He doesn't like it any more than you do," Kyle said, "but it works. Most of the time."

Rob came to her side and pulled her up. She had been crouching, and she hadn't even realized it.

His touch was gentle. He smelled faintly of leather, even though he wasn't wearing any.

"John has never hurt a child in his life," Rob said. "And we won't be gone too long, I promise. John has enough magic to handle the Fates, and your nephew can get home in time to take care of his dog."

"Fang! Dang!" Kyle glanced at his watch. "Aunt Meg, it's nearly emergency time."

She frowned at him. There were more emergencies, and they were planned? How come no one had told her about that?

"No, Aunt Meg. For Fang. If he makes too many messes, he'll cost us extra money, and you know how Dad hates that."

She did know, which was why she had been surprised about the suites in the first place.

She had no idea why the potential dog emergency convinced her more than all the other arguments had, but it did.

"All right," she said. Then she took a deep breath and did the responsible thing. "But I want you to dig another hole in my brain if something goes wrong, all right?"

Kyle wrinkled his nose. "Gross. I can't do that. But I'll broadcast at you, okay?"

That was what she had meant. She hadn't expected him to take it literally. "Okay."

"Good." Rob nodded at her and at John. "Megan and I will do some preliminary work. John, you get those Fates out of here, and get the boy back to his dog before there's a costly puddle. I'll meet up with you when we're done."

Megan's stomach had now tied itself into knots. "How long will we be gone?"

Rob shrugged. "I have no idea, but I'll make sure it's not as long as it seems."

16

Rob mentally shook himself. He hadn't meant to tell this woman that he'd make the time with him seem longer than it was, but that was what he had said. What he'd *meant* was that he would use a bit of magic and move the two of them backward in time if he had to.

But her knowledge of magic was so limited, he wasn't sure she'd understand the explanation even now.

Everyone in the reception area looked like they were emotionally drained. Even the reception area itself seemed out of sorts. The pictures on the wall were crooked, thanks to the Fates' incredible effort to get themselves out of the office. The door looked battered, and the furniture seemed out of place even though Rob didn't think anyone had touched it.

Megan seemed the worst for wear. Her skin was paler than it had been before, and her eyelashes were wet. They stuck together, accenting her eyes even more than they had. Her lips were very red because she'd been biting them nervously, and a tear streak showed him that the lovely red in her cheeks had no artificial component at all.

She'd achieved that much beauty without make-up.

The boy had clearly caused her physical pain with his "broadcast." When they got back, Rob would teach him how to tone that down. Otherwise, if he wasn't careful, he might do some actual damage someday.

The boy looked at him sharply. He'd clearly overheard that last thought.

"We'll work on it," Rob said.

The boy squared his shoulders. Rob was beginning to like him. The kid had courage. Rob hadn't met too many moderns who did.

The door banged again, and this time, the hinges squeaked. The bolts had started to work their way out of their sockets.

"You'd better go if you're gonna go," John said. "I think we're going to release some Fates whether we want to or not."

Rob took Megan's hand. She looked terrified.

"Just hang on tight," he said. "We're only gonna ask a few questions, maybe figure out a few things. Then we'll come back. All right?"

She took a deep breath and then nodded.

She had courage too, considering everything she'd been through in the past few hours. Some people, when they discovered the world had magic, went to bed for weeks and wouldn't get up.

He needed to take care of this Fate problem quickly for her sake as well as his own.

He made a small circle with his left hand and

spelled them to the first person he could think of who would give him a straight answer—Zoe Sinclair.

It was a slower spatial shift than he usually performed, almost as if the magic stream couldn't find Zoe for a moment.

Then he and Megan materialized in a walk-in closet as large as his thatched hut had been. Women's clothes hung from every available post and bar, and Zoe stood in the middle of them, wearing only a black bra, see-through panties, and a large diamond ring on her left hand.

"What the hell?" Zoe snapped. "I thought we had a shield over this place."

He'd learned how to go through magical shields centuries ago, but that explained why the spatial shift had been so slow.

Zoe shoved his chest. "Get out."

Then she saw Megan hiding halfway behind him. Megan's face was so red, it looked like her head was about to explode.

"What in the world is going on?" Zoe asked.

The door to the closet opened, and a tall blond man stepped inside. He was wearing jeans slung low over his hips and nothing more.

Megan covered her eyes. "Travers, jeez."

Travers. Her brother. The one that Zoe was going to marry. He clearly had magical power—Rob could feel it radiating off him—but of an unconventional kind.

"What are you doing here?" Travers snapped. Then he frowned at Rob. "And who are you?"

"You have clothes on, Travs?" Megan asked.

"Yes," Travers said. "My bare chest isn't that disgusting, sis."

He tossed a robe at Zoe, who slipped it on. The robe was as see-through as the panties.

Megan peeked through her fingers. Rob had the sense she wasn't hiding from her brother's lack of clothing so much as she was trying to disappear from the entire situation.

"You didn't tell me we were coming here," she whispered to Rob.

"I told you we were going to find answers," he said.

"But I could have told you not to come here," Megan whispered.

"Because she was the one who said, 'Travers, you and Zoe take your time, wink-wink.'" There was no warmth in Travers's tone. "It was your idea to celebrate the marriage license, sis, and you have no right—"

"I don't think Megan's involved." Zoe had her hands on her hips. She was an attractive woman, but a little too slim. And her clothes were a little too see-through. Rob wasn't sure where to look.

He settled for Megan. Now, *she* was a beautiful woman with appropriate curves. Zoe was too bony, and she always had been.

"Right, Rob?" Zoe asked.

He didn't remember the question. He glanced at Travers, who looked nothing like his pretty sister, and tried to ignore the fury on the man's face.

"You mind telling me who you are and what you're doing here?" Travers asked. "It would be really nice to know sometime before the next millennium."

"Um, sorry," Rob said. He truly hadn't expected this. He was almost as embarrassed as Megan. Maybe he was more embarrassed.

"He's Robin Hood," Zoe said, "and he's here about the Fates, aren't you, Rob?"

"Yes," he said, wondering how she knew about the Fates.

"The question is, how did your sister come to accompany him?" Zoe said.

"Kyle," Travers said. "Kyle was behind it. Wasn't he, Meg?"

"Well, no," Megan said. "I mean, maybe. You see, the Fates needed a ride—"

"And they couldn't take a cab?" Travers asked.

"Kyle said they couldn't. They'd get lost."

"You know they can't, Travers," Zoe said. "It's not safe for them out in the real world."

"Because someone might steal their magic, I know," Travers said, but he didn't sound very sympathetic.

"No," Zoe said. "They wouldn't know the rules of taxicabs."

The rules of taxicabs. Rob looked at her. There were rules for taxicabs, weren't there? And he'd learned them over the years as the taxicabs themselves had evolved.

But if the story were true—or at least if his understanding of the Fates' last few months were true—then they wouldn't know all sorts of things, from taxicabs to slot machines to laptop computers.

Those three women *were* helpless in a variety of ways.

Part of him felt sympathy, and part of him wanted to rub his hands together with glee.

Travers sighed. "So you're Robin Hood."

Rob nodded.

"And you have my sister because . . . ?"

"Because she offered to help," he said, even though that wasn't entirely true.

"Leaving my son with the most incompetent women in the world?" Travers asked a question, but it didn't sound like a question. Something in his phrasing made it sound like a threat.

"And my friend John," Rob said. "He can handle all of them."

"John." Travers didn't sound satisfied.

"Little John," Zoe said. "You know."

"No," Megan said from behind Rob. "He doesn't know. He hates myths and legends. He prefers books on the history of math."

Travers shot her a glare. "Given how myths and legends are working out for me these days, do you blame me?"

Zoe raised herself to her full height. "It seems to me myths and legends are treating you quite well, Mr. Kineally."

He grinned at her. "If these people would leave your closet."

"You're a myth and a legend?" Megan asked Zoe.

"Only in my own mind," Zoe said. "But I spend a lot of time with the real thing. Although we haven't seen much of you lately, Rob. What gives?"

He didn't want to have cocktail party talk in the middle of Zoe's closet. Especially with Zoe in see-through clothing and her half-naked husband-to-be beside her.

"I, ah, just came . . ." Rob stopped himself. That was bad. "I mean, I just got here because I—"

"He wants to know what's going on with these Fate women," Megan said. "He really doesn't want to help them, and I don't blame him."

"I don't blame him either," Travers said, "but not doing something the Fates want is very hard."

"Even when they don't have magic," Zoe added. "You'd think it would be easier, but you'd be wrong."

Rob sighed. "They say true love is at stake."

"I think they're right," Zoe said. "The Faerie Kings have stolen their wheel. The Fates got along without it just fine for millennia, but then they gave up their magic powers because Zeus told them it was a job requirement—"

"For what?"

"They had to reapply to be Fates. They had term limits." Zoe shrugged. "Don't ask me why they believed this garbage, but they did. And now everything's at stake."

"So why aren't you still helping them?" Rob asked.

"They said we're done." Travers reached across a row of cocktail dresses and took Zoe's hand. "I suppose we could have argued more."

"But apparently, it's been a tag-team rescue from the beginning," Zoe said. "You know the Fates. Their main job in life is to ensure that people find their soulmates."

Rob felt that flare of anger again. "Yeah, right. That always works."

Megan put a calming hand on his arm.

Zoe frowned at him. Like most mages, she only knew bits and pieces of his history. "You don't like them."

"I loathe them," he said.

"Oh, great," Travers muttered. "So much for the wedding."

Zoe squeezed Travers's hand. "We'll be fine. Don't worry."

"That's like saying don't breathe."

"They want me to steal that wheel," Rob said.

"They need someone experienced at theft," Zoe said. "I'm not it. Travers certainly isn't. They're the ones who suggested you."

"I'm not a burglar," Rob said.

"You stole from the rich and gave to the poor," Travers said, then stuck his tongue out at his sister. "See? I know some legends."

"You could've called me the original highwayman or something," Rob said. "I certainly wasn't a high-level thief like you see in the movies."

"Are there high-level thieves like you see in the movies?" Megan asked softly.

"Not magical ones," Zoe said. "We don't need all that gadgetry."

"Except when you're stealing a spinning wheel," Megan said.

Rob shook his head. "The wheel's in Faerie, right?"

"Right," Zoe said.

"So high-level gadgetry wouldn't work anyway." He sighed. "They said you know exactly where it is."

"Oh yeah," Zoe said. "I can show you a map."

"Later," Rob said. "If I decide to take the case."

"Which you're not going to do." Zoe shook her head. "Rob, you could be our last hope."

"Whose last hope? You two seem to be doing pretty well here." The words sounded almost bitter. He hadn't meant to be bitter, had he?

But it was ironic. The Fates wanted him to save true love when they couldn't save his true love.

Wouldn't save his true love.

"Tell you what," Zoe said, her black eyes narrowing. "You do me a favor. Spell yourself to the Fates. Say literally 'to the Fates' when you do it. Then come back here, and we'll talk."

"Zo!" Travers protested.

She got a cheeky grin and looked at him. "Come back after—what?—four hours?"

"Five," Travers said. "In fact, how about we see you tomorrow? Or maybe in a few weeks."

"The Fates don't have a few weeks," Zoe said.

"Tomorrow," Travers said.

"I have Kyle for the whole night?" Megan asked.

"You don't have him right now," Travers said.

They were bickering. Rob had never seen adult siblings bicker, except on television.

"I know where he is," Megan said.

"I know where he is too," Travers said. "That doesn't mean I'm comfortable with it."

"John's competent," Rob said so that Megan wouldn't get into any more trouble.

"No one's competent around the Fates," Travers muttered.

"Just do what I ask," Zoe said, "then take Megan to the hotel and wait for us. We'll come to you."

Rob sighed. He hadn't meant for any of this to

happen. He glanced at Megan. The flush that had overwhelmed her face was gone. She looked up at him and shrugged.

"All right, Zoe," he said. "I expect to see you later tonight. But don't have any expectations of me."

She grinned. "Don't worry," she said. "I know exactly what you'll do."

He was afraid of that. He took Megan's hand. It was cold. Then he waved an arm and said, "To the Fates."

And the closet disappeared.

17

This whirlwind travel was starting to make her dizzy.

Megan clutched Rob's hand. It seemed like they existed in a void for half a second, which was better than the inside of Zoe's closet, particularly with Zoe dressed like a Victoria's Secret model (and looking like one too, dammit!) and Travers with his jeans unzipped.

Megan blushed just thinking about that.

No one wanted to imagine their brother doing what her brother was probably doing right now.

She shuddered, and then, suddenly, she was in a library. A large, old library covered with beautiful shelves that ran up several stories. The library didn't smell like musty books, though. It smelled like old dog pee mixed with bad pizza and bubblegum.

She had never been to a place like this. It was too big to be real. The rooms seemed to go off this main area for ever and ever. They even disappeared into a fog-shrouded distance.

Rob squeezed her hand, but he was frowning. He sniffed loudly, obviously taking in that hideous pee and pizza smell. He touched the dust-covered surface of a nearby book and shook his head.

"Something's very wrong here," he whispered.

"We can hear that!" A young woman's voice floated in from the next room.

"Why does everyone materialize in the wrong place?" asked another young woman.

"Have you ever thought that we're in the wrong place?" asked a third.

Rob's frown grew deeper. He let go of Megan's hand, put a finger to his lips, then stepped over a pile of magazines toward the sound of the voices. Slowly, he peered around the corner, and his frown turned into a full-blown grimace.

Then he reached out his hand, and Megan took it.

She was beginning to trust this man, although she wasn't sure why. Maybe it was the confidence with which he moved, or maybe it was just the mercurial nature of his emotions. Anyone who went through that many moods in such a short period of time couldn't be hiding much.

He helped her over the magazine pile, around a mountain of dirty laundry, and through a stack of open books, all resting on top of each other.

The books had interesting titles: *The History of Finger-Pointing in the Magical World; The Titans through The Powers That Be; Famous Familiars and Their Times;* and, ominously, *The War Between The Kingdoms, Volume 45: Faerie.*

But Rob wouldn't let her linger. Instead, he led her into the next room. Three teenage girls sprawled on lawn chairs. Someone had placed ugly green Astroturf beneath the chairs and set up a wading pool next to one of the floor-to-ceiling oak bookstacks. Several books tottered along the edge of the wading pool, dangerously close to the water.

Megan wanted to move all that interesting paper away from danger, but Rob held her tightly at his side.

He was staring at the girls. They were worth staring at. The one closest to Megan was another redhead—Megan hadn't seen so many pretty redheads in one day in years (which could have been an effect of living in Los Angeles, where she saw too many beautiful blondes).

The redhead had cropped her lovely hair so short that it looked like a crewcut. She wore a green bikini that left nothing to the imagination, and she had half a dozen tiny tattoos—most of them of miniature versions of herself (along with one or two roses)—along her torso. A diamond-studded ring stuck out of her belly button, and a matching one hung on the side of her aquiline nose.

She had large breasts and wide hips, and Megan knew that once she hit her twenties, the redhead would share Megan's plus-size figure and not know how she got there.

Next to her, a petite blonde (why were they always petite?) leaned forward in a way that would desert her 'long about twenty as well. She was painting her toenails fuchsia. The girl wore three seashells covering the most strategic locations and tied in place with hot pink cord. If she had had only one quarter of the redhead's figure, she might have been able to pull off the look. But she didn't. She looked like a little girl experimenting with her sexy older sister's clothing.

The last girl wore her hair in cornrows. White beads dotted the ends, clicking with her every movement. She wasn't wearing a bikini at all—or if she was, it wasn't visible beneath her long white t-shirt.

She was the only one with a book on her lap, and in her right hand, she held a pencil. The eraser end had been chewed off. Another pencil was shoved behind her left ear.

Only the redhead looked up when Megan and Rob entered the room.

"Hey, guys," she said, "we have more idiots."

Rob flushed. Megan tightened her grip on his hand. She wasn't trying to control him, but she had a sense that antagonizing these girls wouldn't be a bright idea.

The blonde raised her head. She shoved a piece of hot pink bubblegum in her mouth and started to chew with her mouth open.

"Grrrraaaate," she said. "More blinking work."

"For me," said the girl with the cornrows. She didn't look up at all.

"You should look, Tiffany," said the redhead. "This guy's a dish."

"Yeah, babe," said the blond. "Dump the empath and join us. We need some entertainment, right, Tiff?"

Tiffany tucked an errant cornrow behind her right ear. She still didn't look up. "Daddy's gonna be really mad at us if we don't figure out this familiar thing. He says it's gonna be a crisis real soon now."

Megan frowned at Rob. He shrugged ever so slightly, but that grimace he'd had earlier had morphed into an expression of controlled panic.

What was so frightening about three teenage girls?

Except, of course, that they were teenage girls.

"So that means it's not a crisis right now, right, Brittany?" the redhead glanced at the blonde. Blondes named Brittany. Apparently, they infected every plane of existence.

"Right, Crystal," Brittany said and blew a bright pink bubble.

"Find out what they want and make them leave," Tiffany said. She sounded angry.

"Tell us what you want and then leave," Crystal said.

"Who are you?" Rob sounded like he already knew, like he was afraid of the answer.

Brittany rolled her china blue eyes. *"Every*body asks that question."

"Maybe because they can't believe what they see." Tiffany mumbled as she turned the pages.

"You're in a really bad mood, y'know?" Crystal said.

"Yeah," Brittany said. "Get your nose out of that book for once, and look up. This guy's *hot.*"

Tiffany looked up. Her flat gaze met Rob's. "Hi, hot guy. Do you know how to read?"

Rob opened his mouth, closed it, and looked at Megan as if she had the answers. She wanted to lean back and observe for a moment. These teenagers had issues, and not just with each other. Something was going on here, something underlying the entire scene, that made all three girls unusually tense.

"Of course I can read." Rob sounded offended. "I've been able to read since the Renaissance."

Megan gave him a startled look. She couldn't remember when the Renaissance was, exactly (if she had ever known—history had never been her strong suit), but she knew it hadn't been during Robin Hood's era. He had gone at least a hundred years (or two or three) before he had learned how to read.

No wonder the question made him bristle.

"Daddy sent you, didn't he?" Crystal asked, her full lips turned downward. "This is another stupid test, isn't it?"

"Tell him we're not going to stand for it!" Brittany poked Tiffany. "Tell him that after getting this fake-o lame-o pool as a reward, we're not doing anything he wants ever again."

"You guys are not getting this," Tiffany said. "We would've gotten a real pool if you both hadn't blown the final question."

"Daddy says this is a real pool," Crystal said.

"It says 'pool' on the side," Brittany said.

"'Wading pool,'" Tiffany said with barely masked anger. "And if you knew anything about anything, you'd know that wading pools are for babies, not babes."

"Oh." Crystal's entire body wilted.

"She already told you that, dummy," Brittany whispered so loudly that it sounded like she was shouting.

"Excuse me," Rob said. "I asked a question. Who are you?"

"You're going to irritate Crystal if you keep asking that question," Tiffany said, turning another page in her book.

"Then answer it," Rob snapped.

Megan dropped his hand and walked through the lawn chairs over to the pool. She removed one book from the side, then another.

"What do you think you're doing?" Crystal asked her.

"Whatever it is, Meg," Rob said, "it's probably not a good idea."

"You might want to listen to the hottie, empath," Brittany said.

That was the second time they had called her an empath. Megan had ignored it the first time. She took a deep breath but wouldn't let herself be distracted.

"Thanks," Tiffany said ever so softly and just to Megan. "I've been asking them to clean up for the last two days. We're really gonna get it if we don't fix stuff."

Megan removed the last three books from the side of the pool, set them as far from the water as she could without leaving anyone's line of sight, and sat cross-legged on the Astroturf among all three lawn chairs.

"You girls want to tell me what's wrong?" she asked.

"Meg, you don't know who they are," Rob said.

It was obvious he didn't either, or he wouldn't have been asking them repeatedly who they were. But Megan was determined not to be distracted.

These three girls were in some kind of crisis, and if the only way to talk to them was to settle the crisis first, then she would do that.

Besides, she felt something close to relief. She had been out of her element all day.

But working with teenagers, especially rich, spoiled, and emotionally neglected teenagers, was something she knew more about than maybe anyone else on the planet.

"Daddy did send you, didn't he?" Crystal asked.

"So what if he did?" Megan said.

Rob made little warning motions with his hands. Megan pretended she didn't see them.

"Would it make that much difference if he had?" she asked.

"Well, duh!" Brittany said. "E-yeah. It would."

"How come?" Megan asked.

"They think Daddy's out to get us," Tiffany said. She continued to page through the book, pretending disinterest.

"You don't?" Megan asked.

"Of course she doesn't," Crystal said. "She thinks she's so much better than we are."

"She thinks she's Daddy's favorite," Brittany said.

A lot of issues here. Rob had let his hands fall to his sides. He was watching her as if she was surprising him, but a concern line marred his forehead.

"I'd prefer it," Megan said carefully, "if the girl I asked the question to was the girl who answered it."

"We'd prefer it too." Tiffany finally looked up from her book. Her dark eyes flashed with anger.

"But we haven't talked like normal people since we got this job," Crystal said.

"Job?" Megan asked.

"Y'know," Brittany said. "This stupid Fate job."

"You're the Fates?" Rob put his hand over his mouth after the words came out. He looked surprised, but Megan couldn't tell whether he was surprised by the fact that he had spoken aloud or by the fact that these girls were Fates.

Megan was certainly surprised that these girls were Fates. She had thought the Fates were Fates. Not that she believed the Fates of Greek mythology would be as ditzy as those three women were. But they were more plausible Fates than these young girls.

Although she had noticed that these girls spoke like the three older women, one at a time, all in a specific order.

"Interim," Tiffany said.

"Interim what?" Rob asked, his fingers muffling the words. He got the question out before Megan could.

"Fates," Crystal said. "We're the Interim Fates."

"Why is everyone surprised by this?" Brittany asked.

"Maybe it's because we suck at it," Tiffany said.

"We don't suck at it," Crystal said. "We don't suck at it like those other three did. They made Daddy really mad."

"We're making Daddy really mad," Brittany said.

"Because we're not doing anything," Tiffany said. "They made him mad because they did stuff."

"Which is why it makes sense for us not to do stuff," Crystal said.

"Y'know, like, duh," Brittany said.

Megan felt that same swirling, head turning momentum she'd felt when she'd first encountered the three adult Fates.

She had to work at returning to her own centered place. The key to therapy was listening. And it was hard to listen to these girls because of the way they spoke.

"So," she said gently, "you have to speak in the same order. You can't break that?"

"Would you sound this stupid on purpose?" Tiffany asked.

"You sound quite intelligent to me," Megan said.

"Because she's the brainy one," Crystal said.

"And she's mad at us for making her read all the books," Brittany said.

"I'm mad at you guys for a bunch of reasons," Tiffany said. "And you screwed up the order."

"What order?" Megan asked.

"The speech order," Crystal said. "We tried a spell out of one of the books so we could talk, like, when we wanted to."

"And all it did was make Crystal talk first," Brittany said. "I used to do that."

"Which is really annoying," Tiffany said. "I always start to say something after Crystal, but I can't say anything until Brittany covers us all with her bubblegum breath."

"You used to like bubblegum," Crystal said.

"So did you," Brittany reminded her.

Megan was starting to get a headache. They spoke that way involuntarily? Did they go on tangents involuntarily too? Or was that simply the way these girls thought?

Rob had moved next to one of the bookshelves. He leaned on it, watching the entire interaction. His gaze kept meeting Megan's, sending her warnings that she pretended she wasn't receiving.

"Let's focus," Megan said. "You're all angry. Tell me about that as best you can."

"We're supposed to be doing this together," Tiffany said. "Together doesn't mean I do all the work."

"We make decisions," Crystal said.

"We do?" Brittany asked.

Tiffany closed the book with a bang. She looked directly at Megan. The girl's eyes were so full of fury that Megan could feel it as if it were her own.

"Daddy made this sound like fun, but it's not. It's hard, and no one else is trying, except me. And I don't want to try." She spoke really fast as if she were working to get each word out before the others had to speak for her.

"He said we'd just grow into the job," Crystal said.

"He said all we had to do was what he said," Brittany said. "But he's not saying anything except asking us how come we're not doing our job."

"Does your father live here?" Megan asked.

"Meg," Rob said. "Their father is Zeus."

And you're the King of France, she almost said because she would have said that if he'd been some Los Angeles parent who was interfering with her work. But he wasn't the King of France, he was Robin Hood, and the father of these three young, confused girls could possibly be Zeus.

If the girls were the Interim Fates.

And the other three were the real Fates.

Who had given up their magic to understand their job better and then realized that Zeus had cheated them in a power broker takeover.

And if all of that was the case, then Rob was right: Megan was out of her league.

"No," Tiffany said as if Rob hadn't spoken. "Daddy doesn't live here. He can't. Technically, the Powers That Be aren't supposed to interfere with the Fates."

"Who told you that?" Crystal asked.

"She read it somewhere, I bet." Brittany's voice was filled with disapproval.

"I've been reading because I'm trying to get us out of this mess. It'd be a lot easier if you guys would help," Tiffany said.

Megan's stomach lurched. She looked at Rob. He had the same expression, wary and filled with concern. He hadn't noticed what Tiffany had just said.

"Are you serious about that?" Megan asked.

"About what?" Crystal asked.

"About getting out of this mess," Megan said.

"Yes!!!" All three girls answered at once, their voices so loud they almost—almost—matched the intensity of Kyle's broadcast.

The concerned line on Rob's face grew deeper. He made those funny little movements with his hands again.

"Well," Megan said, "I know how you can get out of this."

Rob's movements became more pronounced. This time, she didn't even make eye contact.

"See?" Brittany said to the others, "I told you this was a test from Daddy."

"No test," Megan said.

"How do we know that?" Tiffany asked.

"Do you have magic?" Megan asked.

"Well, duh!" Crystal said. "What good are Fates without magic?"

Rob rolled his eyes, but Crystal had a point. The three Fates that were with Kyle right now seemed completely out of place. Perhaps they wouldn't be so out of place if they had a little more control.

"But it doesn't do us a lot of good," Brittany said. "There's a lot of rules, and we didn't know that."

"Even though we're supposed to enforce them." Tiffany shoved the book off her lap onto the table beside her. "No one explained that part either."

The no one in question had to be their father, Zeus. The man sounded like a real piece of work.

Megan couldn't deal with him yet. Maybe she wouldn't have to at all if this worked out right.

"Well," she said, "like you three, I don't completely understand the rules of magic. I assume you know them better than I do. Can you use your powers to see if I'm being sincere?"

Crystal and Brittany looked at Tiffany. She nodded.

"You gotta start the spell, then," Crystal said.

"I can do, like, the hand stuff if you tell me what it is," Brittany said.

"I'll just do it." Tiffany made a beatific hand movement. A tiny light formed around Megan.

"Oh!" Crystal said. "I know what you're doing."

"Me too," Brittany said. "All you have to do, lady, is tell us something."

"Tell us again that you know how to get us out of this," Tiffany said.

Megan nodded. "I do know. But it would require secrecy and trust on your part. Can you do that?"

The light around her remained white. She had no idea of whether that was a good or bad thing.

"Sure," Crystal said.

"Yep," Brittany said.

"Of course," Tiffany said.

Megan smiled. Apparently, the whiteness had been a good thing.

"All right," she said. "Here's what I think you need to do."

18

Rob leaned against the bookshelf, his arms crossed. Megan had no idea who these girls were. She probably had a vague understanding—from classical mythology—of who Zeus was. But she didn't know his incredible power in the world of the mages.

"Meg," Rob said before she could go any further. "We may not be able to trust these girls."

Megan, who had been deliberately ignoring him for the past five minutes, finally met his gaze. "Can you do the same spell over them that they just did over me?"

He could do that and a dozen more powerful ones. But that wasn't the point.

"They might be sincere right now," he said, "but their father has a lot more control than you realize. He might be able to warp that sincerity and use it against us."

Megan bit her lower lip. Crystal, the pretty red-head, teared up. Brittany, the scrawny blonde, bowed her head. Only Tiffany, the one who seemed to have a brain, didn't move.

"Daddy can be pretty persuasive," Crystal said in a watery voice.

"Your hottie is right. You probably shouldn't help us," Brittany said.

Tiffany sighed, then nodded. "If Daddy wants to, he can pretty much get us to do anything."

Rob kept his gaze on Megan. He wished he had the abilities her nephew Kyle did because he would send her a message: don't mess with Zeus.

Zeus was one of the Powers That Be. He might actually be the Head Power. There were a bunch of them, almost all of them known as the main Greek gods. They'd been around so long and had accumulated so much power that they were almost like gods.

And for some reason, a reason Rob didn't understand, the rules didn't apply to them. They *made* the rules and let the Fates enforce them.

Only the Fates were locked in his office, and these little girls were supposed to enforce the rules, and they were under Zeus's thumb.

Zeus. Rob couldn't imagine what that man was like as a father. Zeus had hundreds—maybe thousands—of children, breaking yet another rule. When a mage came into his magic, his reproductive capabilities went away.

Rumors were that Zeus had arranged for men to come into their magic young—around the age of 20 or so—and women to come into theirs after menopause. Ostensibly, the argument was that the hormonal activity made it hard to control the magic, but Rob had always wondered if it wasn't a ploy by the old sexist to keep women under his thumb as long as possible.

Except his teenage daughters. Who had magic. And now who had waaay too much power. And obviously had no idea how—or even when—to use it.

"So you're telling me not to trust you as well," Megan said gently.

Crystal's tears spilled over her lower lashes. One tear caught on her nose ring, making her look (rather disgustingly) like she had forgotten to blow her nose.

Brittany glanced at her, then blinked hard, as if she felt the need to cry after seeing her sister cry.

But Tiffany just nodded.

"You feel that you can't stand up to your father," Megan said.

All three girls nodded.

"I understand that," Megan said.

But she didn't. She really couldn't. Only there was no way Rob could explain that to her. No way at all. She was thinking of Zeus as some human father with a little too much control over his daughters.

Zeus was the closest thing Rob's people had to a god, and he had control over everyone.

Except the other Powers That Be, of course.

Which had to be why this scheme had even come into existence.

Rob crossed his arms even tighter so that he was almost hugging himself and frowned. Something else was going on here, something sinister. Something that had to do with power and a lot of it. Zoe had tried to warn him, telling him that Zeus was making a power play, but Rob had ignored that, thinking who cared what Zeus was doing.

Which had to be why Zoe had sent him here—to see the true repercussions.

He loathed the original Fates, but they had kept the systems going. People got their familiars; they learned how to handle their nascent powers; they got their wrists slapped when they called attention to themselves in the mortal world.

What would happen if all that petty stuff got ignored? Magic would go haywire without familiars; mortals would notice out-of-control mages; and the press would learn that half the actors in the business didn't age because they didn't age, not because they had fantastic plastic surgeons.

Rob sighed and tuned back into the discussion. The girls were complaining about Zeus, and to hear them tell it, he did sound like the average father—if the average father had five hundred lovers, a jealous magical wife, and more children than he could count.

"We thought we were his favorites," Crystal said.

"But we're starting to think he hates us," Brittany said.

"Why else would he stick us with all this work when he knows we're bad at it?" Tiffany said.

Megan nodded. She seemed interested. Rob wasn't sure how she maintained that sympathetic expression in the face of all this whining. He was having trouble just standing here.

"Maybe," Megan said, "he knew you were bad at it when he brought you in."

"That doesn't make any sense," Crystal said.

"Wouldn't he want us to do a good job?" Brittany asked.

"No." Tiffany's voice was flat. "He told that superman guy that we were going to change the way everything got done, remember?"

"I just remember that Daddy always comes here when there's tough stuff to be done and does it," Crystal said.

Brittany wrapped a strand of gum around her finger. "Maybe that's why he put us here. So he could really be a Fate without being a Fate, y'know?"

"It would give him a lot more power," Rob said.

Megan started. She had clearly forgotten he was there. The three girls looked at him in surprise as well.

Rob shrugged. "He would be making the rules and enforcing them. They'd no longer be subject to interpretation."

"You say that like that's not good," Tiffany said.

"Do you think it's good?" Megan asked in perfect shrink mode.

"Daddy can be—y'know—moody," Crystal said.

"He forgets sometimes that he said something," Brittany said.

"No, I don't think it's good." Tiffany tugged on her t-shirt, tucking it under her legs. "You said you could help us."

Megan nodded.

"But *he* said not to trust us." Crystal pointed at Rob.

He bristled. He wasn't sure why. "Actually, you said that she shouldn't trust you."

"Only after you did," Brittany said.

"But you were right." Tiffany met his gaze. She was stronger than she looked. He could actually see a bit of Zeus in her—not in her guile—it would take millennia for her to have as much guile as Zeus—but in her native intelligence and in her initial reluctance to use it.

"I'm sure what I'm going to propose will be difficult for you," Megan said, "but I've been in situations like this before—"

Rob snorted. He couldn't help himself. She had never been in a situation like this. Not unless she'd been lying to him, and he knew she hadn't been.

She glared at him, effectively silencing him. Then she continued.

"As I said, I've been in situations like this before, and I've found that if the children truly want something, they'll work at it, no matter how controlling the parent is."

It sounded so good, and it was so full of crap. Rob shook his head. Once again, Megan was spouting the kind of psychobabble that had made parts of the last hundred years living hell.

"You really think we can get out of this?" Crystal asked.

"You really think we can stand up to Daddy?" Brittany asked.

"You really think he won't turn us into warthogs for the rest of our lives?" Tiffany asked. Her tone was as mocking as Rob's mental tone had been.

Megan smiled at all three of them as if Tiffany's tone hadn't bothered her at all.

"Yes," she said, "I really think that. If you all want this badly enough. Do you want to be the Fates for the rest of your lives?"

"For the rest of our lives?" Crystal asked.

"He said 'interim,'" Brittany said. "I looked it up—"

"Actually, *I* looked it up," Tiffany said.

"—and it means short-term," Crystal finished. "Right?"

"That's what I thought it said," Brittany said.

"That *is* what it said," Tiffany said. "I read it to you, remember?"

"Short-term means, like, a week, right?" Crystal asked.

"Only it's been longer than a week," Brittany said.

"A lot longer," Tiffany said.

Rob suppressed a sigh. These girls were grating on his nerves.

But Megan seemed so serene sitting on that Astroturf and looking up at them as if she had no power in the world, even though she was clearly controlling the conversation.

What had the girls called her? An empath?

An empath.

Empaths were rare. He'd only met one other in all of his years. Their magic was subtle, their overt powers slight.

But their ability to control a room—if they knew what they were doing—was phenomenal.

Megan was controlling this room even though these girls were creating all kinds of chaos.

Megan. Not him. Not them.

Megan.

The one without any magic at all.

He tilted his head slightly and watched her. She seemed so at ease. She hadn't seemed at ease when she'd come to the office today. She had displayed a lot of insecurity.

And when he had first seen her inside his bubble, she'd slapped herself to wake herself from the "dream." Certainly not the sign of a secure person either.

Her behavior here was so very different from those other two behaviors. It was almost as if this were a different Megan, one so confident that she could face anything and find a solution.

"Did your father ever give you a time limit on this?" she asked the girls softly.

"No," Crystal said.

"Actually," Brittany said, "he told a lot of people that when this was all said and done, we'd be Fates."

"When what was all said and done?" Megan asked.

"When he convinces the other Powers That Be to forgo the application process," Tiffany said almost as if she were repeating someone else's words.

"The application process for being a Fate, which was why the real Fates stepped down?" Rob asked.

"They didn't step on anything," Crystal said. "They had term limits."

"Those were new. My daddy got the Powers to agree to that," Brittany said.

"On the condition that anyone could apply," Tiffany said. "Aphrodite pushed for that."

"But Daddy convinced everybody that those other Fates were doing a bad job," Crystal said.

"They were," Brittany said. "They let some really mean people loose and stuff."

"But they did better than we are." Tiffany swept her hand around the library. "They'd actually read and understood all these books."

"And remembered them," Crystal said.

"Tiffany can't remember them," Brittany added.

"You can't even read them," Tiffany said and flounced back in her chair.

Rob wanted to grab each girl and tell her to sit still and shut up so that he could think. But Megan hadn't moved.

"But did your father ever say how long you'd be Fates?" Megan asked.

"He said *interim*," Crystal said.

"That other stuff was just junk he told other people," Brittany added.

"Only now I believe it," Tiffany said.

"Me, too," Crystal said.

"Me, too." Brittany sniffled. "I don't wanna do this any more."

Megan smiled softly. "All right, honey. You've convinced me you're sincere. And see? I didn't even need the magic."

Brittany sniffled even louder. Rob couldn't take it anymore. He conjured a handkerchief and handed it to her. She batted her wet eyelashes at him. She was flirting with him. He shuddered.

He retreated to Megan's side and sat beside her. The Astroturf was hard and scratchy.

"Megan," he said softly, "no matter how much you want to help, we can't take on Zeus."

"I'm not asking you to," she said.

"You can't do it without me," he said.

"Sure I can." She smiled, but there was irritation in it.

"Honey, you have no idea—"

"Don't 'honey' me," she snapped. There was the woman he had seen earlier. Not the serene one who'd been talking to the girls. "Ever since we've met, you've been taking responsibility for me or apologizing for not doing it as if I'm some fragile example of femininity. I'm not. I can take on anyone I please. These girls need help, and so do the Fates, and so, apparently, does the group of people my brother's involved with. I know how to help everyone, with or without you."

He gaped at her. He hadn't expected this.

The girls had all leaned forward as if this conversation was a spectator sport. If they'd been actual teenagers, he would have disappeared them—even for just a moment.

But they weren't. They were Interim Fates—possibly the real Fates—and he couldn't have a bad relationship with yet another group of Fates. They might not be as hands-off as the others had proven to be over the centuries.

"You can leave if you want," Megan said. "In fact, why don't you? You can come back for me in, say, an hour."

He wasn't even breathing. He had to remember to breathe. He made himself inhale, and he got slightly dizzy.

What was she doing? Hadn't she noticed how

he'd helped her? He'd explained the magic to her. He'd helped her understand this new world she was in. He'd taken very good care of her in the short time he had known her.

He stood up and almost magicked himself away, and then he heard Little John's voice in his head. John would deride him for leaving her, for abandoning yet another chance.

And, honestly, he shouldn't leave a woman to face the wrath of Zeus alone.

Rob retreated to the bookshelf. He resumed his laid-back posture, crossing his arms and leaning his head against the wood.

"I'm staying," he said.

She frowned at him. The girls all tilted their heads as if he were a new species.

"Continue your little discussion," he said. "I won't interrupt anymore."

"Yeah, right," Tiffany said.

"Like men can ever not interrupt," Crystal added.

"They always butt in," Brittany said.

Megan turned her back on him.

He felt her rejection like a personal loss.

19

Arrogant S.O.B. Who did he think he was anyway, standing against that bookshelf like he didn't have a care in the world?

Megan turned her back on him because she couldn't stand to look at him. He was a mixture of kindness, arrogance, and old-fashioned medieval maleness, and she didn't have the time at the moment to sort through any of that.

She had to remain calm to make her suggestion. She focused on the girls. They looked so young as they stared at her; their faces, which were covered with piercings and make-up in an attempt to look older, only seemed even more vulnerable.

The bikinis, the lawn chairs, and the Astroturf in the middle of their hated library didn't help. Obviously, their controlling father had been trying to placate them.

It hadn't worked.

"All right," she said. "You need to listen to me for a moment, without interruption."

She resisted the urge to turn and glare at Rob just to make her point. She had to forget he was there.

As if that were possible.

"You girls don't want to do this. You were tricked into the position."

All three girls nodded.

"Your father really wants to control this himself, but the others in his group won't let him, so he's manipulating the situation and using you to do it, right?"

Again, the girls nodded. Their eyes were big, and their expressions were identical. Megan hadn't thought the three of them looked at all alike until this moment.

"You were tricked into taking this job. The other three women who had been the Fates were tricked into leaving it."

The girls set their jaws in an identical movement. Megan noted it. They obviously had mixed feelings about the other Fates. She was glad she hadn't called those three adult women "The Fates." It might have lost her sympathy with these three.

"They would like the job back. You would like to leave it. They lost their magic, and they need help recovering it. Would you be willing to do the magic, under their guidance, needed to—"

"No!"

That was Rob. Megan whirled. His hands were fists.

"They will not do anything like that!" He looked angry.

"We can help," Crystal said.

"We'd like to help," Brittany said.

"We can do the magic," Tiffany said. "With help anyway."

"They'll be fine," Megan said.

"NO!" Rob was waving those clenched fists. She wondered if he knew how ridiculous he looked.

Ridiculous and somehow gorgeous. Anger looked good on him. Was that why history remembered him as a lord who, out of anger, took on the entire establishment—and won (at least for a while)?

"They won't be fine. You don't know what you're asking, Meg. The Fates need someone to go into Faerie. Sending these infants into Faerie would be like sending three mice into a pride of lions. You can't do that. The faeries would steal their magic within five minutes and maybe take their souls. And then what would their father do to you? You can't. You just can't."

He was concerned for her. She could feel it. He would have spoken up if someone else had suggested the plan, but the emotion, the vehemence, was all because he was worried about her.

She felt oddly flattered but knew that she couldn't let her own emotions rise too much to the surface. She would lose her ability to help the girls.

"I'm willing to go to this Faerie place," Crystal said.

"Me too," Brittany said.

But Tiffany had grown pale. "The old Fates need something in Faerie? Why?"

Megan shrugged. "They say it'll help them."

"What's wrong with Faerie?" Crystal asked Tiffany.

"I've heard it's kinda wicked cool," Brittany said.

"They've been at war with us for centuries," Tiffany said. "Didn't you guys pay attention in Mrs. Sawtooth's History of the Magical Universe class?"

"Were we supposed to?" Crystal asked.

"Girls," Megan said. She put just a little harshness into her voice. "We were talking about the plan."

"Yeah, but Tiff's worried about it." Brittany spit out her gum and stuck it underneath her lawn chair.

The movement made Megan wince.

"The hottie's right," Tiffany said. "We'd go in there, and they'd win. The faeries would take on Daddy, and he'd have to come for us . . ."

Her voice trailed off. Megan read the expression almost as the thought crossed Tiffany's mind. Their father might not come for them at all, and that would be even worse.

It would prove that he really didn't care about them, that he had been using them all along.

Crystal and Brittany were staring at Tiffany, waiting for her to finish the thought.

Rob came up behind Megan and pulled her to her feet. "We're going to leave now."

"No," she said. "I promised to help these girls."

"We will." His voice was tight and angry.

"We can't go into Faerie," Crystal said. "Not if Tiff's afraid of it."

"Tiff's really our brains," Brittany said. "We tease her because she, like, likes books even though she says she doesn't, but we need her because we'd be really dumb without her."

Somehow, Megan managed not to wince at that.

"We'll help you," Rob said, and there was sincerity in his voice. His hand still clutched Megan's arm, his fingers a bit too tight against her skin. "If we bring Clotho, Lachesis, and Atropos back here and they've already regained their magic, will you three step down?"

"Daddy won't like that." Tiffany's entire body radiated fear.

Megan wanted to shake off Rob's hand, but she didn't. She didn't want to do anything that would alarm the girls. Instead, she willed herself to be calm and said:

"See, this is where you have to decide if you want to live your life or the life your father chose for you."

The girls looked at each other. Crystal and Brittany seemed hopeful, but it was clear they were waiting for Tiffany to make the decision.

Poor girl. She had been in charge from the moment their father had dragged them here.

"What you have to make certain of," Megan said as gently and nonjudgmentally as she could, "is that what you want and what your father wants is in your own best interest."

"I can't stand talking in order like this," Crystal said.

"And we never get to leave this library," Brittany said. "It sucks. That's why Daddy brought the pool."

"He brought the pool to insult us," Tiffany said through clenched teeth. "He promised us a beach on the Mediterranean if we did everything right. This is no beach."

He was manipulating them, using them, and insulting them. Megan felt anger rise inside her. She tamped it down. She had to remain neutral.

But Rob's eyes had narrowed. The anger fairly sparked off him.

"You girls have to make a decision," he said. Megan wanted to elbow him, but it was too late. He'd already butted in. She couldn't stop him from doing more. "The thing is, you have to make it fast because we're leaving."

"We can't, like, think about it and summon you back?" Crystal asked.

"No," Rob said.

Megan was actually glad he'd answered that question because she still had no idea how most of the magic rules worked. Her sympathy rose for the girls. They had no idea how most of the magic rules worked either, and yet they were ostensibly in charge of it all.

"We can get you back if we want to," Brittany said defiantly. "Right, Tiff?"

Tiffany didn't answer her. She was watching Rob.

"If you girls won't agree," he said, "we'll come up with a new plan. And you will probably end up as the Fates if that's truly what your father wants for you."

Rob wasn't shabby at manipulation either.

"What if we tell Daddy about you?" Tiffany said, clutching her knees to her chest. She wasn't wearing bikini bottoms.

Megan wanted to chastise her for that but didn't. Perhaps the girl had never learned modesty.

Rob shrugged. Apparently, he didn't notice Tiffany's lack of attire. "If you tell your father, I'm sure he'll have something to say to us. We'll deal with it. I've handled worse."

That was bravado. Megan heard it in his voice. She wondered if the girls did too.

"You know, that's kinda mean, Tiff," Crystal said.

"Yeah," Brittany said. "They offered to help."

"You think they're doing it for us?" Tiffany turned her head so that her cheek rested on her knee. Megan could no longer see her face. "They're doing it for those other Fates. They don't care about us."

"Those Fates helped kill the love of my life," Rob said. "I have no desire to help them."

"And I just met them," Megan said.

"We only came here at the request of a friend because she thought that things were out of control." Rob let go of Megan's elbow and slipped his arm around her back, pulling her close. He was going to leave soon whether those girls wanted it or not. She could just tell.

"Things *are* out of control," Crystal mumbled.

"Daddy says they never were in control," Brittany said.

"But those other women, they could stand up to Daddy." Tiffany's voice was muffled. She still wasn't looking at anyone. "We sure can't."

"It takes practice," Megan said.

Tiffany nodded but didn't move.

"We'll step down," Crystal said. "I promise."

Brittany looked at her, eyes wide. Tiffany raised her head.

"You didn't ask Tiff," Brittany said.

"Yeah, who put you in charge?" Tiffany sounded offended.

"You weren't making any decisions," Crystal said. "I know I can stand up to Daddy. Can you?"

Brittany's eyes grew even wider. They looked like they were going to pop out of her head. Rob's arm grew tight around Megan's waist. She slipped her own arm around his.

The entire room was full of fear.

"I don't know if I can," Brittany whispered.

"None of us can." Tiffany lowered her head.

"*I* can," Crystal said, "and it takes three of us to be Fates, right, Mr. Hottie?"

"Right," Rob said, and Megan suppressed a smile. She'd bet he'd never been called Mr. Hottie before in his life.

"So you're quitting?" Brittany asked.

Crystal nodded.

"Until Daddy shows up," Tiffany said.

"Even then." Crystal squared her shoulders and looked directly at Megan. "Can you guys hurry up about getting those other Fates their magic stuff back? Because I don't know how long these two can keep a secret."

This time, Megan did smile. The girls did work as a team. They just didn't recognize it yet.

"I think they'll surprise you," Megan said.

"But yes, we'll hurry up," Rob said. Then he snapped his fingers, and the library disappeared.

20

Rob's Las Vegas office had never looked so welcome. He appeared on the two-toned rug, his arm around Megan's back and her arm around him. The trip had been so quick that she hadn't even had time to grab on tighter like she had before.

She blinked in surprise. Apparently, she hadn't expected to come here.

But he wanted the magical trail to end here, particularly if Zeus were pursuing them. The entire interaction with the Interim Fates had terrified Rob—and he couldn't remember ever being terrified before.

"Is Kyle still here?" Megan was getting used to interdimensional travel, but it still clearly unnerved her.

"I told John to take him back to wherever the dog was. I recall that there was dog emergency." That conversation seemed like a long, long time ago.

So much had happened since then. So many dangerous things.

Megan had no idea what she was playing with by advising the Interim Fates to defy their father. This was nothing like advising some rich Hollywood brat to defy the head of a major studio.

Zeus had real power, life-destroying power, and no qualms about using it.

And, apparently, no Fates to get in his way.

"Then what are we doing here?" Megan slipped her arm from him, pushed her hair away from her face, and sighed. She looked drained. Being calm for those children had taken something out of her.

"Laying a false trail." Rob went to his desk. Since he was here, he might as well get his car keys. No sense in using magic when he didn't have to.

"A false trail. From those children?"

"From their father."

"Zeus." Megan shook her head. "He sounds like quite a piece of work."

"He is that all right." Rob wasn't going to try to explain Zeus to her, at least no more than he already had. If she didn't have an inkling about Zeus from her mythology and cultural history classes, then trying to teach her in a few hours wouldn't work.

Besides, she'd had enough shocks for one day.

Rob's keys were beneath a stack of papers that a secretary must have put on his desk. He glanced at them. Three more CEOs had pledged money to a fund they thought would bring in more oil from the Middle East. Instead, the money went to a corporation named for a major oil baron, a corporation that helped children eat.

"Do you think John took my car?" Megan asked. "Because if he didn't, I'd like to go back to the hotel."

Rob looked up. She was studying his face as if she wasn't sure of him any longer.

He wasn't sure of himself either. He always went to an intellectual position when faced with danger. He would separate from his emotions, move to a tactical place, and then live there until the danger had passed.

Only there was no way to know when this danger would pass.

"Are you all right?" she asked gently.

"Fine," he said, and the word sounded curter than he wanted. He wanted to speak to her tenderly, to ease that emotional roller coaster she'd been on. But he felt very far away from his own emotions at the moment. He had no idea how to reach hers.

"The car?" she prompted.

"I'm sure he didn't take the car," Rob said.

"Good." She headed toward the door, then stopped when she put her hand on the knob. "It's been . . . unusual."

She was going to leave. As quickly as she had appeared, she was going to leave. As if there were nothing between them.

Had he imagined that? Or was it all on his side?

"I'm coming with you," he said.

"No," she said. "That's fine."

In the past, he would have let a woman get away with that sentence. But this wasn't the past, and she wasn't just any woman. He didn't want her to leave.

Besides, they had unfinished business.

"I told Zoe we'd meet her at your hotel, re-member?" Rob said.

He wanted to tell Megan that he wasn't going to let her out of his sight, that she was probably in danger from Zeus, that she had probably of-fended all of the Powers That Be, but he couldn't. He would sound alarmist and somewhat crazy and more than a little overprotective.

At this point, he had no idea what she thought of him, but he hoped it was none of those things.

"You can just snap yourself there, right?" Megan asked. "Because I have to drive. I can't afford to stay in that parking garage overnight."

Snap himself there. What a way to describe it.

"I'd prefer not to use any more magic than I have to," he said.

She looked skeptical.

"Besides, driving from here to the hotel wouldn't leave a magical trail."

"Oh." Apparently, that convinced her. Not the pleasure of his company, not the warmth of his presence. "I guess you can come then. If you want to leave now."

She looked pointedly at the papers in his hand. He set them down.

"Now's fine," he said.

They were being so oddly formal with each other, as if they didn't know each other.

Of course, they really didn't. They hadn't met before last night—if that even counted in the realm of meeting anyone. After all, they hadn't had much of a conversation last night, and today, they'd mostly dealt with the Fates.

He'd only assumed she was as attracted to him as he was to her.

And that was probably a false assumption. Considering his lack of experience with modern women and considering her ability to turn on the compassion when she needed it, he had probably misread every single signal she'd sent.

"Let's go then," she said and led him out the door.

He followed her through the hallways of his own company. He tried to imagine what it looked like to her. It consisted of cubicles and neutral brown walls covered with tasteful prints picked by his interior designer fifty years ago.

Someone had recently told him that those prints were worth money—collector's value, hard to come by—but he had ignored it. Everything half-a-second old in America was considered an antique. Even the office equipment here, except for the ugly cubicles, of course, and even those were ancient by American standards. He'd bought them at the insistence of his team almost twenty-five years ago when the Age of the Cubicle was just beginning.

But Megan didn't seem to notice any of it, not the art; not the Eames chairs; not the gray, functional desks with the state-of-the-art computers. She didn't even nod at the employees as she passed them. Instead, she kept her head slightly down and headed toward the stairs and, ultimately, the exit.

Those Interim Fates had called her an empath, and her abilities in that library had seemed uncanny. Now she was acting like an empath as well:

in room after room, all filled with emotion, she was walling herself off.

Just like he had done when he had returned from the Interim Fates. He had walled himself off so that he could fight an important battle.

She walled herself off just to get through a crowd.

His heart went out to her again. Did she know that her discomfort around large groups of people came from her natural magic talent? Or did she assign something else the blame?

And how could he explain to her that the abilities she'd shown—the way she had talked to those girls, the profession she had chosen—were as much a part of her as that mind-reading ability was a part of her nephew?

She hurried down the art deco staircase that he had installed against the advice of his first designer, a man he had hired when this building was being built. That man had had no idea that deco was going to be classic; if Rob had taken his advice, the place would be an outmoded curiosity instead of one of Vegas's hidden architectural wonders.

He had always gone his own way. Always. Even when he'd fallen in love with Marian.

He'd married her toward the end. But in an era when everyone married, remained chaste, or had mistresses in other towns to hide the bastard children, he had lived in sin with a noblewoman in the forest, no less.

For centuries, everyone had told him to date, and he'd tried on occasion, only to fail.

And now he was falling for an empath nearly

eight hundred years his junior who had no idea what kind of windmills she was tilting at.

Was that why he was falling for her? Because she was tilting at windmills?

Hardly anyone did that. The true idealists were as rare as empaths, and just as fragile.

"Megan," he said, "wait."

She stopped at the main glass doors. The security guards watched him approach her as if they'd never seen him like this.

Maybe they hadn't. He felt vulnerable again.

Somewhere in that walk from his office to the front of the building, his emotional walls had crumbled.

She looked over her shoulder at him. "Wait for what?"

He didn't know the answer to that. He just wanted to be beside her. Walking with her instead of behind her. At her side.

For as long as she would have him.

He didn't say any of that. He was afraid he would scare her.

"For me," he said simply. "I just wanted you to wait for me."

21

Wait for him.

Megan had waited for a man like Rob all of her life.

And, in this postfeminist era, she was embarrassed to admit it, and even more embarrassed to admit that she was attracted to a man whose attitudes were so out-of-date that they had been old-fashioned in the medieval era.

She was tired. And very confused.

Those Interim Fates had taken all of her energy, and she still wasn't sure she'd helped them.

She wasn't sure she had helped anyone.

The doors in front of her were warm from the Vegas sun. Above her, an air-conditioning vent sent chills down her spine. She needed to move.

She pushed on the doors just as Rob caught up to her. He slipped a hand onto the small of her back, sending a different kind of chill up her spine.

Maybe she was attracted to him because he was so very handsome. He moved beautifully, and she was always attracted to graceful men. Then he had that melodious voice, with its unusual accent, and she was lost. Just lost.

He could be a Neanderthal and have those qualities (although a Neanderthal wouldn't have those qualities—not in the looks department or the movement department, but maybe in the voice department [although the accent would be completely different, provided, of course, Neanderthals had the physical ability to speak a complicated language like English]) and she'd still be attracted.

The bottom line was, simply, that the combination of looks, brains, movement, and accent was just lethal, at least for her, and he could think she was property, hit her over the head with his club, and drag her away by her hair, and she would let him.

She'd probably even enjoy it.

And that just made her even more disgusted with herself.

They stepped outside into the blazing afternoon heat. It didn't matter that there was an awning above them or that the nearby building pumped cool air onto the street; it was still the middle of the desert and so incredibly hot that she felt as if she would melt at any moment.

The chills from the air-conditioning dissipated immediately. The chills from Rob's hand remained.

She walked at her normal pace to the parking garage, forcing him to keep up with her. She had blamed him all day for having emotions that ran the gamut from anger to kindness, but her emotions had been all over the place too.

Too many times, she'd let a man's kindness blind her. A man who treated her with respect, a man who listened to her, a man who acted as if she were important; she used to misread those signals and think that he was falling for her.

She rounded the corner into the parking garage. It smelled of old gasoline, and wasn't really much cooler than the sidewalk.

Rob had managed to keep up with her and keep his hand against the flat of her back. She liked that.

She liked it a bit too much.

Even if she discounted the fact that he believed women needed to be taken care of, even if she ignored the way that he had stomped all over her in the conversation with the Interim Fates, there was still the matter of their eight-century age difference.

Yes, he might have a love for Maid Marian that had lasted for the ages, but she had died ages ago. And in that time, he had to have known other women.

Maybe this was how he met them, charming them, showing flashes of himself, using his magic to woo them, and then getting what he wanted— whatever that was (could a man who had lived 800 years still think with the wrong part of his anatomy? She'd always heard that older men started using their upper brain 'long about fifty, but did that apply to men who aged slowly over several centuries? And who could she ask? She didn't know anyone else who had met someone as old as Rob. Except Zoe, whom she didn't know well either).

"You're very quiet," he said, his voice echoing against the concrete dividers.

"It's been a difficult day."

That was an understatement. She had discovered that her brother was not only magic, but engaged; that her poor nephew had been able to read minds ever since he could remember; and that there was not one, but two, groups of Fates—ditzy women/girls who somehow controlled the universe.

Anyone would be stressed after all that.

Her Mini Cooper sat alone in the section of the parking garage designed for small cars. Hardly anyone owned a small car anymore. Across the divide, dozens of SUVs vied for space.

She waved her hand at the passenger side—she didn't even want him to think he could drive her car—and unlocked the doors. As she crawled in, she watched Rob fold himself into his seat.

He looked comfortable enough.

She closed her door, put the keys in the ignition, and started the car. Rob turned toward her.

"I make you nervous, don't I?"

She wasn't sure how to answer that. He did make her nervous, but not in the way he thought. She wasn't nervous because she was afraid of him. She was nervous because she was attracted to him, and how could she admit that to a man who was famous not only in his own time but also throughout generations?

And, under another name, he was famous in this time too. Only as a billionaire playboy who jetsetted from place to place.

So she decided for bravado instead. "I was just thinking that I must make you nervous."

"Me?" he said after a moment. "You? Make me? Nervous? I—"

Then he laughed.

"I guess you must," he said.

She grinned at him. She hadn't expected him to make her smile.

Then she backed out of the parking space. The car turned easily, and she didn't even come close to the SUVs. She probably should have checked her bumper before backing out, though. One of those monstrosities had probably hit her.

She clicked the air-conditioning higher, not that it would do any good yet, and rolled down her window. Rob's was already down.

She turned left, trying to remember exactly how she had gotten here.

It felt like a lifetime ago. In fact, she could hardly remember how to operate the car. Of course, that probably had something to do with the man beside her.

He was a powerful distraction.

"You know," he said, looking out that open window, "the Interim Fates called you an empath."

"They called you a hottie," Megan said.

"Well, in your case, it's true."

What an obscure compliment to give her. At least he wasn't repeating tried and true lines.

Lines tried and proven true over centuries.

She shivered. The air coming from the blowers had grown chilly. She rolled up her window and turned the air-conditioning on full blast.

"What they said about you is true in your case too," she said.

He grinned at her sideways. "I'm not trying to butter you up."

"I'm not trying to butter you up either. They're right. They're too young for you, but they're right."

And there it was, in the open. The age thing.

"They're too *immature* for me," he said. "I've learned over the course of my long life that age really doesn't matter."

So there had been other women, probably hundreds of them.

"I would think it would have to." Megan came to an intersection, thankful that the stoplight ahead of her was red. She needed a moment to remember the route to the hotel. "I mean, after all, what do people have in common anyway? A shared history—not just the time they spend together, but the time they spend on the planet—accumulated wisdom, and years of observations—"

"Does my age bother you?" he asked.

"Um . . ." It was her turn to stammer. For a moment, she wished she was an interim fate and could say, *well, duh!*, with impunity. "Sure. I mean, yeah. I mean, shouldn't it?"

"I don't know," he said. "Should it?"

"You were in the Crusades," she said. "Not on a crusade, but *the* Crusades. You know, the historical event. And I'm sure the more I talk to you, the more historical events I'll learn about. You've lived like 25 times longer than I have. And that doesn't bother you? There's no way I can be as 'mature' as you are."

"That's a kind way of saying that I'm an old fart." He grinned. "If the hotel's anywhere near the Strip, you just missed your turn."

She cursed, fought with the wheel, and glanced in the rearview mirror. How could he tell? In this stretch of Vegas, all of the neighborhoods looked alike.

But the Eiffel tower and the Empire State building were suddenly on her right, instead of slightly to her left.

"Turn here," he said, "and you'll be fine."

She nodded, feeling dumb. Here she was talking about maturity, and she suddenly felt like she was on a practice drive with her driver's ed instructor.

She followed his advice and found herself on a six-lane road filled with cars with the Strip glowing like a neon mirage ahead of her.

"I wasn't saying you're an old fart," she said, wondering if she had implied it. She had trouble picking the right words while she was also driving and pretending not to be lost. "I'm just saying that a person like me has got to be dull to a person like you, no matter how mature I am for my age."

"It doesn't work that way," he said. "After a certain point, all adults have a lot in common."

"Whatever that means." She turned again. The streets were starting to look familiar.

"After a while, who you are is more important than how long you've lived." He shrugged. "Think about it. With the exception of your parents, don't you feel like you're the same age as most people who are over thirty and not obviously frail and elderly?"

She did. She gave advice to people twenty years older than she was without thinking about it, and talked to people who were in their sixties as if they were the same age as she was.

She let out a small breath. "I understand the 'you're only as old as you feel' concept, but it has nothing to do with eight hundred years of living versus twenty-five."

His eyebrows went up. "You're only twenty-five? Well then, forget it. You're much too young for me."

She opened her mouth, shook her head, and then realized she had no response to his comment at all. None.

"We're just going to have to wait until you're thirty," he said.

She reached the hotel and turned left into the parking garage. The attendant waved at her. She waved back.

"Wait for what?" she asked as she pulled into the same parking space she'd had that morning.

"A relationship."

She shut off the car and shook her head again. "A relationship?"

She couldn't quite believe that. Why would he be interested in a relationship? A friendship, a one-night stand, but a relationship?

He chuckled. "You actually believe me."

Her face grew so warm that it almost hurt. He had tricked her into admitting her feelings. How could an eight-hundred-year-old man make her feel like she was in high school all over again?

He frowned. "I meant about being twenty-five instead of thirty. Not about the relationship."

She nodded, made herself breathe, then popped the car door open. "It's hot in here, don't you think?"

He took her hand. "I'm actually interested in you, Megan. The relationship comment wasn't a joke. Seriously."

"Sure," she said and got out of the car, slamming the door so hard that the sound echoed in the concrete bunker that was so like the one she had just left.

He got out too. "I mean it. I haven't met a woman who has attracted me like you have in centuries."

"See?" she said. "There it is again. Centuries."

"You want me to say years?" he asked. "That's trivial in the context of my life. I mean centuries. Since Marian."

The last two words hung between them. He looked appalled by them; she felt helpless, as if she were floating against a tide she had no control over.

"Is that a line you use on all the women?" she asked after a moment.

He shook his head. His expression was tight.

She regretted her question suddenly. She had wanted him to feel as uncomfortable as she did, and she had clearly achieved that. In fact, she had made him feel more uncomfortable.

She had hurt him.

"I'm sorry," she said. "That was rude of me."

He blinked and seemed to get control of himself, but his eyes were wide and pain-filled. Still, he forced himself to smile.

"I deserved it," he said. "I guess it's odd to think that someone like me, someone who has been around forever, would fall for someone else in less than a day."

Her breath caught. Fall for? He wasn't lying. She would be able to sense it if he were lying.

Wouldn't she?

"It does seem improbable," she said, and her words sounded lame. Worse than lame, they were slightly cruel.

Why was she hurting him? Because she was afraid of him?

Not him, exactly.

She was afraid of the powerful emotions he was drawing up from inside her. She had worked for most of her adult life at masking her emotions, hiding behind the screen she'd learned, being as calm as she could be.

She was anything but calm around Rob.

"Yeah," he said and smiled again ever so slightly. "It does seem improbable. But everything about me is improbable."

She had to give him that. She had to give him more than that. She had to stop fighting whatever it was between them.

"Everything about this day has been improbable," she said.

"I'm moving too fast for you." He leaned against the car and rested his arms on the roof, staring at her.

She resisted the urge to look around him to see if the attendant was listening.

"Everything is moving too fast for me," she said. "I'm not good at surprises."

"It seems to me you are," he said. "You were

able to handle the Interim Fates better than I could have."

She shrugged. "I work with teenagers."

"Not teenagers who have enough magic to destroy the planet."

"Oh," she said softly, "some of them think they do."

"I mean literally."

She nodded. "I know that. But there's not a lot of difference between thinking you have that power and actually having that power."

"Unless you use it," he said.

"With their father around, do you think they would?" she asked.

He grinned. "You see, you do really well with surprises. You have a lot of this figured out."

"And a lot of it is just me swimming upstream." She was used to swimming upstream. When her parents had adopted her, they'd already had Travers and Vivian. Megan had felt like she was behind the curve from the moment she had arrived in that house.

The world had always been an inexplicable place, and she worked hard at not being noticed.

And here was a gorgeous man—a gorgeous, accomplished man—a gorgeous, accomplished man in many countries and many lifetimes— noticing her.

More than noticing her.

Wanting her.

For whatever reason.

"So," he said. "I was right. I scare you."

Megan nodded. It was difficult to be honest

with him, but it felt good at the same time. Still, she wanted out of the conversation.

"I scare you," he said, "because of who I was."

She shook her head. "Because of who you are."

He raised his eyebrows. "Rob Chapeau, Billionaire Playboy? I already told you that's made up for the press."

"Magical, good-looking, a little—" (a lotta, but she wasn't ready to say that) "—old-fashioned, smart, and strong."

He smiled, clearly flattered and a bit bemused. "Why would that frighten you?"

Honesty time. She had promised herself. "Because you're interested in me."

"Why wouldn't I be? You're beautiful—"

She snorted.

"—smart, strong, and intuitive. I like all of that."

"I'm sure there were countless women in your past with all of those traits."

He nodded. "But none of them with the ability to see me, and see me clearly."

Her gaze met his. "I don't know if I see you clearly."

"You walked into my magic circle last night," he said.

"Drove in," she said.

"And your questions this afternoon kicked my magic enough out of control that I showed you parts of my past no one has ever seen. Then you were able to talk with the Interim Fates. That's amazing. I've never met anyone like you."

"So," she said, trying not to let disappointment

into her voice. "It's all about that empathic ability you were talking about. That rarity."

He shook his head. "It's about you. I find you fascinating, and I want to protect you, and I want to hold you—"

"I don't need protection," she snapped. She hated it when he brought this up. If he persisted in this attitude, there would be nothing between them.

"Ah," he said, leaning his chin on the back of his hands. It almost seemed like he was part of the car this way. "But you do need protection, Megan. You—"

"I can take care of myself. I have for twenty-five years. I'm a very strong woman, you said so yourself, and I can—"

"I know you're strong," he said. "I know you can take care of yourself. But no one has looked out for you, have they? Not once. No one told you that you have a special ability. No one showed you your magic like they showed your brother his."

"My brother had no idea until this week." She was glad the car was between her and Rob. She needed the shield. She was getting more and more unsettled.

"But you're so sensitive about how you look and your own abilities," Rob said gently. "That comes when someone has to take care of herself, when she has no one to defend her."

"My family's great," she said. "It's just weird. I have a pretty, petite sister and a brother who looks like a 1950s version of an All-American basketball player, and then there's tubby little old me."

Tubby. She winced when she said that word. It just came out.

"Was that what your parents called it?" Rob asked gently.

She shook her head. "They said it was baby fat. They said I'd grow out of it."

"You're voluptuous. Bottitcelli's *Venus,*" he said. "So incredibly beautiful. Women need to celebrate their looks, their femaleness. You do."

"I don't," she said. "I'd give anything to be a size six. But I could starve and never fit into anything smaller than a ten. I'm big-boned and big-hipped and big, big, big."

He could probably hear the self-loathing in her voice. Her counselor had told her to work on body image, and she tried. But that meant accepting she would never be small, she would always be short and round, and nothing she could do would ever change that.

"Womanly," he said.

"Fat," she said.

"In today's culture," he said, "I can see how you feel that way. But women like you were rich in most of the years I lived through. Rich and strong because you had to be lush to bear children, to live through the hardships. Women like you represented the ideal female beauty, warm and soft and curvy."

She stared at him but continued to lean against the car so that he couldn't see her body.

He actually seemed to mean those words. He said each one as if it were a sensual detail, as if he were describing the best meal he'd ever had or the tastiest bottle of wine.

"You believe that, don't you?" she said.

He nodded. "My Marian was built like you, not like the thin things that portray her in the movies. She was a great beauty. Like you."

Megan shook her head slightly. "I'm not beautiful."

"Half the cultures in this world would think you are. And most of the cultures in the past. America has a sickness. It has infected you so that you believe you have no beauty at all. You are stunning." Then he smiled. "This is what I mean by protecting you."

She frowned. "I'm not following."

"I mean that like all of us, you have damaged places, hurt places, and those places need a champion, someone to help them heal. I don't want to take over your life and diminish you. I would like to be beside you, and keep those harmful attitudes from hurting you worse. There is nothing wrong with having someone strong beside you, to give you added strength."

She tilted her head slightly. She'd never heard anything like this, and she wasn't sure if it was true. It certainly wasn't anything she'd been taught in her courses, although it had a certain validity for her practice.

If she had been able to go home with some of her patients, to defend them—protect them—against the verbal battering they received from their parents, or to point out the neglect, the lack of love, then she would have been those children's champions. And she would have been able to help them strengthen. Maybe their parents wouldn't have changed, but the kids might have seen where their parents were deficient, where their home life was deficient.

"Everyone needs a protector," Rob said. "Even me."

"I couldn't protect you," Megan said softly. "You're a bona fide hero. There are books dedicated to all you've done."

"And yet," he said just as softly, "in order to do those things, I've had to separate myself from my heart. I thought that heart was gone. But you found it."

Her gaze met his. His eyes were warm, sincere.

"We can protect each other," he said, "if we but try."

He was winning her over, and so quickly. She wasn't sure she wanted to be won.

She needed a little time, time to reflect, time to see if this was real or as ephemeral as that trip to the Interim Fates had been.

He stood, obviously feeling her change of mood.

"First," she said quietly, "I need to see if Kyle's all right."

"Then we have to save the world for true love." Rob's words were mocking.

"We did promise to help the Interim Fates," Megan said.

"You promised," he said. "I just agreed to help you."

"You don't think they're worth helping?"

"I think Zeus will destroy us for trying." Then Rob grinned.

Megan felt even more confused. "What's the smile for?"

"You truly are an empath," he said. "You know how to manipulate me."

She shook her head slightly. She didn't like this empath talk. "I didn't mean to manipulate you."

"Maybe not consciously," he said. "But you did."

He was right; she hadn't been aware of what she had done. "How?"

His smile widened. "The best way to get me to join any cause is to ask me to defend the powerless against the powerful."

"Zeus's daughters," Megan said.

He shrugged eloquently. "How much more powerless can you get?"

22

Megan was good at distraction—or at least at distracting Rob. Not only had she taken the conversation off her own insecurities, but she had also gotten him out the parking garage, up the elevator, and to the door of a suite.

It was almost as if she had magical powers as well as the powers of empathy.

She rang the bell, biting her lower lip as she did so. He thought it odd that she wouldn't have a key to her own suite, but he didn't say anything.

He'd been saying enough.

The hallway was wide and empty. Rows of suites ran along the side. This wasn't as upscale as he was used to—John insisted that Rob always stay in five-star hotels to impress the marks.

This place felt cheap. The floorboard echoed as he walked on it, the door seemed thin, and even the doorbell that Megan rang sounded like a duller version of what he was used to.

Obviously, he'd been spending too much time with the wealthy again.

A chain rattled inside, followed by the click of a deadbolt, and the snick of a smaller door lock. Then the door opened, and Kyle peered out.

"Haven't I told you to leave the chain on when you open doors?" Megan asked, sounding irritated.

"Why?" Kyle asked. "I heard you coming a mile away."

Rob hoped not. He had to put some shields back up if he was going to be around the psychic kid.

Kyle gave him a cool glance as if he'd heard that thought (and he might have) then pulled the door the rest of the way open. Megan walked in, wrinkled her nose, and stopped in the entry.

Rob followed.

The entire suite smelled of garlic, potato chips, and diet soda. Beneath those smells was the faint odor of pee.

Was everywhere he went today destined to smell of pee?

The place was large, with a living room on one side, a full kitchen, and a full dining room. At least two bedrooms were off the hallway.

An obese dachshund came up to Megan, its tail wagging. It raised itself on its hind legs, put its front paws on her calves, and gave her a doggy grin.

She stiffened. Rob came up behind her and put a hand protectively on her shoulder. For once, she didn't back away.

"That's Fang," Kyle said to Rob. "He doesn't hurt anyone, but Aunt Megan was badly bit by a dog so she tends to forget that they can be nice."

Rob squeezed her shoulder slightly in support.

"Are you here alone?" Megan asked.

"Mr. Little went to get some food," Kyle said. "The Fates are in the bathroom helping each other with make-up. I'm having lunch."

Hence the garlic-potato-chip-diet-soda smell. Megan walked into the main room. Light from the television set reflected onto her shirt. She picked a container off the coffee table.

"You're having chips and dip for lunch?"

Kyle shrugged. "I got hungry."

Megan shook her head. "Your dad's not home yet, right?"

"How'd you guess?"

"Just lucky," she said.

Rob glanced at her. The dog had followed her into the living room like she was its answer to everything.

"How come it smells like pee in here?" she asked.

Kyle chewed on his lower lip. That had to be a family habit. On him, it looked painful. Parts of his lip looked chewed through.

"Dunno," he lied. He wouldn't look up at Rob.

Megan still had her back to him. She was picking up potato chips and wiping up dip. She certainly had managed to distract herself—and Rob—from the conversation they'd been having earlier.

"We didn't get you here in time to solve the pee emergency, huh?" Rob asked as quietly as he could. He was almost subvocalizing, knowing Megan couldn't hear that, but Kyle could if his psychic radar was on.

"Is it that bad?" Kyle whispered.

Rob nodded. "Didn't John notice?"

"He was fighting with the Fates. They were mad you took Aunt Megan."

"What're you talking about?" Megan came into the hallway, carrying the potato chip bag and the empty dip container.

"Nothing," Kyle said.

"How amazing you are," Rob said.

"Liars," Megan said, and went all the way into the kitchen itself.

"Why were they mad?" Rob asked in that quiet way.

"They thought you took her to Faerie. You didn't, did you?"

Not yet, he thought. But he might, considering what he had to do there. Empaths could distract most faeries, which was why empaths were so rare. In the long ago Mage–Faerie wars, the faeries, for self-protection, had wiped out entire lines of empaths.

Kyle was staring at him, alarmed. "You wouldn't do that to Aunt Meg, would you?"

Kyle had misunderstood him.

"Do what?" Megan came out of the kitchen, brushing her hands together. Her gaze met Rob's. She was looking even more tired than she had in his office.

"Put you in danger," Kyle said before Rob could speak up.

Megan smiled. "Apparently, I did a good job of that myself today."

Kyle looked even more panicked. The boy reached for Megan as the front door opened. John came in, carrying six grocery bags. He staggered past the group and set all of the bags on the kitchen counters.

Rob caught the scent of ripe tomatoes and fresh peppers. "I thought chili wasn't on the Atkins Diet," he said.

"Ah," John said. "You have to make exceptions for special occasions."

He'd learned to make chili two hundred years ago, and he had never given out the recipe. The meal was spectacular. Rob had been missing it, though, since John had ruled out chili as a viable Atkins food about six months ago.

"Why is this a special occasion?" Megan asked.

John grinned at her. "Because I declared it one."

But his expression said enough to Rob. It was a special occasion because of her. Because she was the "best thing" for him.

If she would let him talk to her.

If she would let him convince her that he really did think she was the most special woman he'd met in generations.

"Dad's gonna be really mad," Kyle said to Rob in a conspiratorial tone.

Rob jumped. The boy hadn't heard that last thought, which was good. Rob was blocking his thoughts better than he'd hoped.

"About Megan?"

Kyle shrugged. "I was talking about the pee emergency."

Rob smiled. "I can make it go away if you want."

"Isn't that dishonest?" Kyle asked. "I heard Zoe telling Dad that magic was only for the right uses. We were late getting back."

"So it's okay to use magic to return here, but not okay to use it to clean up the mess?" Rob asked.

Megan looked his way and frowned slightly. Had he spoken too loudly? He didn't want to get Kyle in trouble with her or his dad.

"I dunno," Kyle said. "I'm really confused by all the rules."

Like the Interim Fates. Like Megan. Like everyone, it seemed, except the Fates themselves.

"Let's take care of it," Rob said. "It was my fault you were late. If you get in trouble, blame me."

Megan walked to the doorway of the kitchen. She leaned against the door frame and crossed her arms. "Are you bribing my nephew to make points with me?"

She had, apparently, heard everything.

Rob felt vaguely guilty. Had he been doing that? He hadn't been aware of it. But he wouldn't normally use his magic to clean up dog pee.

"I don't know," he said. "Would it impress you?"

She smiled. "I'm sure it would make my brother angry. Anything that annoys Travers pleases me."

Rob frowned. "Is that true?" he asked Kyle.

"Dad says it's a typical brother–sister relationship, but his relationship with my Aunt Viv isn't like that, so I don't know." Kyle was very serious as he answered.

Poor kid. Didn't he have a childhood?

"And yes, I did. I do lots of kid stuff."

Rob felt a real heat in his cheeks. He was blushing almost as much as Megan had.

"I didn't mean to insult you," Rob said.

"You didn't. But Dad's on his way, so if you're gonna do something, do it soon."

Apparently, the kid was really tuned into his father to know that he was on his way home.

Rob glanced at Megan, silently asking her approval.

She shrugged, then grinned, and said, "I'm sick of places that smell like dog pee."

"You were somewhere else that smelled of dog pee?" Kyle asked.

"We saw the Interim Fates," Megan said.

"Oh." Kyle smiled. "If it still smells like pee there, that's because of Fang too. That's where Zoe rescued him from."

"Fang was their dog?" Rob asked, feeling a little frisson of worry. More things for Zeus to be angry at.

"No," Kyle said. "They were supposed to do something with him—like give him to somebody or something like a familiar—only they didn't understand that. And they didn't know that dogs need to go outside sometimes or that they need baths. He was pretty grody when Zoe brought him back."

"I'll bet," Rob said.

"He's, like, in the parking garage," Kyle said with sudden urgency. It took Rob a moment to figure out that he meant Travers, not Fang.

"Right." Rob waved a hand, then cupped his fingers into a ball and willed the doggy stains— all of them—into stain oblivion.

The suite instantly smelled better.

The fact that John had just put onions and garlic in olive oil helped.

"Thanks," Kyle said.

Megan shook her head. "From saving the world to saving my nephew's dog from my brother's wrath. You're quite something."

Rob smiled at her.

"He's more than something," John said from the kitchen. "He's smitten. He wouldn't've used magic for something that small before."

"Why didn't you clean up the pee?" Rob asked.

"I'd like to say I was going to leave it for you, but I had my hands full of Fates for longer than I wanted," John said.

Rob opened his mouth to comment, but John shook a wooden spoon at him.

"And get your mind out of the gutter. Those women don't do anything alone."

"I thought that wouldn't bother you," Rob said.

"Gentlemen," Megan said gently, "there is a child present."

"Yeah." Kyle sighed. "But I had to learn about all this stuff a long time ago, Aunt Meg."

She looked alarmed. "What stuff?"

"Y'know, like how Fates do everything together. If you think about it, it can be really icky. Like this make-up thing. I mean—"

"Okay," Megan said, putting up her hands. "I see what you mean."

Kyle still had his back to her. He gave Rob a sideways grin, and winked. Did the boy really know what Rob had meant?

Megan would have thought such things were bad for the boy, but back in Rob's day, children were around parents all the time. Many people slept in one-room huts and had huge families.

The human race survived.

Kyle's grin widened. He snapped his fingers, and Fang fell in beside him.

"Me and Fang want to finish watching the anime that we ordered up. Is it okay to watch in my room? You guys are gonna talk about grown-up stuff."

"It's okay," Megan said. "So long as you grab an apple from the kitchen to chase away that chips-and-dip lunch you had."

"That won't make my lunch healthier, Aunt Meg," Kyle said.

"But it'll make me feel better," Megan said.

Kyle rolled his eyes, and went into the kitchen. John tossed him an apple, which he caught, and then he headed down the hall, Fang trailing behind him.

"That's one special kid," Rob said.

"We think so," Megan said with obvious pride.

"Your brother must have been really young when he was born."

"Why?" Megan asked.

Rob glanced at her. John shook his head, then made a show of turning on the tiny television the hotel had thoughtfully provided on the kitchen counter.

Apparently, he didn't want to hear their conversation any more than Kyle did.

"Because," Rob said, "my people can't have children once they come into their magic. Men usually come into it around twenty or so."

"Travers couldn't have been magic that long," Megan said. "I would have noticed."

"I have a hunch he hadn't noticed," Rob said.

Megan gave him a soft smile. "Travers is good at being oblivious sometimes. But you couldn't ask for a better brother."

She was being loyal after the sharp comment she'd made about him earlier. She did seem to adore her family. She had defended them when Rob had criticized them, and she had shown over and over again how much she loved Kyle.

Rob approached her and reached out a hand for her. "Let's finish that discussion."

Her eyes suddenly seemed guarded. "Let's not."

"Megan, I . . ." And then he just decided to stop talking. Talking wasn't getting him anywhere.

So he leaned forward, and kissed her.

She stood very still for a moment, then leaned into him ever so slightly. He wrapped his arms around her waist and pulled her close.

She tasted of sunshine and lip gloss and something sweet, something he'd never tasted before, something uniquely Megan. She was so soft and warm, and she leaned against him as if she were drawing strength from him, her arms wrapping around his neck and bringing him even closer.

He wasn't sure how long they kissed. All he knew was that when he finally broke it off—to tell her that he wanted to go to a more private area, just to talk (and maybe do something more)—he was surprised to see that her eyes were closed and tears dotted her cheeks.

He touched one and stared at it in awe, a shiny drop of water against the ridges on his forefinger.

"Megan?" he whispered.

She didn't open her eyes. Instead, she squeezed them even tighter. Her eyelashes were wet.

He placed both hands on the sides of her face, and used his thumbs to wipe away the remaining tears. Then he kissed her damp, salty skin.

She let out a small moan. Her eyelids fluttered open. Her eyes seemed even greener than they had before.

"I'm sorry," she whispered. "I didn't mean—"

"Oh, look."

"Kissing!"

"Perfect."

Rob felt a thread of irritation. Couldn't those three women leave him alone?

He looked over Megan's shoulder. The Fates had crowded together in the hallway like they were posing for the opening credits on a sitcom. He half expected to hear theme music—*Here's a story about three strange ladies*—and was relieved when he didn't.

"This is private," he said.

"We can tell." Clotho smiled. "Everyone who wants privacy stands in the most public place in the suite."

"You could get a room," Lachesis said. "You can afford it."

"I thought Megan had a room," Atropos said.

They were wearing tasteful but glittery make-up that somehow made their jeans-and-blouse outfits from earlier in the day look very glamorous.

He had to ignore them. Megan's cheeks were flushed, her eyes closed again, an expression of pain on her face.

"You have a room?" he asked, wondering which of the rooms off the hallway was hers.

She nodded.

"Let's go there," he said.

She didn't answer. Then she sighed deeply, opened her eyes, and smiled as if she had never done that before.

She kept her face averted from the Fates and took his hand.

To his surprise, she led him out of the suite and into the hallway. Then she reached into her pocket and removed a keycard.

She opened the door to the adjoining suite as the other door swung shut.

Before it snicked closed, he could hear the Fates.

"I do so love true love," Clotho said.

"It's nice when it works out like it's supposed to," Lachesis said.

"Let's hope that they don't get too distracted," Atropos said. "We need them to keep true love alive."

Rob didn't hear the response. But he did frown. *It's nice when it works out like it's supposed to?* What did that mean?

Marian had been his soulmate, not Megan.

Right?

He shivered once and followed Megan into her suite, not sure he wanted to know the answer to his internal question.

23

He probably thought she was a basketcase.

As Megan stepped into her own suite, she wiped her face with the back of her hand. Tears. She'd never cried before when she'd been kissed.

But she had never felt so inexpressibly sad before, like a part of her was mourning something that she hadn't even known was there.

And then there was the part that had gotten all shuddery, the part that knew she had never been kissed like that before and was afraid she never would be again.

Her suite was colder than her brother's. She walked to the temperature control and adjusted it upwards.

Rob stood in the entry.

"Sorry about all that," he said. "I just had to get away from those women."

Megan nodded, feeling hideously embarrassed. She didn't want to turn around, but she couldn't monkey with the temperature controls all day.

Rob came up behind her and slipped his arms around her waist.

"Where were we?" he muttered. "Ah, I remember. I had decided that talking was no way to convince you I'm attracted to you."

Then he kissed her bare neck right where it met her shoulder, and a delicious shudder of desire ran through her.

The tears threatened to come back too.

She didn't want that, but she didn't want him to let go either. She turned around inside his arms. He looked up in surprise—his entire face seemed alive with passion—and she kissed him.

He pulled her so close that she couldn't quite tell where she ended and he began. He kissed her mouth, her damp cheeks, her eyes. He kissed her neck, and that shiver ran through her again.

And she was kissing him back, her hands finding the jacket on his suit coat and helping it slide off, and then the buttons on his shirt, and the fly on his trousers, and then somehow, she was leading him toward the bed she hadn't yet slept in.

He had a magical mouth that managed to find every part of her that could arouse her, and he hadn't even gotten past her shoulders yet. First, his hands were busy with her shirt, then the clasp of her bra, and then the button on her jeans.

She tripped and fell backwards on the bed, pulling him on top of her. His pants came off easily, and she helped him with hers, and all the time, he kissed her, finding the sensitive areas on her breast, her stomach, her hips, his fingers finding even more sensitive places in even more sensitive areas.

He brushed against her leg, and she bent down, grabbing him and moving him exactly where she wanted him. He slipped inside, his face between her breasts, her legs wrapped around him, forcing him deeper and deeper.

He murmured her name, then raised his head, and she kissed him.

She had never felt so beautiful, so desired.

So loved.

Her eyes closed again, and the tears threatened.

He moved inside her and she could feel the pressure building in both of them and it was like she wasn't one person anymore.

She could feel his passion and hers, his need and hers.

There were no barriers left.

They were one person, and when she—they—couldn't take it any more, and the climax came . . .

. . . she couldn't tell if it was his or hers or theirs.

She couldn't tell, and she wasn't sure if she wanted to. She drowned in sensation—their sensation, two bodies that had somehow—magically—become one.

24

He had never felt like that before. Not once in eight hundred years.

Rob clasped his arms around Megan, holding her to him, pulling her with him as he fell to her side.

He didn't want to lose the togetherness. He didn't want to lose that sense of being more than himself, of being inside her body and her mind at the same time.

He had no idea how a woman felt during love-making—until now—and it was even more arousing than he had thought. If he weren't so tired, it would arouse him all over again.

He kissed that sensitive place on her neck, gently this time. He would never ever be able to be with another woman, not after this.

Megan stirred, her hand caressing his back. But she didn't seem to want to separate from him either. Her face was buried in his shoulder, her warm body tucked against his, so soft, so precious.

Intellectually, he knew what had happened. He

had just made love to a true empath, an empath who had lost her guards—if she ever really had any—and had let him so deep inside her that her magic had flowed both ways.

For that moment, anyway, she had been as attracted to him as he had been to her because she had felt his emotions.

He knew he should tell her that, but he wasn't sure how. He would be telling her to question her own emotions—and yet, he was doing that. He was questioning how she felt.

He didn't want her to regret this, to think that somehow, this was some sort of aberration for her.

Although he had a feeling it was.

He smoothed her hair back. "You okay?" he asked softly.

She raised her head. Her eyelashes were still spiky from those earlier tears. "I've never felt anything like that."

His heart skipped a beat. He brought her head closer, kissed her forehead, and sighed.

"Why are you suddenly so sad?" she asked, and gave him his opening.

He sighed again.

"Is it Marian?" she asked.

He froze. Marian. He hadn't thought of her since he had stepped into the apartment, since he had found himself wondering about great love.

Megan had given him an answer to his earlier question. He had loved Marian with all of his heart. It had been a true love, a union of like minds.

But he was different now. Older. Centuries past the boy he'd been. And this woman that he held now, what she had just given him was so much more than he'd ever had with Marian.

And this relationship was just beginning.

Or so he hoped.

"Robin?" There was a thread of fear in Megan's voice, and she started to pull away.

He kept one arm wrapped around her and stroked her hair. "Is it always that intense for you?"

He made sure his question was very gentle, nonthreatening. He tried to keep his fears and doubts in check.

"Sex?" she asked.

He nodded.

A tear landed on his chest. Then she wiped it off, smearing the wetness.

"It's always—strange for me," she said. "I usually feel so distant."

"And this time?" His worries suddenly changed. Had the intensity only been there for him?

"This time," she said, and her voice trembled. "This time, I almost lost myself."

She said that as if it were a bad thing. He made himself take a deep breath before saying anything more.

"Do you regret it?" he finally asked.

"Do you?"

She wasn't going to answer. This was one of the places in which she'd been hurt. She'd felt mutual passion—maybe too young to understand that young men have stronger sexual urges than young girls—and had gotten attached when the young man hadn't.

He shifted slightly inside her, then smiled at her. "I don't have any regrets."

Her answering smile was radiant. "I'm not sure anything could surpass that first time."

He felt her joy—or maybe it was his own. He couldn't tell. They were still linked, and he was aroused all over again.

He kissed her, and she kissed back—this woman loved to be kissed—and he rolled all the way over so that she was on top of him.

She sat up, his hands resting on her hips, guiding her gently.

The magic started all over again—

And that was when some idiot pounded on the door.

25

Megan was off him in half a second, scrambling for her robe, before she realized that she wasn't in her condo. That knock made her feel like a high school girl caught necking by her parents.

She threw open the closet door and found a terry cloth robe provided by the hotel. As she yanked the robe off the hanger, she turned.

Rob hadn't moved. And he was as aroused as he had been a moment ago.

How had she attracted such a handsome man? She still couldn't believe that.

He smiled, and patted the bed beside him. "It's okay, Megan. They can leave."

She shook her head. "I'm supposed to be watching Kyle."

"Kyle's got John and the Fates. They'll take good care of him, just like they did before."

She pulled the robe on, suddenly embarrassed by the whole thing. He could see her naked. He could see every single flaw.

The knock came again. "Megan! You okay?"

It was Travers.

The flush in her face traveled down her neck into her chest. She hadn't blushed that deeply since she was in middle school.

"Coming, Trav," she said, and then bit her lower lip.

Rob laughed. "That was a few minutes earlier."

"This is serious," she said. "That's my brother. He'll be mad."

Rob's smile faded. "Let him."

"But I'm supposed to be—"

"I think he's mature enough to understand," Rob said. "After all, we interrupted him and Zoe."

That was true, and even more embarrassing. Megan shook her head. "They're engaged. We just met last night."

"I don't think they've known each other very long either," Rob said. "It usually doesn't take mages long to recognize their true love."

Megan put a hand in front of her face. Everything was moving too quickly for her.

"Meg!" Travers shouted again.

Then she heard a key card in the door. She hurried into the hallway and yelled, "Trav, it's okay," but by the time she'd finished the sentence, he had entered the suite, Zoe behind him.

He let the door swing closed behind him. "You're flushed."

"Travers." Zoe grabbed his arm.

"Are you all right?" Travers asked. "Did you get too much sun?"

"Travers." Zoe tugged on his arm.

Megan was mortified. Even more mortified than she had been when she had interrupted them. Or more specifically, when Rob had interrupted them.

"You don't look well," Travers said.

She didn't feel well, at least not now. Before she had felt spectacular, like a completely different woman, and now, she had no words for the sense of loss that was coming over her.

"Travers." Zoe tugged again. "I think we should leave."

"I'm not leaving. Something's happened to Meg—"

"I happened to Meg." Robin came out of the bedroom. He had found another robe. It barely fit across his chest, and it left his legs bare.

They were sexy legs, athlete's legs. And his feet were perfectly shaped.

She really hadn't taken the time to look at him, and she should have. He was so gorgeous.

"You?" Travers strangled the word out. "You took advantage of my sister?"

That got Megan's attention back on the situation. She turned toward her brother.

His blue eyes were blazing, his skin pale. He looked ready for battle.

"Trav," Megan said. "Calm down."

"Calm down when this pervert seduced you? You barely know each other."

"He kissed me," Megan said.

"It looks like a lot more than kissing happened here." Travers put his fists against his hips.

"Travers, stop," Zoe said.

"She's my sister. She doesn't need anyone to take advantage of her."

"He didn't take advantage," Megan said.

"You may think that," Travers said, "but he's old enough to be your—great-great . . . ancestor."

"So?" Megan asked.

"So older guys, younger girls. That's always a bad combo, Meg. You *know* that."

Zoe let go of Travers' arm and crossed her own.

"What about older women and younger men?" she asked. Her question was deceptively calm. "Is that a bad combo?"

"We're different, Zoe, and you know it," Travers snapped.

"Explain to me how," Zoe said. "I'd really like to know."

"We're in love."

"Who says we're not?" Rob asked.

Megan shivered. That feeling earlier. Had that been love? She had thought so in the middle of it all, but she'd learned so often that what she thought was permanent, others thought was ephemeral.

Travers glared at Rob. "I say. You haven't known her long enough."

"How long have you known Zoe?" Rob asked.

Travers let his fists drop from his hips. Zoe stood back, a skeptical expression on her face.

Megan moved between her brother and Rob. Her lover.

"You know, this isn't going to get any of us anywhere," she said, dropping into her psychologist persona. "Robin and I are consenting adults. And I most certainly consented. In fact, I was consenting again when you came barging in the door, and I must say that I'll consent any time in the future if each time is as absolutely spectacular as this first time."

Travers blinked once, looked at Megan, then at Rob, and then closed his eyes. Then he rubbed his thumb and forefinger on the bridge of his nose and said in a pained voice, "Waaay too much information."

"Yeah," Megan snapped. "Like seeing you and your fiancée in full—whatever that was. We're even now."

Zoe grinned. "I do like you."

"Then tell my brother I'm not thirteen."

Travers opened his eyes. They were still blazing blue. He didn't look at Megan. He looked at Rob.

"But you see, that's the problem. She is thirteen inside. She doesn't understand men for all her fancy education. She gets too involved and then gets hurt, and you—you have a history, and probably thousands of women, and *my sister isn't somebody who can be loved and left*. You got that? Because she deserves better."

Megan's breath caught.

"You have quite the protector," Rob said softly.

"I tried to tell you I didn't need one," Megan said.

Rob put a hand on her shoulder and pulled her against him. His body felt solid against her back.

"Zoe's been teaching me spells," Travers said. "I may not be as old as you or as famous as you, but I can take you on if I have to—"

"Travers," Megan said again. "I consented."

"And he'll hurt you," Travers said. "They always do."

"Have a little faith in me," Megan said, but those tears were threatening again. He was right. They always hurt her. Everyone seemed to, even without meaning to. "I know what I'm doing."

"And so do I," Rob said. "I love your sister."

Megan felt her heart flutter. She felt cocooned in emotion, the same emotion that had touched her when she and Rob were in bed.

"You don't know her well enough," Travers snapped.

"I think you should stop now," Zoe said. "You probably don't want to say much more."

"She's my sister. He's some thousand-year-old legend."

"Eight hundred years," Rob said tightly.

"I thought you said age doesn't matter," Zoe said.

"She's my sister," Travers repeated.

"When he doesn't have an argument," Megan said as calmly as she could, "he gets louder. I think he doesn't want to think about me and Rob naked. I certainly think he doesn't want to think about me and Rob having fun while naked. And I absolutely think that he doesn't want to think about us having fun naked again any time soon. So he's going to do what he can to stop it—"

"Jeez, Meg, give it a rest," Travers said. Then he cursed and stomped into the living room. "I hate it when you're right. I'm going to have to wash out my brain now."

Because she was mad beneath her professional

calm, she said, "Not until I tell you exactly what we did."

He let out a yelp and flopped onto the couch, his hands over his ears. Zoe gave her a sideways grin, then went into the living room to comfort her fiancé.

Rob stood perfectly still for a moment, and then he chuckled.

"You're really quite brilliant, you know," he said.

"Well, I have to be to make up for my brother," Megan said. "He's an ass."

"He loves you."

She nodded.

"He's seen you hurt before."

Those tears again. Dammit. Would they always be there, right below the surface?

Rob turned her toward him, put a finger under her chin, and lifted her face to his. Then he kissed her. He meant it as a calming kiss—she could sense that—but it went beyond that. The passion that had been interrupted moments before returned, as strong as ever—

"I'd tell you to get a room," Travers said, "but you already have one. Still, can this . . . utterly disturbing moment wait for, say, half an hour. We were supposed to talk with you about the wheel."

"We waited for you," Megan said, deliberately wrapping her arms around Robin. She was still mad at her brother, and she didn't care what he saw.

"Well, yeah, you have a point." Travers sounded nervous, but Megan wasn't about to turn around and look at him.

Instead, Rob was the one who broke out of the embrace.

"We do need to discuss the wheel," he said.

Megan frowned at him. "You're the one who didn't want to be involved," she said.

"And you're the one who pissed off Zeus," Rob said.

"Zeus?" Zoe sounded scared. "How did you make him angry?"

"We have no idea whether I did or not," Megan said.

"She promised to help the Interim Fates," Rob said to Zoe.

Zoe's eyes were wide. "Help them with what?"

Megan sighed and pulled her robe tighter. "They have an emotionally abusive, controlling father who doesn't care about them at all. They've been thrust into a job that they have no training for, and they're expected to perform well. They have no abilities to take care of themselves, let alone others, and they're frightened. Someone has to help them."

Zoe just stared at her. Travers let his arms drop. He sighed and leaned forward on the couch, then shook his head.

"You can take the psychologist out of her practice," he said softly, "but you can't take the practice out of the psychologist."

"I don't think switching the cliché really works," Megan said, "but you made your point. And you're wrong. I wasn't being intrusive. Those girls need help."

"Those girls have more power than all of us combined," Zoe said quietly.

"Power means nothing," Megan said. "I've counseled teenagers who've had more money *and* more power than I have, but that still didn't stop them from being screwed up. These girls need a lot more than a pile of magic books and some instructions on running the world. They need someone to care for them."

"You said you'd do that?" Travers asked slowly.

"I said we'd help them get out of that job," Megan said. They were still staring at her. She was glad she couldn't see Rob's face. She already knew how he felt about this. "I figured we can do it since we know where the real Fates are."

"She did get the Interims to agree to step down if the real Fates come back," Rob said, "but whether they do that or not remains to be seen."

"You think they won't," Zoe said. It didn't take a psychologist to infer that, considering his tone.

Travers had his hands stuck through his hair. He was still shaking his head. "You know, sometimes I think I'm going to wake up, and find myself in front of my computer, doing Mrs. Jacobson's taxes. And sometimes, I think I'd be happy doing just that."

Zoe gave him a sideways look. "Having second thoughts?"

He grinned up at her. "Not after this afternoon."

It was Megan's turn to moan out loud. "Too much information."

"It's not even close to the information you gave me earlier," Travers said.

"I can give you more," Megan said.

"Enough!" Rob had a spectacular bellow. It shook his body and Megan's. "We have to resolve this. Megan did make promises to the Interim Fates, and, it seems, Kyle has made promises to the Fates. We all will come to the attention of Zeus sooner or later—he's not as dumb as his daughters when it comes to tracking magic—so I suggest we do something."

"We've already done something," Zoe said. "It's in your ballpark now, at least according to the Fates."

"What is?" Megan asked, not sure she really wanted to know.

"This entire scheme—with your lovely, added Zeusy fillip—can't go any farther until the Fates have that wheel. It's the only way they can reclaim their magic without the help of the Powers That Be," Zoe said.

"They can't ask the Powers That Be," Travers said to Megan, "because Zeus is one of those Powers."

Megan nodded. "I got that from Rob's paranoid reaction."

Rob's hand left her shoulder. "I'm not paranoid. I'm just practical."

"This from a man who tried to take on the Fates," Megan said.

"I was dumb," he said, "and lucky."

She sighed. Then she turned to Zoe and Travers. "Why can't you guys get the wheel?"

"Because," Zoe said, "the Fates took us off the case."

"So we'll put you back on."

Travers stood, put his arm around Zoe, and pulled her close. "She nearly died in Faerie," he said. "I'm not letting her go back."

"As if he has any say," Zoe said. "But I do agree with him. I'm not going back inside, even if the Fates wanted me to."

"So you're going to send us?" Megan asked.

"Actually," Zoe said, "the Fates only wanted Robin."

Rob nodded. "So then it's Robin they'll get."

26

Rob's kind of thievery wasn't really suited to a heist. He'd never done one. He'd started out as a highwayman, and then had become a master con artist.

And he did continue along his old lines. He still found ways to take from the rich and give to the poor.

Only now, he made the rich believe they were going to get a good return on that investment. Of course, he never promised when that return would happen—or even if it would happen. And he made certain that the rich knew they were investors in high-risk businesses. Most of the time, that was all he had to say.

The rest of the time, he threatened to expose his investors who wanted to pull out. *We're building hospitals in the poorest countries in the world,* he would say. *Do you really want the press to hear that you believe building hospitals isn't a worthwhile investment?*

He had a dozen variations on that theme, and

it always, always brought compliance from his rich investors. A few of the savvy ones never invested with him again, but the rest had no idea what they were getting into.

Legal highway robbery. When he'd come up with this at the turn of the last century (and somehow managed to survive the U.S. stock market crash in '29), he had been proud of himself. It had gotten rid of the risk, at least for him, and had enabled him to keep the haves from completely breaking the backs of the have-nots.

But this—stealing something from someone else, something physical—he hadn't done that in more than a hundred and fifty years.

"I suppose," he said softly, "there's no way to get this wheel out of Faerie."

He was thinking of some sort of broad-daylight truck hijacking or a spinning-wheel snatch in the middle of the Vegas strip.

But Zoe shook her head. She reached into what passed for a pocket in her skin-tight leather pants, and removed a piece of paper.

The paper glittered with magic.

"I have a map of Faerie," she said.

He whistled.

"We have to be very careful with it," she said, "because it has its own magic. If we touch it too much, someone's going to know what we're doing."

"Gotcha." He'd seen maps like that before. Usually, he tried to stay away from them. It'd been relatively easy, since he'd never been the kind of thief looking for real treasure.

He'd always just wanted to equalize the playing field between those with power and those without.

Zoe held the map gingerly between her thumb and forefinger as she walked into the dining room. Rob followed her, cinching his robe tighter. He would rather have spent the afternoon with Megan, but his conscience had gotten in the way.

His conscience and his concern about Zeus. Zeus's punishments were legendary: this was a man who had destroyed his own father, and who had taken true heroes, like Hercules, and made them into slaves. He was the one who had come up with the whole Sisyphus-pushing-a-rock-uphill-for-eternity thing, and who had once decided that mortals were so wicked, he had to flood the Earth to rid the world of them. (Fortunately that hadn't worked.)

And that was long before Rob's time. He'd tried hard not to pay attention to the things that Zeus had done since. They were equally icky, but a lot more covert.

Megan stayed at Rob's side until they reached Travers. Travers stood and glared at his sister.

"I don't think this should be clothing optional," Travers said.

"You don't want me to hear this," Megan said.

"It doesn't concern you," he said.

"I'm involved, thanks to you and Kyle, and now Rob. I'm staying." She pushed past him.

Rob grinned at Travers. "She's not going to listen to you."

Travers shook his head. "Doesn't stop me from trying," he said softly. Then he gave Rob a sideways smile. "You know, it's hell being an older brother."

"I can only imagine," Rob said truthfully.

Zoe spread the map over the entire surface of the dining room table. Lights flickered and spun, making the entire suite seem like it was part of a casino.

"Hey," she said, beckoning them, "we've got a world to save here."

"Or at least a spinning wheel," Rob said, then sighed. How had he gotten into this? Ah, yes. A beautiful redhead, a silly promise, and some sort of buried nobility.

"This is amazing." Megan had bent over the table. The colors from the map illuminated her face. She was bathed in light.

"Don't touch it," Zoe said.

"It's hard not to," Megan replied.

"That's part of the magic," Zoe said. "It's a Faerie map. Usually only faeries can have it, and then only for a short period of time."

"How'd you get it?" Rob asked as he reached the table.

Zoe grinned at him. "I have strange friends in low places."

"Some of them quite helpful." Travers reached Zoe's side. He squeezed her waist and pulled her close. "Which reminds me. Has anyone heard from Gaylord since last night?"

Zoe shook her head. "I'm sure he'll show up when we least expect him."

"Gaylord?" Rob asked.

"A friend of Zoe's," Travers said. "He's a faerie."

"Man," Megan said, "I'm not sure I can get used to that word in its old-fashioned context. It makes me bristle."

"Faeries make mages bristle," Zoe said. "Historically, we don't get along."

"But you get along with them?" Rob asked, feeling odd. He had never heard of such a thing.

Zoe shrugged. "People are people. Magic people even more so."

"Whatever that means," Megan said softly.

Rob slipped his arm around her and hugged her to him, then moved her slightly. He didn't want her to have any chance of touching that map.

It had sunken into the tabletop. The colors on the map constantly changed, moving and floating around as if tracking moving objects. Some parts of the map had runes on them; other parts were written in Old English, a language he'd grown up with but never learned to read well. It made his brain hurt. A few parts of the map had directions in Celt, and one or two other parts had something written in the Cyrillic alphabet.

"This thing is pretending to be old," he said, "but it isn't."

"I have no idea about its age," Zoe said. "I bought it from a shaman a few days ago."

"And left it in her car last night," Travers said. "I'm amazed no one stole it."

"The car was parked outside a casino," Zoe said to Rob. "Everyone knew better."

"Why?" Megan asked.

"Most of the casinos lead into Faerie," Rob said.

Megan frowned.

Poor thing. She had to learn about the great wide world all at once. No wonder she was getting confused.

"This map," Zoe said, "shows Faerie as it is at this minute. It constantly changes. The entrances, the exits, the location of the magical items."

Rob nodded. He'd seen a few other maps like this, but never one of Faerie.

"You need to look up from it," Zoe said to Megan. "You can lose yourself in it."

Megan looked up slowly and blinked. "Wow. I still see a reflection across my eyes."

"This map is really dangerous," Zoe said. "I'm told that its power will only last a month, but I'm not sure of that. I do believe the warnings I got, though. They went like this: don't look at it too much, or you'll lose time. Don't hold it too long, or you'll end up at a place of the map's choosing. And don't try to take magic from the map, or it might kill you. Is that clear?"

Rob shivered. Faerie magic. The most dangerous kind. "Very."

"No," Megan said. "How can a map do all that?"

"At this stage, Meg," Travers said, "just accept. Believe me, it makes things a lot easier."

"And saves us all from pink elephants," Zoe muttered.

"What?" Megan asked.

Zoe grinned. "Your brother was very hard to convince about magic. We had an incident with a pink elephant."

"And too many five-dollar bills," Travers said.

"After seeing you guys this afternoon," Megan said, "I'm not sure I want more information."

"I *know* I don't," Rob said.

The map showed all sorts of warrens and tunnels. It also showed a wide expanse marked

Faerie. Entrances were all over Las Vegas, with a few in Mississippi, one in Connecticut, and a handful more in Atlantic City. The rest were scattered across Europe. Past Italy and Spain, the entrances to Faerie faded out. The Middle East, Africa, Asia, Australia, and unsurprisingly, Greece had no entrances at all.

He couldn't commit the map to memory though; every time he looked at it, something changed.

"How're we going to find anything in there?" he asked. "It's different from minute to minute."

"Well," Zoe said, "finding the wheel is actually pretty easy. Getting it out is going to be hard."

"Why?" Rob asked.

"Because," Travers said. "The wheel is the very heart of Faerie."

Rob wasn't sure he'd heard this right. "What do you mean?"

"It's in the center of Faerie," Zoe said, "and it powers everything."

"And you want me to go in there and take it out?"

"I don't," Zoe said. "The Fates do."

"One man, alone, taking down Faerie."

"If anyone can do it, you can," Zoe said, and smiled.

Megan slipped her arm through his. "I'll come with you."

"No, you won't," he said.

Megan squinched up her face like she did when she thought he was controlling her. He really wasn't controlling her, but he did have centuries more experience dealing with magic than she did. He knew a lot more about it than almost everyone in the room.

"She probably has to go with you," Zoe said. "That's how the Fates work. What's your prophecy?"

He felt a trickle of irritation. "I have no idea."

"You don't know your prophecy?" Zoe sounded shocked.

"I don't believe in that nonsense," he said.

"Then why are you helping?"

Megan had her arms crossed. Travers was pointedly not looking at the map and was, instead, watching Rob. Zoe was the one who was frowning.

"I'm helping," Rob said, "because I got talked into it. Let it go at that."

"He's helping because you sent him to the Interim Fates," Megan snapped, "and he thinks I was stupid. You all think I was stupid."

"Misguided, maybe," Zoe said. "No one takes on Zeus."

"At the expense of his children?"

"Do you know how many children he has?" Zoe asked.

Megan shook her head. "I gather no one does."

"That's right," Zoe said. "Hundreds, maybe thousands, some with magic, some without."

"Over the centuries, I trust," Travers said.

"Yeah," Zoe said. "I'm sure a lot are gone now."

Travers shook his head. "I have trouble enough raising one. I can't imagine raising hundreds, maybe thousands."

"That's the point," Megan said. "He isn't raising them. He's using them."

"Why is that our problem?" Zoe asked.

Megan seemed to grow taller. Rob had never seen anything like it. "You see, *that's* the problem. All you people thinking that other people should be allowed to raise their kids however they want. We pay for that dysfunction in increased crime rates, suicides, and just general misery."

"From Zeus?" Zoe asked.

"From all dysfunctional parents," Megan said. "And this society. We abandon our kids. Everyone figures they survived their rough childhood, so these kids can too."

Rob felt his face heat. He'd said something similar to her earlier.

"Yet, if you really think about it, imagine how you would've felt if someone had stepped in and helped you when you needed it."

"You can't save the world, Meg," Travers said softly.

"Oh, really?" she said, putting her hands on her hips and whirling to face her brother.

Her robe started to pull open. Rob would have liked that, but he knew it would create another familial scene, so he reached over and tightened her belt.

She acknowledged him with a small nod.

"It seems to me," she said to her brother, "that this mission is all about saving the world. Because the world isn't worth living in without love—"

"My thoughts exactly," Zoe said.

"—and Zeus and everything he stands for is getting in the way of love. I have no idea why you people are balking at helping in any way you can." Megan was shaking.

Rob wanted to pull her close, but this time, he realized, he didn't dare. She was very upset, and part of that upset was at him.

"We did help," Travers said.

"Then you took a break for some nookie," Megan said.

"I'm not the only one."

"No," Megan said, "*nookie* takes two."

"Oh, really?" Travers asked. "Is that a technical definition? Because I know you know that there are some things that can be done alone—"

"You're mean!" Megan said, obviously remembering an old slight.

"And your bedroom always had thin walls."

"Not as thin as yours—"

"And that," Zoe said with finality, "is too much information for me. How about you, Rob?"

Rob was actually enjoying this exchange. He would ask Megan about it later. "Well—"

"Saving the world, remember?" Zoe said. "The prophecy that you don't believe in. What was yours?"

He shrugged. "I don't recall much about a conversation I had hundreds of years ago."

"You *forgot* your prophecy?" Zoe asked.

Megan frowned at both of them. "Is this important?"

"It could be," Zoe said. "The Fates always hand out a prophecy about each person after they're born. Sometimes it has death information in it, sometimes it has other stuff, but it is *always* about how that person will find true love."

"Your prophecy told you about Travers?" Megan asked.

"Yes, it did," Zoe said.

"Let it go, Zoe," Rob said. "I promised I'd help with the wheel. That's enough."

"It's not enough," Zoe said. "What happens if your prophecy says you could die in Faerie?"

"Then I'll have to find a way to survive. The prophecies don't always come true."

"You do remember yours," Zoe said, eyeing him suspiciously.

He shook his head. "I never let them tell me."

"Why not?" Travers asked.

"Because," Rob said. "Marian was already dead. I knew I had no chance at true love, so why hear a stupid prophecy about what had already happened?"

Megan made a small squeak. Rob looked at her. Her face was pale, her eyes dark hollows against her skin.

"I, um, need to get dressed," Megan said, and hurried out of the room.

"You're a first-class idiot," Zoe said, watching her leave.

He knew that. He hadn't meant to be so blunt.

"You know that prophecy couldn't have been about Marian if they wanted to tell you after she had already died," Zoe continued.

The bedroom door slammed shut. It took Rob a moment to focus on Zoe.

"What do you mean?" he asked.

"The Fates," she said. "They only give out prophecies of the future, not portends of the past. If they wanted to tell you after Marian died, then they thought you hadn't met your true soulmate."

Two days ago, he would have yelled at her for that. But after this afternoon, he was beginning to realize that there was a lot in this world he didn't understand either.

"You think Megan is his soulmate?" Travers asked.

"My people fall in love fast," Zoe said. "Rob is hooked. I can tell."

"Well, you've got a way to go with Megan," Travers said to Rob. "Because right now, you just fit into her classic pattern. You seduced her and hurt her. And I don't care who you are. Hurt her any worse, and you'll pay for the rest of your long and unnatural life."

27

Megan leaned against the closed door and stared at the rumpled bed. The scene of the crime, as it were. Only it hadn't been a crime.

As she had so forcefully told her brother, she had consented. She hadn't just consented, she had initiated. She had pulled off Rob's clothing, brought him into this room, and jumped him.

They hadn't even pulled down the coverlet—something she always did in hotel rooms because who knew what other people had done on top of those things?

She winced.

Other people probably just did what she and Rob had done.

Her clothes were scattered around the room, and so were his. Some of his still had to be in the entry, but she hadn't really noticed as she had hurried in here, her stomach twisting and her eyes so dry that they hurt.

Ironic that her eyes were dry now. The way her

heart was feeling, she would have thought those eyes would have been filled with tears.

Yet, if she looked at things calmly and rationally, she had no reason to be upset. She knew about Marian. Hell, she had known about Maid Marian as Robin Hood's Truest Love since she had been a little girl, reading books of legend and lore.

She had known; she had always known.

So why did it hurt?

Because, for about two hours, she had felt cocooned in such a deep love that she had actually believed it when a man who had known her for less than twenty-four hours had said that he had fallen in love with her.

A man with an amazing and unusual accent and a deep, sexy voice had told her in no uncertain terms that he could love her, and then he had enumerated the reasons.

A man who was the most attractive man she had ever met, a man who had decided that words weren't enough and that he needed to use his body to convince her.

She had been convinced.

And then he had made it a lie.

Although he had never said she was his soulmate. He hadn't said she was his true love.

All he had said was that he loved her.

Which should have been enough.

She sighed and grabbed her clothes. She tossed them on the bed—as far from the rumples as she could get—and dropped the robe. Time to come back to reality. Time to figure out what was really going on.

What would she counsel her patients to do?

Wait, that wasn't fair. Kids often didn't have life experience to make good choices. Both she and Rob had life experiences—he a few thousand more than she had.

What would she counsel an adult?

She would ask: *What do you want in this relationship?*

And she would answer: *I'm not sure it is a relationship.*

All right, she would say, *do you want to be a relationship?*

And her heart answered for her: *Yes.*

Do you love him? she would ask.

I don't know.

And she didn't. That was the center of it. Because this had happened before. She had gotten overwhelmed by desire, desire that seemed to radiate from the man, desire that she would reciprocate—and then that desire would fade. Friendship or respect or a sense of fun might replace it. But that *feeling*, that warmth, would be gone for good.

Only she had felt that strong, overwhelming sense of belonging when Rob had pulled her close in the middle of the discussion with Zoe and Travers. His desire had continued, and so had hers.

But did she want more from him than sex?

The sex was pretty good. (Pretty good? The sex was the most spectacular of her life. The sex would have been enough to sustain any relationship, for anyone, for as long as the sex worked.)

Which was probably her answer.

She wanted more, but would settle for the sex.

And if some teenager had told her that, she would have said it was pretty pathetic.

But she doubted any teenager would ever, ever experience sex like that.

She smiled to herself and pulled on her clothes. Then she grabbed her brush from her overnight bag and straightened her hair.

Rob was a complicated man. He claimed he wasn't controlling, but he would make blanket statements, like when he had said that he didn't want her to go with him.

Yet he could be sensitive and caring.

Was she in love with him?

She didn't know. She didn't believe in love at first sight.

But if she did believe in it, would she claim she was in love with him?

Her heart warmed. From the moment she had seen him, she had been attracted to him. She hadn't been able to get him out of her mind.

And no other man would ever compare to him.

Was that love?

She didn't know.

Unlike Rob, she had never experienced it. She had no idea what it felt like.

Was it this confusing?

Her patients always said it was, and she believed them.

Hell, she had experienced the confusion part herself.

But never the all-enveloping warmth. Never the complete and total merging with another person. Never the certain knowledge that no other person would ever measure up to this one.

She sighed.

Her training had made her analytical. This was a question for her heart.

And her heart was hiding, terrified of being hurt.

28

Megan wasn't coming back.

He had hurt her and he hadn't meant to.

"Excuse me," Rob said, and headed toward the room. Neither Zoe nor Travers tried to stop him, which told him that they agreed: he had screwed up.

He stopped outside the bedroom door, half expecting sobs. The women from his past, with the exception of Marian, would have been wailing by now.

But it was silent in there, except for a quiet rustling. What was she doing?

He knocked.

"Come on in, Rob," she said.

He opened the door. "You knew it was me?"

She was fully dressed. Her lips still looked swollen from being kissed, but her hair was combed and her clothing was straightened.

"Who else would it have been?" she asked. "Travers hates strong emotion, and I don't know Zoe all that well."

"She's a good person," Rob said.

"I'm beginning to figure that out," Megan said. "Did she send you here?"

It was a trick question, and fortunately, he'd had enough experience with women *not* to admit that Zoe had told him he was an idiot.

"Coming after you was my idea." He held out his hands in a what-was-I-thinking gesture. "I'm sorry."

Megan shrugged. "I'm the one who's sorry. I overreacted. You've lived for centuries without me. To think that I'm the most important person you've ever met is arrogant, particularly since the whole world knows about Marian."

He sighed. She sounded so reasonable, and yet he worried that she wasn't. "You are important."

"You told me that," she said.

Which wasn't the answer he expected.

"But do you believe it?" he asked.

She nodded. "Oddly enough, I do. And if you'd asked me at noon yesterday whether I would have believed that people could come to mean so much to each other that they were as involved as longtime lovers, I'd have said not outside a wartime situation."

"A wartime situation?"

"You know, like being hostages together or being the only two survivors on a battlefield."

"Wow," Rob said sarcastically, "you have a romantic view of love."

She smiled. "I was raised to be practical."

"But you're not practical, Megan," he said, "or you wouldn't have spent time with me this afternoon."

She met his gaze. Her green eyes seemed clearer than they had before. "Oh, yes, I am. What I felt today is something I've never felt before—and I liked it. So I asked myself: Did I want to experience that again or ruin it by having the wrong expectations?"

He frowned. He had never heard anything like this.

"And I realized that I'd rather be with you as long as I can, and experience whatever it is that we have until we're both tired of it, rather than letting John's rather blanket statement about me being the best for you and all this talk of Fate and soulmates make me overreach the relationship."

"Overreach the relationship?" he repeated. He'd never heard anything like that.

"This relationship is going to be what it's going to be," she said. "No amount of wishing can make it anything else."

There was a certain amount of logic to her statements, but there was no logic in how he felt. And there had been no logic in how he'd felt about Marian, either. At some point, a man had to realize that sometimes he lived through his heart and not his mind. And that living through the heart was just as valid—if not more valid.

"Did they train you to think like this in your profession?" he asked.

Her smile widened. But it looked cooler than he'd ever seen it.

"Yes," she said. "It's my job to see what's beyond the emotion, to understand it, and to help the patient understand it as well."

"And in this case, you're the patient and the therapist?" he asked.

"It worked, didn't it?"

"And they call economics the dismal science," he muttered.

"What?" Megan frowned at him.

He shook his head. "Nothing. It just seems like a sad way to look at the world, analyzing each emotion good and bad, and figuring out the logical approach to that emotion. Sometimes, it's better to follow your feelings."

"Says the man who once defied the Fates," Megan said.

"I don't regret that, even now," Rob said. "I followed my heart."

"And they could have imprisoned you for it."

He smiled. "I'm beginning to understand why they didn't. They knew how I felt about Marian."

Megan nodded. "We all know."

He felt his cheeks heat. He wasn't going to get past this. "Megan, I have been honest with you from the beginning."

"I know that," she said. "And I think that we have tremendous potential."

The word stung him, and he wasn't sure why. It was a dismissive word, one that undercut what he already felt. He grabbed his pants, which were in a pile on the floor, found his shirt, and tossed them on the messed-up bed.

Then he took off the robe.

Megan's cheeks heated. She wasn't as dispassionate as she pretended to be.

He grabbed his pants and slid them on, then

put his shirt over them, buttoning it quickly. He preferred not to feel naked any more.

"For the record," he said as soon as he finished dressing, "what I feel—and have felt—for you since I met you is the most quick and intense emotion of my life. Is it true love? I don't know. But I do know that two weeks ago, I would have told you I had already experienced true love."

Megan watched him, her eyes glittering.

"I don't know how you feel, but I do know you don't value yourself much," Rob said. "You're willing to settle for whatever I have to give, where me, I want this to be the best relationship of our lives. And since I've already had a fantastic, deep, and mutual love with a marvelous woman, I know I'm asking a lot."

He opened the door, finally identifying what he felt. Anger. He didn't like the way she had somehow dismissed him.

"But I'm asking a lot," he said, "because I don't settle. I never have."

He stepped out of the room, grabbed his suit-coat, and headed back into the dining room.

Megan wasn't following him, and he pretended he didn't care. He had made a promise to get that silly wheel.

And he would.

29

Megan stood inside the bedroom, and watched Rob walk across the suite. He was barefoot, which made him seem oddly vulnerable despite the expensive suit he wore.

He was right: she was settling—and she had thought that good news.

But he was also right about something else: he didn't settle. She had known that about Robin Hood as long as she had known about Maid Marian.

If he'd been the kind of man to settle, he never would have gone into the woods and assembled his now-famous band of Merry Men. He never would have taken on the Sheriff of Nottingham, and the Pretender, King John.

He would never have taken on the Fates.

Megan sighed. Rob was talking to her brother and Zoe as if nothing had happened. But he was slightly turned so that he could see her.

She felt a connection to him, even now.

How strange was that? Feeling connected to a man she hadn't even known two days ago?

Maybe it wasn't strange at all. Considering all she'd learned in the past several hours, perhaps it was normal. Perhaps that was why she hadn't hooked up with anyone—not really—because Rob had been out there, waiting to meet her.

What had he said? She had slipped into his magic—driven into it, she had said—and no one, *no one*, not Marian, not the Fates, had done that before.

Megan could accept the idea that someone like him could love her. But she had a lot of trouble accepting that he would make her the most important person in his life.

She hadn't been the most important person in anyone's life before. She'd always been an afterthought: the third child, the younger sister, the second aunt, the trusted friend.

She squared her shoulders. The one thing Rob hadn't said, the one thing no one had said, was something she would tell her patients sometimes.

Love took courage. To love someone—anyone, even a parent or a family member—was a risk. You gave your heart, your very being, to that person, and you risked rejection, or worse.

You risked complete destruction of every warm emotion you'd ever felt.

All she had done from her earliest memories was protect herself from emotion. And even though her own therapist had mined her background, searching for a single traumatic event that caused Megan to shut down like that, she had never found it.

Her therapist had even interviewed her parents to see if the event was preverbal.

The only thing anyone could come up with was that Megan had been abandoned as an infant. Had that been the traumatic event? That someone—the person who had birthed her—hadn't loved her enough to keep her?

Or had Megan, as an older child, responded emotionally to the news of her abandonment?

But that had never felt right. Megan wasn't sure she believed in preverbal memory, and she didn't remember a time when she had ever felt unloved.

Her family—the Kineallys—had loved her as much or more than her biological family could have.

She sighed. She was just reserved, that was all, and risk-averse, and afraid.

Very afraid.

And there was Robin, gesturing over a map of a place so dangerous, the danger spilled into the map itself. Her own brother, whom she loved dearly but never thought of as mighty courageous, had rescued his fiancée from that place. (Even though Megan still wasn't sure how. Had he added and subtracted the faeries to death?)

Her nephew had taken care of three of the zaniest women Megan had ever met, had heard adult thoughts since childhood, and still had the sweetest personality of anyone she had ever met.

And Rob. Rob had lost the person most dear to him centuries ago, and yet he kept living. Not only kept living, but was willing to try again.

There was something wrong with her if she didn't give this her all.

Not many people got a chance like this.

She slipped on her shoes, and crossed the suite's floor. The conversation was about embedded spinning wheels and transforming lights. She felt behind already.

"All right," Rob was saying as she approached. "So the Faerie Kings stole the wheel from the Fates, and they were able to continue on, even though the wheel was their source of power."

"Someone told me," Zoe said, "and I can't remember who because this has been a strange few days, that the Faerie Kings became a lot more powerful after that. In fact, the expansion of Faerie happened after that."

"So they're not going to want to let the wheel go," Rob said.

"The way the Fates made it sound," Travers said, "they won't have any choice."

Rob frowned. "Why is that?"

"Because," Zoe said, "even Fates have prophecies, apparently, and the wheel and the Faerie Kings and someone named Great-Aunt Eugenia are all involved in theirs."

"Only my great-aunt died," Travers said.

"This Eugenia is related to you?" Rob asked.

"And me." Megan entered the conversation as if she had never left. "She was the one who found all three of us, and helped with the adoptions."

Travers looked at her in surprise. "I never knew that."

"I checked the records. Great-Aunt Eugenia put Mom and Dad in touch with the agencies where we all were, and actually pointed Mom to each one of us."

"But she was dead before the Fates lost their powers," Travers said.

"Murdered, remember?" Megan said. "And Viv and her new husband caught the murderer."

"Fascinating," Rob said. "So technically, your aunt was involved in all this, but as a catalyst."

"I hadn't thought of it that way," Zoe said.

"You know," Travers said, "something strikes me, though."

They all turned toward him. He had moved away from the table slightly, probably so that he wouldn't be staring at the map the entire time.

"You mentioned to Rob, Zoe, and you've told me in the past that all the prophecies are about true love."

Zoe nodded.

"Would that apply to the prophecies about the Fates as well?" Travers asked.

"True love for them?" Rob asked as if the concept were as foreign as trees on the moon.

"Why not?" Travers asked. "They're part of the magical community, right?"

"But who made the prophecy for them?" Zoe asked.

"Whoever were the Fates before them," Travers said. "Or maybe they made it for themselves."

Megan saw where he was going. "Which would explain why they were so willing to give up their magic. They thought they were going to fulfill their destinies."

Rob's gaze met hers. His expression was cool. He seemed very distant from her. But he nodded.

"Do you think they'll tell us about it?" he asked.

"It doesn't matter if they do," Zoe said. "Prophecies are deliberately obtuse. We'll understand it after everything is done. No need to muddy the waters before we finish this thing."

"Before *I* finish this thing," Rob said, then sighed. "Although I'm not sure how. If this wheel powers all of Faerie, then I don't have the magical abilities to remove it."

"We need to figure out how to create a Faerie-wide blackout," Zoe said.

"Or not," Travers said. "Look, when I tried to get Zoe out of there, I used the wheel."

Megan slid her hands behind her back. Everyone else was so comfortable discussing fantastic things, and she still felt like she had walked into the middle of a movie set.

Only the hero was in love with her, and she'd actually experienced the magic.

Rob took Travers' arm and led him away from the map. "Fold that thing up, Zoe. I think we're done with it for now."

Megan understood what he was doing; he was afraid that if the magic spilled off the map, it would allow someone in Faerie to hear their plans.

Zoe nodded, grabbed the map, and rolled it up like a poster. For a moment, the table rolled with it, then Zoe slipped her fingers between the wood and the map, and the table bounced back to its normal shape.

"You used the wheel?" Rob asked when he and Travers reached the living room.

Travers nodded. He sat on the edge of the couch. Rob sat on a nearby chair. Megan perched on the chair's arm. Rob put a hand on her leg, and the warmth of his skin through the cloth of her pants reassured her somehow.

He wasn't quite as distant as he seemed.

"I was afraid I wouldn't have enough power to get Zoe out of there," Travers said. "Then I remembered the Fates saying that they didn't need the wheel after a few centuries. All it did was augment their existing power, and they learned how to do that on their own. So, I figured, I could use it to augment my power. I reached out for it—mentally, if that makes sense—"

"It does," Rob said.

It didn't, Megan thought, but she didn't say that. They didn't need to explain more to her.

"—and drew power from it, literally. My magic became stronger—I became stronger—and Zoe and I got out."

Rob nodded. "It still strikes me that it'll be hard to remove if it is the power center."

"But what Travers is saying is that he thinks you can use the power of the wheel to remove the wheel," Zoe said.

Megan was really frowning now. "Is it, like, plugged into something? The power has to come from somewhere."

Travers waved his hand dismissively. "In a scientific world, maybe."

"I believe in a scientific world," Megan said in a small voice.

"So do I, most of the time," Travers said, "but not in a place like Faerie."

"There is a science to magic," Rob said. "I've just never studied it. Power does come from somewhere, just like electrical current. But walls aren't imbued with electricity. They're wired, and the wires are attached to a series of lines that are ultimately attached to a place where the power is manufactured. Magic has a similar system, which I don't entirely understand—and that's my own people's system. Faerie may use a completely different one."

"The wheel has to be mobile," Zoe said. "The Faerie Kings stole it from the Fates. They had to do that somehow."

"Maybe we should ask the Fates how," Megan said.

Everyone looked at her as if she had just suggested jumping off a cliff.

She shrugged. "They probably know more about that wheel than we ever would."

Rob sighed. "She has a point."

"I know she does," Travers said. "But I was hoping that I wouldn't have to talk to them any more. It's confusing."

Zoe gave him a fond smile. "They're not confusing. Just breathtaking sometimes."

"And not in a good way," Rob added.

Megan nodded. "But last I remember, John was cooking chili, and Kyle was watching anime, and the Fates had told us . . ."

She stopped herself and flushed.

Rob grinned at her. "They told us to get a room. But you already had one."

"Oh, not this again." Travers stood up. "Now I'm voting for a conversation with the Fates."

He marched toward the front door.

"Wow," Zoe said softly to Megan. "You really do know how to push his buttons."

"Twenty-five years of practice," Megan said with pride.

Zoe shook her head. "Maybe I'll have to take lessons."

"Naw," Megan said. "I just irritate him. You want to get under his skin in other ways."

Zoe grinned. "Truer words have never been spoken."

She followed Travers to the door.

Rob stood, but Megan stayed seated. She reached for his hand, and somehow missed.

"I wanted to say—"

"Later," he said. "Let's finish this spinning wheel thing first."

"But it worries you," Megan said. She could feel it, an amorphous concern, a sort of in-over-his-head kind of anxiety.

"Of course I'm worried," he said. "I think they're all asking the impossible."

"But you're going to try," she said.

He nodded. "I've always liked the impossible," he said, and headed out of the room.

30

The moment Rob entered the hallway, he realized he had forgotten his socks and his shoes. But he wasn't about to go back for them.

He felt a low-key irritation with Megan, one he didn't want to thrash out with her at the moment. He'd never been attracted to someone who settled before. That bothered him more than he cared to think about.

The carpet in the hallway was cold and slightly damp, probably from the air-conditioning. He walked to the next suite over, and heard Kyle's voice, mixing with his father's, John's, and the barking of that silly obese dog.

Then the door beside him clicked shut.

He didn't want to look. Megan was probably sitting inside her suite, trying to make sense of the day.

Not that he blamed her. Everything had changed for her, and he had made it worse, pressuring her into something she apparently wasn't ready for.

And he didn't know how much of his own

emotion had bled over. How much he had coerced her—in an inadvertent way—just because she could feel what he had been feeling?

He would have to discuss that with her when—if—he got out of Faerie with the wheel.

"Forget something?"

He started, and looked beside him. There was Megan, holding his shoes, his socks stuffed inside them. She looked charming, her own feet bare, her hands clinging to his ridiculous, expensive twenty-first century leather shoes.

In spite of himself, he smiled at her.

"Thanks," he said, taking the shoes from her.

"You know, those probably aren't world-conquering shoes," she said softly.

"That's not what the salesman said." Rob stepped inside the other suite. It smelled of chili—rich and thick and enticing—and fresh baked bread.

Megan walked in with him. "The salesman told you the shoes would help you conquer the world?"

"The well-dressed man always controls his environment," Rob said in a modern, stuffy, upper-class British accent. "Shoes make the man."

"Really?" Megan said. "Because I'd think that world-conquering shoes would be some kind of miracle boots or tennies."

"Never tried conquering the world in tennies," Rob said. "It might work."

He pulled the door to the suite closed. John was still in the kitchen, removing the bread from the oven. The Fates were setting the table, going around it in circles and placing settings down as if they were playing a game of Duck, Duck, Goose.

Kyle was talking animatedly to his father, and Zoe was petting that overweight dog.

The entire scene in front of him should have made him calmer. Instead, it made him tense.

All of these people were counting on him because of some historical misunderstanding of his skills. If he could, he'd recommend some famous cat burglar, only he couldn't think of any.

Apparently, among his people, he was the world's greatest thief.

He sighed.

"You can do this," Megan said.

He glanced at her.

"You have done a lot of amazing stuff in your life. I'm beginning to understand how this new world works. If the Fates believe in you, then you have the ability to do whatever they ask."

Rob smiled. "You still don't understand all of it. Just because there are prophecies doesn't mean they'll come true."

"Good thing we don't know what they are, then," Megan said.

He shook his head, went into the living room, and set his shoes beside the chair. He had no real desire to put them on yet.

Zoe saw him first. She patted the dog one last time, then sat down on the couch. She nodded to a nearby chair.

"We have to do some planning," she said in a loud voice.

"At dinner," John said from the kitchen.

"Some of it now," Zoe said.

The Fates looked over at them, all movements in unison. Rob hovered near the chair. He didn't want to sit down. He didn't want to be comfortable here, not yet.

He needed more information, and Megan had been right: that information had to come from the Fates.

"Before we have dinner," Zoe said, "I want to show you what the wheel looks like now."

"You can't do a magic spell into Faerie," Clotho said, leaving the dining room.

"It isn't safe," Lachesis said.

"They'd know where to find you," Atropos said.

"They know where to find me now," Zoe said. "We're all safe so long as we don't threaten them."

"And they have no idea what we're up to," Travers said. "At least, not yet."

Not until Rob went into Faerie and took the wheel, that is.

He sighed. Megan stood near the door. Kyle looked nervous, which meant everyone in the room was nervous.

"This can't wait until I serve dinner?" John asked.

No one answered him.

Zoe beckoned with her right hand. "Gather 'round. You in particular, Rob. You need to see this."

The Fates set the remaining dishes down and took over the couch. Rob found an armchair similar to the one he'd been sitting in inside Megan's suite. She came up beside him, and he pulled her next to him.

She opted for the arm again, and not his lap, like he'd hoped.

"I'm going to show you my memory," Zoe said

with a pointed glare at the Fates, "not the actual wheel itself. Because this is Faerie, they've probably moved it—"

"They haven't," Clotho said.

"How do you know?" Rob asked.

Lachesis shrugged. "We are able to stay in touch with parts of our past, even though our magic is gone."

"Or perhaps it is our future," Atropos said, and all three Fates giggled.

Travers rolled his eyes. Rob felt that thread of irritation grow, but Megan looked at all three of them, her head cocked.

"Do they remind you of someone?" she whispered.

"Thank heavens, no," he said, not bothering to whisper back.

She gave him an exasperated look, then folded her hands in her lap, and looked at Zoe.

Zoe raised her eyebrows at him. "This is for your benefit, Rob. Are you going to pay attention?"

"Did you have a school marm somewhere in your background?" he asked, not liking the pointed way she asked the question.

She shook her head. "We don't have 'marms' in France."

"France?" Megan whispered.

But Rob didn't explain it to her. He had first met Zoe in France nearly a century ago. She had just come into her magic, and she was quite frightened of it.

"Watch," Zoe said, and raised a closed fist.

Then the suite faded. The beeps of slot machines, followed by the soft roar of conversation, snuck into the emptiness. Then the glare of artificial lighting mixed with flashing signs and too much neon.

A casino.

And not just any casino: a Faerie casino. He recognized the language around him. It was Elvish, mixed with medieval English and Gaelic—the Faerie's version of their own language.

Faeries played video games, stood next to each other and had real conversations—not the kind they had when they were worried about mages overhearing—and something glowed in the distance.

Signs—in English—announced concerts, comedy shows, and the amounts in progressive slots. So, occasionally, the Faeries brought humans down here, probably to pick them clean of their luck.

Rob shook his head. Megan had grabbed his hand and was clinging to it tightly, as if she had never seen anything like this.

And, of course, she hadn't.

She was biting her lower lip, her eyes as wide as a child's.

The scene around them shifted as the memory did—Zoe had gone toward that glow.

The floor throbbed beneath Rob's feet, almost as if he were in a big machine. Gradually, the Faeries around him disappeared, although he could hear voices whispering. He wanted to turn around, to face them, but he knew this was a memory—and not his memory.

Zoe's.

He couldn't see the actual Zoe through all the slot banks, video poker machines, and craps tables. The slots didn't have the usual cherries and sevens, but instead listings of human traits—a way of betting on and manipulating human lives.

"Why do they allow that?" Clotho said.

Her voice was very distant.

Someone shushed her, and the illusion rose again.

That whispering made his hair stand on end.

Ahead of him, the machines parted, showing a great pit. It was bathed in light, so much so that he couldn't see in front of it. He went forward and nearly tripped down a flight of clear stairs.

They were lit from beneath. He glanced up, saw himself sitting in the armchair, Megan still clinging to his hand—and yet he was standing on the floor of the pit, all alone.

He was actually inside Zoe's memory.

He wondered if the others were too.

She had a powerful magic to do this. He was impressed.

Then he focused on the scene before him. His eyes had finally adjusted to the light.

The pit was round and seemed designed for gaming. Blackjack tables stood next to craps tables, which were near poker tables. A giant roulette wheel dominated the entire pit. The wheel shot out red and black lights that didn't seem to affect the white light that glowed in the entire area.

Rob frowned and started toward the wheel, only to be held in place. It was Zoe's memory, not his; Zoe's magic, not his. He had to wait until she had gone forward—if she had.

She hadn't, but she had focused on the wheel itself. And that was when he realized that it looked odd, not like a classic roulette wheel at all. Beside it were three empty chairs.

"They couldn't hang around and wait to see what was going on?" Lachesis asked, startling Rob.

"This is a memory, remember?" Atropos said, and again someone shushed them.

Rob tuned everyone out and stepped toward the wheel. This time, the magic-memory let him. The wheel had spokes—no real roulette wheel did—and didn't have built-in slots for a ball. Those slots had been added onto the edge as if they were an afterthought, and if he looked at them closely, he thought he could see light through them, but he wasn't sure.

The base of the wheel was covered in cloth, and then he realized that he was looking at it wrong.

The base wasn't covered in cloth. That was the part of the spinning wheel where the unspun material was before it was spun into threads. If he looked hard enough, he would find the spindle, and the real base of the wheel—the legs.

He tried to peer around the wheel, but he couldn't. The memory had frozen him in place. Apparently Zoe hadn't moved from here. He could only look, and not touch, nor could he actually examine the real base or the chairs or the platform on which the wheel rested.

He couldn't see how to take it out.

Still, he reached for the thing, and it all vanished.

He had dropped Megan's hand, his own hand extended across the room as if he were a child, reaching for something he couldn't have.

Everyone was staring at him.

He cleared his throat, brought his hand down, and took Megan's again. She covered it with her other hand.

"Um," he said, trying to think about this entire mission, "where was that?"

"We can look on the map," Zoe said. "It's supposed to show us where everything is in real time."

"No." Rob blinked. His eyes still ached from the bright light. "What I meant was . . . was that deep in Faerie or near the surface? We seemed to be in a casino."

"We were," Travers said, "but it's deep, and it's not like those casinos on Boulder Highway that the Faeries own. It's an underground cavern, almost, a secret place that took me a long time to get to."

"I went through some kind of long fall," Zoe said.

"Me, too."

That's what Rob was afraid of. "Once you landed, how far did you go?"

"That's the tough part," Zoe said.

"Everything changes down there," Travers said. "The entire place works on a mathematical system. Do you know what fractals are?"

"Not a clue," Rob said.

Travers sighed. "No one does. Am I that weird?"

"You're that weird, Dad," Kyle said.

Travers grinned at him, then looked back at Rob. "It works on a pattern that has a mathematical base. Like slots, only more complex. It works without some overall mind adjusting the pattern all the time. But you have to be able to see it."

"Math has never been my strong suit," Rob said, wondering how this applied.

"That's a problem," Travers said. "Because if you can see the patterns, you can go directly to the heart of Faerie. Otherwise, you'll get lost, and you might not come out for years."

"À la Rip Van Winkle," John said. Rob started. He hadn't realized John was behind him. "I always wondered how that guy could lose so much time bowling."

"The games weren't as sophisticated then," Zoe said.

"All right, let's assume I can see the patterns"— which Rob doubted he could, but for the sake of argument, he'd assume it—"then how far is the wheel from the entrance?"

"It didn't take me long to get there," Travers said, "but I was hurrying. I thought Zoe would die."

She gave him a fond smile.

"Time estimate?" Rob asked.

"I don't have any," Travers said. "I'm not sure time exists down there."

"It exists," Clotho said, "but it's Faerie Mountain Time."

"Which is better," Lachesis said, "than Faerie Midnight Time."

"Although you're better off," Atropos said, "with Faerie Solstice Time."

"Okay," Rob said, suppressing another sigh. "I get it. We have no way of measuring how far the wheel is from any exit, which, I have to admit, makes it impossible to make a plan. Add that to the fact that the thing looks too big for one man to carry—"

"That's the effect of the magic," Clotho said.

"Really, I could carry it," Lachesis said.

"Any one of us could," Atropos said.

"When you had your magic," Rob said.

All three Fates shook their heads in unison.

"Even without," Clotho said.

"It's made of the lightest wood," Lachesis said.

"It's designed so that even a child can carry it," Atropos said.

"A real child or one of those, y'know, magical kids?" Kyle asked. He was sitting on the floor, one hand on the obese dachshund's back. The dog was looking into the kitchen, tail wagging. Apparently the creature hadn't forgotten about the food on the counter.

Neither had Rob. His stomach was growling.

"A real child," Clotho said, sounding somewhat indignant. "Magic did develop over time, you know."

Rob didn't even know that. He just assumed it came into being when the Earth came into being. Of course, history—like math—wasn't his strong suit, unless he'd lived through it.

"If I don't know how hard it is to remove," he said, "and I don't know how long it'll take me to carry the thing out of the casino, and I don't know if I can even lift it, then I can't plan this heist."

"I think heist is the wrong word," Clotho said.

"We weren't thinking of anything armed," Lachesis said.

"You watch too many movies," Atropos said.

He hardly watched any movies, except late at night, and often on pay-per-view or Turner Classic Movies. He usually fell asleep in the middle of whatever he was watching, so the plots really didn't stick with him.

But he knew better than to contradict the Fates.

"I have to get it out of there somehow," he said, "and my magic isn't enough to take on the entire Faerie Kingdom. My theft skills weren't really skills. They were bullying and thuggery, and always with a political aim. I'm not really the man for this."

"Oh, you're precisely the man," Clotho said.

"If only you'd stop denying it," Lachesis added.

"After all, this is political," Atropos said.

"Because of Zeus?" Rob asked.

All three Fates shook their heads again. He was getting an image of those bobblehead dolls that were sold in stores all over Vegas, and he wasn't sure he could keep a straight face about it.

"Because of the Faerie Kings," Clotho said.

"The initial rivalry was between magic systems," Lachesis said.

"What's it between now?" Megan asked.

Rob glanced at her. She seemed involved in the conversation and not out of her depth like she had before. If anything, the vision of the wheel seemed to calm her.

It had simply convinced him he had no idea what he was doing.

"We do have to deal with Zeus, that's true," Atropos said.

"He will destroy everything we've worked for," Clotho said.

"He doesn't believe in true love," Lachesis said.

"And if you were married to Hera, would you believe in it?" Atropos asked.

Clotho waved a hand. "Of course, that relationship is not our fault."

"We would never allow a man to marry his sister," Lachesis said.

"His sister?" Megan sounded appalled.

Travers put his hand over his face. And Kyle wrinkled his nose.

Apparently, some parts of Greek mythology were left out of modern schooling. Among the ancient gods and goddesses there was a lot of what would be called incest now, which Rob found just as disgusting as he had when he first heard of it, however many centuries ago.

"The Titans arranged that marriage," Atropos said, "for reasons we'll never understand."

"And then put Hera in charge of married women which," Clotho said, holding up a single finger as if she were giving a lecture, "we never would have done."

"The woman is supremely unhappy," Lachesis said. "Her husband is the most unfaithful creature ever created, and she blames it all on the women he gets involved with."

"Which," Atropos added, "is why so many married women are bitchy, in my opinion."

"Huh?" Zoe said, twisting her new engagement ring.

Rob suppressed a grin, although Travers looked alarmed. Megan had leaned against Rob's leg, watching the entire proceeding as if it were being staged for her benefit.

Rob wished he could remain as detached. He had to bring everyone back to the real topic soon enough.

Clotho reached over and patted Zoe's leg. "It's not that married women are unhappy, dear."

"It's just that occasionally Hera sends a little discontent their way," Lachesis said.

"Simply to stir things up," Atropos said.

"She believes it brings passion to a relationship," Clotho said.

"And it does," Lachesis said, "but the wrong type."

"Why haven't you stopped her?" Megan asked.

All three Fates turned toward her. Even Zoe looked shocked.

Megan shrugged and extended her hands. Rob put his hand on her shoulder, leaning her back against him.

"I misunderstood something again, didn't I?" she asked.

"Hera's one of the Powers That Be," Rob said. "Technically, they're the Fates' boss."

"Although I note you don't give them obeisance any more," Zoe said to the Fates.

The Fates looked down at their hands. This was the moment, then, that Rob could turn the conversation back to his so-called heist. They had to know that this wouldn't work. Why were they sacrificing him?

"Are you trying to kill Mr. Hood?" Kyle asked.

Rob glared at him, then cursed silently. He must have broadcast that last thought.

Everyone looked at Kyle. He was staring at the Fates.

"That's what he thinks. He thinks you're sending him in there so that the Faerie Kings'll catch him and hurt him. He thinks you don't like him." Kyle sounded indignant. "You should be nicer to him. He's in love with my Aunt Megan, and she needs someone like him, someone who really loves her. She's the nicest person I know, and she gets all the bad breaks—"

"Kyle!" Megan hissed at him.

"We don't hate Robin," Atropos said, sounding shocked.

"We consider him one of the good guys," Clotho said, sounding even more shocked.

"We have asked him to be our champion," Lachesis said. "We only do that with the best of the best."

"Well," Rob said, "I'm flattered, ladies, but I really am the wrong man for the job. Maybe you shouldn't look for a champion and a good guy, but for someone slightly shady, someone who can actually pull this off—"

"You know, I never thought I'd hear that kind of nonsense coming out of you." John spoke up. He was standing near the kitchen door and looking very disgusted. "Not the man for the job, 'someone slightly shady'—what the heck do you think you are? Mr. Clean? Rob, you still steal from the rich and give to the poor. The only difference now is that they pretend to like what you're doing."

Rob's cheeks grew warm. "I've learned a few tricks."

"You *are* more than slightly shady," John said.

"You always have been. And you're tough, and you have a lot of magic. You've just forgotten who you are."

Megan frowned. Rob glanced sideways at his best and oldest friend.

"What are you referring to?" he asked. "I'm a lot of things. I'm a displaced lord, a retired highwayman, a former Crusader, a widower, a billionaire playboy, and—apparently—someone slightly shady. What else?"

"For heaven's sake, man," John said. "You're not just those things. You are a hero and a champion just like the Fates say. And you're a leader of men. You always have been."

Robin shook his head. "If there's anything I'm not, it's a leader of men, John. I've fought those creatures."

"No, sir," John said. "You've led me and Will Scarlet and Friar Tuck and dozens of others. You've led regimens and corporations. You're a leader, Robin, and you always have been. All you need is the modern equivalent of the Merry Men."

31

Robin should have thought of that all on his own. He leaned back in his chair, Megan still touching his side, everyone in the room staring at him.

He had been the one who had been approaching this as if he had to go in alone, and he hadn't thought of his usual team. Of course, everyone from his usual team—with the exception of John Little—had been dead a very, very long time.

Rob rubbed a hand over his face, mostly so that he had something to do so that he wouldn't have to look at the Fates. He could still feel them, though, staring at him expectantly.

They thought life and death rested on this. They did say politics was involved (and that was pretty plain, now that he thought about it), and they claimed they needed a champion, not that he really wanted to champion those women.

But he could champion Zeus's daughters—not for their own sake, of course, but for Megan's. She really believed in him.

She was gazing at him fondly, as if she was already a step ahead of him. And of course, it made sense that in this, she would be. It had to do with emotion, which was her forté. At the moment, it certainly wasn't his.

"So how do you suggest I recruit these men?" he asked John. "There aren't any forests around Las Vegas. And I have a hunch that if I walk around the city looking for enemies of the Faerie Kings, most people will think I'm referring to a rock band."

John was glaring at Rob as if he were particularly obtuse. Then he shook his head. "I'm putting food on the table. If no one wants to eat, fine. I'll eat it all myself. But you're welcome to join me if you want."

He stomped into the kitchen.

"What did I say?" Rob asked.

Megan smiled at him. Her smile was gentle. "You've already recruited."

"Technically," Travers said, "Rob was recruited."

"Into a preexisting band," Zoe said.

"I thought you guys were out of this because of your wedding," Rob said.

"We have planning to do, that's true," Travers said.

"But we got our license." Zoe smiled at Travers. There was deep love in that gaze. It made Rob smile, even though he hadn't felt much like smiling in the last few hours.

"Travers and Zoe aren't the central focus, but you do need a team," Clotho said.

"We expected you to get one," Lachesis said.

"And John Little is right. You already have one," Atropos said.

John walked past them, carrying a steaming pot of chili. Kyle got up and headed for the table, grabbing a trivet off a nearby counter on the way.

"I don't see how Travers, Zoe, and John are a band," Megan said. "You had more than that initially, didn't you?"

That question was aimed at Rob. He was watching John and Kyle, and noticing how well they worked together.

"Yeah," Rob said, feeling distracted. A plan was coming together in his head whether he wanted it to or not.

"Won't it take more than four people to take on an entire kingdom? I mean, you had more to go after a sheriff."

"He was in the pocket of the Pretender, King John," Little John said as he marched back through the living room. "You people gonna eat or what?"

The Fates all stood up. Kyle was already at the table, fending off the obese dog. Travers stood, and extended a hand to Zoe, who took it.

"Why aren't you participating in your own rescue?" Rob asked the Fates.

They smiled prettily at him, and oddly, not a one answered.

John came back through, this time carrying fresh baked bread. Everything smelled heavenly.

Rob's stomach rumbled again. He stood, and took Megan's hand. She squeezed his.

"I wish I could help," she said softly.

"Oh, but that's part of the plan, dear," Clotho

said from the table. She had sat beside Kyle and was petting that misnamed dog.

Rob frowned at her. "Megan can't go near Faerie, and you know it."

"We know nothing of the kind," Lachesis said, sitting on Kyle's other side. Didn't that make the poor kid nervous? It would have made Rob nervous, and he'd known these women for centuries.

"Why can't I go with you?" Megan asked. "Surely there's something a mere mortal can do."

"You're not a mere mortal, dear," Atropos said. She sat beside Lachesis and reached for the bread without waiting for the others to get to the table. "Whoever told you that is just wrong."

Megan let go of Rob's hand, although he kept holding hers. Her fingers were limp in his hand, but he didn't let go. He was almost afraid to.

She didn't need to learn about her skills like this. He made a small gesture with his free hand, but no one seemed to see it.

Travers sat next to Clotho, and Zoe sat beside him, which put her at the head of the table.

"No one told me I'm a mere mortal," Megan said as she slipped her hand from Rob's grasp. She headed for Zoe's free side. "I figured that one out on my own."

Rob stopped, clenched his now-empty hand into a fist, and then walked a bit more slowly to the table.

Travers was looking at Megan as if he'd never seen her before. "You know, the more I'm learning about Great-Aunt Eugenia and our entire family, the more I'm thinking maybe the Fates are right."

"Of course we're right," Clotho said.

"Have we ever been wrong?" Lachesis asked.

"You dumped your magic for a really dumb reason," Kyle said.

All three Fates glared at him. Rob's breath caught. If they still had magic, Kyle would be a toad now.

"I agree with Kyle," John said, coming in from the kitchen again, carrying butter and some Tabasco sauce. He sat down at the foot of the table, leaving the chair next to Megan open. "You guys really let Zeus pull one over on you."

"We . . ." The Fates all started that sentence in unison, then looked at each other and sighed.

"We know," Atropos finished for them. "You have no idea how embarrassing it all is."

"I know how dangerous it is," Travers said. "I'm not letting Zoe go back into Faerie, no matter what's at stake."

"Like you're in control of me," Zoe said.

He looked at her. "Are you going back in?"

"Are you crazy?" she said. "I didn't want to go in the first time."

Rob shook his head. He sat down next to Megan. John was already ladling the chili into bowls. It was thick and dark red, filled with beans and big hunks of roast beef, just like John's chili always was.

Rob's mouth actually watered. He hadn't had this in so long, and it was one of his favorite meals.

"I can't go in with a skeleton team," Rob said. "I'd need Travers to guide me to that wheel, and I'm going to need John's help to get it out."

"Wait," Megan said. "I'm still not sure what you all mean by the fact that I'm not mortal. I don't have magic."

"Women come into their magic after, y'know, menopause, Aunt Megan," Kyle said, his face as red as the chili. "Didn't anyone tell you that?"

"You haven't come into your powers yet?" Travers asked. "That's why you never turned me into stone like you always threatened."

"She's got her powers," Clotho said. "You all have never noticed."

"I noticed," Rob said.

"We know." Lachesis waggled a finger at him. "And thank heavens you're soulmates, or you would get a lecture on using her talents to your advantage."

Rob felt fear rise in his stomach. He didn't want Megan to find out this way. "I didn't—"

"What's she talking about?" Megan asked.

"Darling," Atropos said. "You're the rarest of the rare."

"All of magic is only blessed with one a generation," Clotho said.

"If we're lucky," Lachesis said.

"And no matter how hard they try," Atropos said, "not a single one has ever been born in Faerie."

Rob glanced at Zoe. He wanted her help to stop this. But she was watching with fascination, and he realized that she was such a young mage, she had probably never met anyone like Megan before.

She had no idea what she was looking at.

"One what?" Megan asked in exasperation.

"You're an empath, darling," Clotho said.

"The most vulnerable, and most powerful, of us all." Lachesis smiled at her.

"Blessed and cursed among women," Atropos said.

"And," Clotho said, "the center of the magical universe."

Rob looked at her. She hadn't noticed when the Interim Fates had called her that. But she was noticing now.

Her eyes were lined with tears. "Don't make fun of me."

"We're not, darling," Lachesis said.

"You're rarer than Kyle," Atropos said.

"Kudos to Eugenia," Clotho said. "She knew how to assemble the perfect family. We had our doubts."

"But she proved us wrong," Lachesis said.

Megan turned to Rob, her cheeks red. "What are they talking about?"

He took both of her hands. Damn the Fates for doing this in public. Damn them for putting him in this position.

"You absorb emotion, Megan," he said. "You probably always have."

Travers's face had gone pale. "Is that why we fight? Because you feel how pissed off I am, and then you get pissed off?"

Megan shook her head. "This can't be true. If it were true, I couldn't be a psychologist."

"Actually, that's what makes you a good one," Rob said. "Somewhere along the way, you've learned to block some of that emotion, but you still feel it. So when someone tells you how he feels, you know whether or not he's lying."

Megan frowned. Was she comparing what he had just said to what he had told her before? Rob wondered.

"The Interim Fates told you what you were," Rob said. "But you didn't ask me about it."

He was feeling a little panicked. She was being so quiet.

"I thought they were being snide," she said.

"Because they called me hottie?" he asked, forcing a smile.

She shook her head. "You are. But they weren't the most polite people."

"Oh, dear," Clotho said. "Fates should be polite."

"On what planet?" John asked, and this time, Rob's grin was real. His gaze met his best friend's, and John shrugged, a smile dancing at the corner of his lips.

"Why, this one, of course," Lachesis said.

"Contrary to popular opinion," Atropos said, "we have no interest in other planets."

"What?" Zoe asked.

"You're side-tracking them," Travers stage-whispered.

"We've been accused of paying more attention to other planets than our own," Clotho said.

"We've been accused of many silly things," Lachesis said.

Rob tuned them out and turned toward Megan. She was staring at her chili as if she'd never seen it before.

"Are you all right?" he asked, even though he knew it was a silly question. She wasn't all right.

She was probably as far from all right as she could be.

"What did they mean?" she asked softly. "About you using my talents?"

He closed his eyes. He didn't want to have this discussion in public. "Can we talk about it after dinner?"

"No." The word was forceful. The conversation around them stopped. "We have the discussion now."

He opened his eyes. The tears were gone from hers. Her expression was cool.

"Really," Atropos said, "we have more important things to deal with."

"Like who rules other planets?" Travers shook a spoon at them. "Sometimes you people just don't know when to quit."

"Stop it," Megan said. "I just asked a simple question. I want one straight answer."

She looked at Rob, and she was going to ask it again.

"How did you use my talents?" she asked.

"Oh, child," Clotho said, "it's not as devious as it sounds."

"Unless, of course, he thought of it first," Lachesis said, mostly to the other Fates.

"Which we're sure he didn't," Atropos said to Megan.

Rob held up a hand. He wanted them to stop talking. He wanted to tell her this.

"You felt his emotion, dear," Clotho said. "Which is a danger of being an empath. You can be seduced by someone whom you're not attracted to."

"But that's not the case here," Lachesis said.

"After all," Atropos added, "you are soulmates."

Megan's cheeks had grown so pale that Rob thought she was going to pass out. "Is this true?" she asked—not him, but Zoe.

Zoe met his gaze, and he saw panic in her eyes. Then she looked at Megan and shrugged. "I'm new to this. You're the first empath I've ever met."

Which was no help at all. It felt like a dodge, which, of course, it was.

"It's true," John said. "But Rob's not like that. You might've met some other guys who were, but not Rob. And honestly, you can't blame the other guys either, especially if they were mortal. I mean, if they were mortal, then they couldn't manipulate like that because they had no idea what you are."

"What I am," Megan repeated. She nodded. "What I am."

She set her spoon in her dish of untouched chili.

"I'm going to leave the table," she said. "I need to think. Don't talk about important things until I come back."

Then she grabbed a piece of bread and stood up.

"Megan," Rob said.

But she didn't look at him. She didn't look at anyone. Instead, she put her head down and walked from the room, very slowly, as if her entire body hurt.

The dog followed her, its tail at half-mast,

almost as if her need for comfort was more of a draw than his own desire for food.

Travers stood, set his napkin beside his plate, and started after her. Zoe caught his arm.

"Let her go," Zoe said.

"But—"

"Let her go," Zoe repeated.

"She needs space, Dad," Kyle said. "She always has. Remember?"

Because she was an empath. Because the only way she knew her true emotions was to distance herself from other people's.

Somehow she had learned that much. Despite her lack of training, she had learned a little.

"I'll go," Rob said.

"I think you've done enough," Travers said.

Rob felt the anger he'd been suppressing rise. "What does that mean?"

"Using my sister's abilities to seduce her? That's pretty low, even for a billionaire playboy."

"It wasn't like that," Rob said.

"Sure it was," Travers said. "She was easy, wasn't she? I've read about you. You like to have women dripping off you, and you took the first available one on this little adventure. My sister."

Rob clenched both fists. He was leaning over the table, facing Travers, whose fists were also clenched.

Rob wanted to leap across the table and strangle that arrogant man.

"If you guys spill my chili, I'll never forgive you," John said.

The break was just enough to hold Rob back.

He could almost hear John in his head: *Words, Rob. We have to learn to work with words.*

All right. He would work with words, then.

"Do you think so little of your sister that you believe I'd take advantage of her, and she'd let me?" Rob said.

"She's been taken advantage of before," Travers said.

"Maybe because her family never took care of her." Rob was leaning on the table so hard that it moved slightly.

"We always cared for her," Travers said.

"Yeah," Rob said, "that's why you fight with her so much."

"I fight with her because I love her," Travers said.

"And don't respect her."

Travers reached across the table and stuck a finger in the center of Rob's chest. "I wouldn't talk about respect if I were you, pal."

"I can talk about respect if I want to," Rob said. "I've shown her nothing but respect."

"Oh yeah?" Travers poked his finger into Rob's chest once more. Travers hadn't trimmed his fingernail, and the movement sent a small, sharp pain through Rob. "That's not what I'm hearing."

"Your sister is an amazing woman," Rob said.

"I know." Travers kept his finger against Rob's shirt. Rob was doing his best to ignore the provocation.

"I wouldn't be standing here if it weren't for her."

"Because you can manipulate her," Travers said.

"Dad," Kyle said. The boy sounded agitated.

"Because I respect her," Rob said.

"You have a funny way of showing it," Travers snapped.

That comment made Rob catch his breath. Travers was right, but not for the reasons he thought—Rob had not deliberately manipulated Megan, not once. No, Rob wasn't showing her respect now by standing here, arguing with her brother when she was in distress.

Rob pivoted, a military movement, and walked away from the table.

"Hey!" Travers yelled. "Where are you going?"

Rob could hear chairs move, Kyle making a distressed noise, and Zoe saying, "Trav, don't!" but Rob kept walking.

He heard footsteps behind him. Let that man come near him. Let him, and see what would happen.

"Leave her alone," Travers said. "You've caused enough trouble."

Rob kept walking.

"Touch my sister again, and I'll—"

Rob turned. Travers was right behind him. Travers stopped speaking the moment that Rob faced him.

"You'll what?" Rob asked softly. "Take me on? You? An untrained mage?"

Travers stopped. He was holding his ground rather admirably, considering.

John had stood up. Kyle was watching, his eyes wide. Zoe was still sitting, shaking her head. And the Fates, bless them, were eating as if this was all for their entertainment.

That angered Rob even more.

"Or will you resort to the manly defense?" Rob asked. "Are you just going to hit me? Because I've been spoiling for a fight for weeks now. You want to accommodate me?"

"Dad," Kyle said. "He's a good guy, really."

Travers met his gaze. The man was rethinking his impulsiveness. "You know how many times she's been hurt?"

So that was it. Travers was angry because he finally understood why his sister had gotten into a variety of bad relationships—all impulsively, it had probably seemed to him.

"Yeah," Rob said softly. "I'm beginning to realize that."

"Then you understand why I don't want you near her."

"No," Rob said. "I don't understand that. Because if I don't go to her now, I'm no better than those other guys. I have to explain what's going on and how I didn't manipulate her, at least not intentionally. If I don't, then everything falls apart."

Travers bit his lower lip. His frown deepened, but his anger seemed to be fading—or at least the impulse to hit Rob was.

"She's fragile," Travers said. "You be careful with her."

Rob shook his head ever so slightly. "She's not fragile, Travers. If she were fragile, she'd have broken long ago under the weight of everyone's emotions."

Travers raised his chin. Was that the anger coming back? The urge to argue?

"But," Rob said to stave him off. "I will be careful. I promise. I have more at stake here than you do."

Travers studied him for a long moment. Rob wasn't sure if the man was going to hit him or spit at him. But Travers did neither. Instead, he nodded once.

"I'm not sure I like you," Travers said.

Robin smiled. "That's okay," he said. "I'm finally beginning to like you."

32

Megan let herself into her suite and then leaned on the closed door. The place was a mess—the coffee table moved, the chairs to the side, her shoes still on the floor.

But it was quiet here, and the emotions that had her so agitated seemed muted.

An empath. That explained so very much.

Her earliest memories were of drowning in emotion. She had always felt out of control. Her moods would swing wildly—happy, sad, frightened, angry—and often without reason.

She could remember her mother saying, *I don't know what to do with you, Meg, honey. Your reactions never make any sense to me.*

And her father picking her up one day—she was maybe three and so happy to see him—and as she had been pressed against his wool jacket, she'd burst into tears.

The sadness had been his that day, not hers.

She might not have made it through the day to day if it hadn't been for Great-Aunt Eugenia.

That woman frightened her (or maybe she had frightened her great-aunt? Wow. That was a concept), but just before Megan had gone to school, she had managed to have a quiet moment with her great-aunt.

Megan, you're a very sensitive little girl.

And Megan had nodded.

You need to make walls between yourself and the world. Let me show you.

Great-Aunt Eugenia had touched her head and her shoulders and had helped her bring up shields—that's what Megan eventually called it. Later, her therapist called it a *Star Trek* metaphor: whenever Megan didn't want to deal with something, she raised shields.

But there had been more to that day than simple shields. Her great-aunt had smiled at her and cupped her face.

You need the walls, honey, just to get through the day. But remember, never ever wall off your heart.

Had she done that? She wasn't sure. It had certainly been hurt enough.

She walked toward the living room and sank into the chair where Rob had been sitting before dinner. She ran her fingers over the arm, remembering how his hand on her thigh had soothed her.

All those men. She had tumbled into bed with some of them because their lust had infected her. But she had stayed away from just as many—or more. Some of them had seemed like they had a cloud around them, a cloud of confusing emotion—part lust, part hatred, part admiration.

Stalker emotions, she'd told her friend Conchita. *There's something off about these guys.*

How do you know? Conchita would ask.

Megan would shrug. *I just know.*

And that was the worst part. Quantifying things. She had always been intuitive, always relied on her gut and not her head. That was the main reason she fought with Travers. He was all logic—at least until he met Zoe—and Megan was all emotion.

Only Megan's emotion had logic, and beneath Travers's logic, there was always a little too much emotion.

But Rob, Rob had seemed pure to her from the beginning. Not pure in a sexual sense—he clearly wasn't (she smiled)—but his reactions were clear, his emotions untainted.

He had been intriguing from the first, in that weird outfit in the desert after all the streetlights had gone out, then in his office, and in her apartment, and finally here, when he had decided to prove to her how he felt.

How could he think he had manipulated her when he was being so honest? He had just wanted to show her how he felt.

And she had known it. She had felt it, all of his emotion, *all* of it, and had almost gotten lost in it.

Then she had separated from it and tried to figure out her own—

And couldn't.

Because she had walled off her heart, despite what Great-Aunt Eugenia had told her? Was that why Megan had never ever fallen in love? Because she had blocked every opportunity?

Was that why her eyes had teared up when Rob touched her? Because her heart was struggling against a wall, trying to break free?

Raised voices came to her from the next room—Rob and Travers—and bits of emotion. She was good at blocking out emotion from room to room—she had learned that from Great-Aunt Eugenia too.

Megan actually had to concentrate to see what the emotion was: a mixture of fear and panic and anger—and guilt.

She closed her eyes and concentrated. She could actually separate out the emotion by person. She had never really tried that before, although she had done it in counseling sessions. If she focused on a person, actually looked at them, she could get a sense of them.

But she had always thought of that as part of her concentration, not as a magical gift.

Both men were feeling the anger, and both, oddly enough, were feeling guilt. But Rob was feeling the fear, and Travers was feeling panic.

Because of her? Why?

She let the emotions go, stood up, and walked as far from the other suite as she could. She touched the edge of the table where the map had been, and frowned.

Rob had always been up front with her. Why, then, was he so adamant about her not going into Faerie? Every time he had said that, she had gotten angry because he had used the word control.

(And oh, boy, did that make sense now. Always, always people accused her of being out of control, of needing control, of needing help, of needing someone else to take charge because she was too emotional.)

He knew what she was, so he wasn't trying to

get her to control her emotions, and while he was being protective, he hadn't treated any other woman in the room paternally. So something else was going on.

She closed her eyes and remembered, trying to see if she could sort out the emotions that had been flying through this room.

And what she got, again, was fear.

What would terrify the great Robin Hood?

She opened her eyes. She had already seen what terrified him. It was the very thing that had closed him down for so very long. For centuries, actually.

Robin was afraid of loss. He had lost Marian. He was afraid of losing Megan.

Really?

Or was that her ego talking?

And why would going into Faerie mean that he had lost her?

Someone knocked on the suite door. She frowned, resisting the urge to get a sense of who it was. She had separated herself long enough. She needed to get back to Travers's suite to make sure her brother and her lover didn't kill each other.

She went to the door and pulled it open.

Rob stood there, his head bowed. He looked almost boyish, like a child who expected to be yelled at for something he had already done.

"May I come in?" he asked.

She nodded and backed away from the door. Despite her resolution, she was having difficulty opening her heart. It almost felt like something blocked her, something reluctant inside her kept her boxed in.

Rob stepped into the room and closed the door behind himself. He started to reach for her and then stopped. "I just wanted to say I'm sorry."

"I know," she said.

"I didn't mean to manipulate you."

"I know that too," she said.

His brow furrowed, just a little, as if this wasn't going the way he'd expected. "I really do love you."

"I know," she said again.

He shook his head slightly. "Then why did you leave?"

"A few minutes ago?" she asked.

He nodded.

"I needed time to think." Away from the noise, away from the untidy emotions. Away from Rob.

"Do you want me to go, then?" he asked.

She shook her head. "I want you to answer a question."

"All right," he said cautiously.

"I want you to tell me what would happen to me if I went to Faerie."

The fear that rose from him was palpable. She could actually feel him work to tamp it down.

She decided to try something, something she used to do impulsively with some of her more distressed clients.

She touched his arm, and sent soothing warmth his way.

His fear lessened.

His eyes widened. "Who taught you that?"

She shrugged. "I think I picked it up on my own. It works then?"

"It's part of your magic."

"I thought women don't have magic until they get older."

He smiled. "It's a rule designed by Zeus. But a few things got missed. Like empathy. That's not an emotion he understands, so he doesn't recognize empaths as magical."

"Strange," Megan said. "So he has that much control, then?"

"He has more than you can imagine."

"But I thought he ruled with all the others."

"He does," Rob said, "but he leads them, and he manipulates them. He's not a good man."

"I've figured that out." She let her hand drop from Rob's arm. The fear he had felt was gone now. "You still haven't told me about Faerie."

And the fear bobbled back, just a little, and then it stayed constant.

Rob sighed. "You're not going to just trust me on this, are you?"

"I'm curious," she said, "and besides, if it's something I should worry about, I'd rather know about it."

His entire expression changed. Somehow those words calmed him. Perhaps because they made sense to him.

"Let's go sit," he said.

He led her into the living room, and he took the armchair again. She didn't sit on the arm because she wanted to see his face. So she sat on the couch, her hands threaded together and resting between her knees.

"Faerie," Rob said. "It's a scary place."

"I'm gathering that," Megan said. "It looked kind of familiar."

"The Faeries get some of their magic from luck. They steal as much of it as they can."

She nodded, knowing he was still hesitating.

"But it's also a cold place, Meg." He sounded like a man who knew. "There are rumors—and I don't know if they're true—that the faeries themselves don't understand emotion. They can't experience it. Or won't."

"Aren't they—human?—like you guys?" She asked. "Or us? I am one of you guys, right?"

He smiled. "Right."

"So, we're human, right?"

"Kind of," he said. "I don't want to use the word superhuman because that has all kinds of terrible connotations. We're more than human, I guess. Enhanced humans. Or maybe human is just normal, and we're a little more than normal. You know, like intelligence. People have a range of intelligence, but most fall in the average category. We're above average, I guess. I'm trying not to make us sound better because we're not. We're just different. And amazingly the same, at the same time."

Surprisingly, his words didn't confuse her. He valued regular people—he had fallen in love with one and still loved her, even though she had been gone for centuries. He thought of himself as having more gifts, but not as being better.

And Megan's heart opened at that. Warmth flooded her, almost overwhelming her.

She did love him. She had loved him from the moment she met him, but this—this realization that he cared about all kinds of people, and on a deep, deep level—this somehow broke down that last wall.

The wall that said she wasn't good enough or thin enough or smart enough or—as she had learned in the last few hours—magic enough for him to love her.

These distinctions didn't matter to him. He valued people, just like she did, whether they were rich or poor, fat or thin, smart or dumb.

Magic or not.

Her eyes filled with tears again.

"Did I say something wrong?" he asked.

She shook her head, and then wiped at her eyes with the back of her hand. "Go on."

He frowned, then blinked at her. Then said, "I lost my place."

She let out a small laugh—mostly because she had been nervous—and then said, "I sidetracked you. I asked if faeries were human, but then I asked if you and I were too."

He smiled. "Oh, yeah. And yes, I think faeries are. But I don't know. We all look different— redheads, blondes, brunettes, different skin colors, just like the rest of the human race. But faeries all have black hair and pointed ears and upswept eyebrows. They look different, and they might be different."

Then he shrugged.

"But," he said, "that could be good old-fashioned prejudice speaking. A lot of what I know about faeries is pretty old, from before we learned that people are the same under the skin."

"If you're right," Megan said, "and they don't feel emotion, then they're not the same."

"But I don't know if that's true or a myth," Rob said. "I've stayed clear of Faerie as much as I can. I do know that some humans have fallen in love with faeries. I've also known a few faeries who quit their kind and came to live among us. They claimed they did it for love."

"You don't believe them?"

He opened his hands and studied his palms. "They didn't sound like they believed it themselves. It was almost like they aspired to love, does that make sense? They tried to act like someone in love, so that maybe they would fall in love."

"Could it be a spell?" Megan asked. Then she frowned again, feeling a swirling confusion. She knew so very little, and it was beginning to annoy her. "We do do spells, right?"

"I do. Zoe does. Travers does," Rob said. "But you don't, not in the traditional sense, and neither does Kyle, although he might when he gets older. Some magicks are different."

"Like the faeries?"

"I don't know," he said, "and yes, they could be under a spell. But if it affected all of them, I think that would be more properly considered a curse."

"It would have to be powerful to do that," Megan said.

He nodded. "Yes, it would."

Megan stood and stuck her hands in the back pockets of her jeans. She paced around the living room, wishing she had learned most of this stuff long ago. She couldn't help because she was so far behind on the information scale.

"All right," she said. "You say that faeries have

no emotions. So I'm confused. Wouldn't that make me safer? Why am I in danger from them?"

"Because," he said, "you are the repository for many emotions. Emotion is much more powerful around you. You're like an enhancer. Faeries covet you."

"Why?" she asked. "If they don't have it, how can I be of use to them?"

He leaned back in the chair. It was a strange movement, not a relaxed one, but one that was supposed to make him seem relaxed.

"Here's what I know," he said. "I know of at least one empath in the past who got trapped in Faerie. They magicked her somehow—enslaved her, the story goes—and they would send her into the world to collect emotion so that she could then distribute it to the faeries."

"Like luck," Megan said.

"Hmm?" He blinked at her, obviously confused.

"You said they collect luck. They collect emotions too."

"I guess," Rob said.

"Do you personally know of this empath? Or is this just a story?"

"All stories have a basis in reality," Rob said.

"I'm sure they do," Megan said, not being sure at all, "but if you're just repeating something you heard, then—"

"I'm not risking you!" he snapped.

"I'm not yours to risk," she snapped back, and then gasped. The power behind those words had been his, not hers. It had been his fear coming through as anger, being reflected back at him through her.

Although she believed that she controlled her own destiny.

"What I mean is," she said, "should I chose to risk my life, it's my decision, not yours."

"And I have to live with it," he said, once again deceptively calm.

She nodded.

He cursed, and she could feel real distress behind the word.

"What?" she asked.

He shook his head.

"Robin."

He closed his eyes. "I said the same thing to Marian. More than once."

"And yet she was the one who died," Megan said.

"Oh," he said quietly, "but I left her first. And I did it by choice."

33

Fear. Fear was an amazingly powerful emotion, more powerful than love, if one let it be.

Rob shook his head and closed his eyes so that he couldn't see Megan. He had been so terrified of losing Marian that he had left her first, going off to fight in the Crusades, and then learning that no matter what he did, he couldn't shake how he felt about her.

Nor could he shake the fear.

So he had gone home, only to find that she was angry with him, and the relationship had changed. They had patched it up as best they could, but it was never exactly the same.

And that had been his fault.

"Robin?" Megan asked gently.

He opened his eyes. She was studying him.

"You know how I know you didn't manipulate me?" she asked.

He shook his head, wondering why she was telling him this now.

"Because," she said, "from the first moment I saw you, I've loved you too."

He couldn't respond at all—there were no words—so he didn't say anything.

"But what I've learned, in a life as a closet empath"—and then she smiled, amused, apparently, at her own choice of words—"is that even though emotions are powerful and can overwhelm you, the only thing that'll save you is hanging onto yourself."

He wasn't sure he understood that. His confusion must have shown on his face, for she crouched next to him and took his hand.

"The only way *I* can love you," she said as gently as he'd ever heard her speak, "is for there to be an 'I' in the first place."

She was right. He knew that. He had given up everything for Marian after he had come back, and it hadn't made things better. They were all right, but they had never achieved that passion and perfection of the early years.

"You want to go to Faerie, don't you?" he asked.

"If I can distract them so that you can steal the wheel, why not? It doesn't sound like I'll die."

"But you could get trapped there," he said.

She smiled at him. "I'm in love with Robin Hood, and wasn't it said of him that no walls could hold him? No prison could keep him out?"

"Of me, yes," he said. "But not of the people around me."

"Didn't you rescue everyone who'd been captured?" she asked.

"When I was young," he said.

"Did anyone get captured when you were older?"

"No," he said, "but I'd gone up against mere mortals. Faeries are powerful."

"And yet my newbie brother defeated them," Megan said.

"He escaped them," Rob said. "That's a different thing."

She shook her head. "It seems to me escape is all we're discussing. And I believe it's completely possible."

She did believe it, he could see it in her eyes. She believed it with all the naïveté of a new mage. And yet she had an argument.

And he was reacting out of fear.

"Can I be part of your plan to get the wheel?" she asked quietly.

His heart—his fearful, newly reopened heart— trembled as he said, ever so softly, "Yes."

34

It felt like the old days. Rob was at the top of his game. John liked the plan. Everyone had a part, even the kid.

John stood still while Zoe put the finishing touches on his disguise. Apparently no one could enter Faerie looking like a civilian—the faeries would encircle them, use their magic against them, and steal whatever luck they had.

Invisibility spells didn't work either because the faeries could track them. Sometimes, they let mages with invisibility spells go very deep into Faerie before trapping them there and making them lose years.

Some, Zoe said, lost their lives.

Although John hadn't heard of it. He stood in the middle of the giant bathroom at the back of Travers's suite. Travers sat on the edge of the bathtub watching the entire procedure. Rob peered into the mirror, looking at his newly blackened hair, his upswept eyebrows, high cheekbones, and brand-new pointed ears.

"It looks weird," he said. "They'll see right through it."

"They didn't see through me," Travers said. "But a faerie actually did mine."

He'd been done up to look like a faerie in order to rescue Zoe. She had put him right just that morning, which he reminded her as they all headed toward the bathroom.

"If we could find Gaylord," Zoe said, "then we'd use him. But I think he heard that I had been rescued and went off on his own again. He does that."

"You're doing fine," John said through clenched lips. It actually hurt to have her do this magic on him. His face was stretching, and his bones were creaking.

She had insisted on doing the magic because she'd been around Faerie her whole life (apparently, from what Travers said, her prophecy had been about Faerie), and because she thought that John and Robin wouldn't "go the distance."

She didn't explain that, but John knew what she meant. There was a certain delicacy to all faeries that he didn't have—he was more the linebacker, break-a-few heads type—and for this to work, he had to willow out a little.

Zoe couldn't change his mass, but she was moving it around some. He was actually going to get taller and thinner, which was initially what he wanted (that Atkins diet), but not like this.

Apparently, there were no fat faeries. John tried to think of a counterexample and couldn't come up with any.

Not that he was fat. He was large, big-boned, and strong. Fat never figured into it.

Except when he stood on his own scale, and realized how much weight he'd put on since he'd been a young man.

Of course, food was more widely available now than it had been in the twelfth century.

"Don't smile," Zoe said, still working on his cheekbones. This took a delicate magic, the kind that was almost like sculpting.

Rob looked oddly like some of the paintings made of him centuries ago. Put him in green and add a feather in his cap, and he'd look a little like Errol Flynn—and John hadn't seen any resemblance before now.

"I'm still not sure I should go back in," Travers said forlornly. "I'd be happier if I stayed up here."

"I'm lousy at math," Rob said, "and John's only slightly better."

"Who does the books for your corporations?" Travers asked.

"A series of accountants who never see all of the books. It's a checks and balances thing," Rob said, "since I really can't oversee it well."

"Sounds like a major handicap," Travers said.

"I've coped for a long time." He shrugged, turned around, and rested his hands on the counter, peering at John. "You look more like an oversized leprechaun."

"Faith and begorrah to you too," John grumped.

"Stop moving," Zoe said. "I'm almost done."

"The three of us have to go in," Rob said. "I need you to get us to that wheel as quickly as possible. John and I'll get it out, but again, you have to lead."

Travers sighed. "Leaving Zoe to guard the Fates."

"I'm not guarding anyone," Zoe said. "They're going to help me monitor."

"Which I don't entirely understand," Travers said.

"Done." Zoe took her hands off John's face. It still ached, but not as badly. He looked at himself in the mirror. He looked a lot more like the Jolly Green Giant than an oversized leprechaun, but he wasn't sure that was an improvement.

"You don't have to understand," he said to Travers. "Rob's in charge. He never tells us the entire plan."

"Great." Travers muttered.

Zoe smiled fondly at him. "Come up here," she said and pointed to the chair that John was just vacating.

John went and sat by Rob. "Aren't we a pair?" Rob asked. "I'd rather wear green and smear mud on my face than do this."

"It's the same idea," John said, hearing his jaw crack as he spoke. This was going to be a painful few hours.

"I suppose," Rob said.

"It's the team that worries me too," John said. "Zoe doesn't have enough firepower if we all get trapped."

"But she has the Fates," Rob said. "They know some magic tricks that we don't."

"And don't, at the moment, have the skill to execute them."

"It'll work," Rob said, but he looked worried too, and John knew why. Megan had talked him into letting her be involved. The Fates thought that was a good idea—that was why, they said, the adventure was happening now, because of Megan.

But Rob didn't want to put her at risk.

All of them would be at some kind of risk. John wasn't really sure what the faeries could do to him besides steal some of his magic and make him lose a few decades, but he also knew he didn't want to find out.

"Yeouch!" Travers said. "It didn't hurt when Gaylord did it."

Zoe shrugged. "He's had more practice, I'm sure."

"Smuggling people into Faerie? I don't think so."

John rubbed his hands over his weirdly shaped face. "How long do you think this'll take us?" he asked Rob softly.

"Too long," Rob said. "That's my biggest worry— that it'll take much too long."

35

Megan sat nervously in her car, staring at the luminous dial on her watch. Seconds sure took a long time to pass when she tracked each and every one of them.

She was three parking lots away from her target, an unnamed casino on the Boulder Highway. She had driven by the place just to make sure she was in the right area, and, judging by the description Zoe had given her, she was.

Apparently the ancient casino with the neon sign that said CRAPS, SLOTS AND BEER was the faeries' main casino in Vegas. Megan found that hard to believe, particularly with all the fancy casinos around, but Zoe insisted.

In fact, she said there was an entrance to Faerie inside.

She also said Megan would have to work hard to ignore it.

Megan was working hard to ignore a lot of things, mostly the feeling that she probably should have listened to Rob. He had been afraid for her

because of abilities she hadn't completely understood. He had also been afraid for her because she
was getting in over her head.

And it wasn't until she saw that rundown casino,
with the ratty cars in its parking lot, that she
sensed he wasn't overreacting.

Still, she had Kyle on her side. Kyle, and Zoe,
and the Fates. Apparently they had set up some
kind of command system. Zoe had enhanced
Kyle's mind-reading ability to pick up any signal
from Megan, although she had to be really specific
about it. They had given her instructions—all five
of them had (well, the Fates probably counted as
one person in this case, since their instructions
were broken down into parts)—and had made
her repeat those instructions back to them.

She had even practiced a little. Enough that Kyle
frowned at her and said, "I *heard* you, Aunt Meg."

A little bit of petty revenge for that moment in
Rob's office, where Kyle had broadcast to her.

Still, she was very much on her own, and she
had been instructed not to panic when the faeries
noticed her. The only time she really needed to
call for help was if they tried to take her to Faerie
or if she felt physically threatened.

Otherwise, she was to wait until someone came
to get her or until dawn, whichever was sooner.
No one had quite figured out how she would
know when dawn was from the inside of the
faerie casino, so they tried one small trick.

They magicked her watch, protecting it from
faerie time manipulation. The Fates believed the
magic was too small for the faeries to notice, and
Zoe believed Megan could explain it all by simply

saying she had purchased the watch at an odds 'n ends store in North Vegas. Apparently, a place there did sell magical items to the nonmagical. The faeries often stashed things there so that they could trace particular marks.

Finally, the hands on her magicked watch showed 9 p.m. She started the car and drove out of the parking lot, heading down the street to the faerie casino.

Her stomach clenched.

Zoe had tried to explain this to her: the faeries had had casinos here since Vegas had been founded. Time was irrelevant to them (although the Fates argued that it simply moved differently for them) so they didn't notice that their place was out of date.

Zoe actually believed that the faeries kept the casino out of date on purpose to capture the gambling addicts and the long-timers, not to attract tourists. The faeries were pure businessmen through and through, according to the Fates, and maybe part of a mob, according to Zoe.

All Megan learned was that she had to watch her own back.

With people who had more magic than she could imagine, and had (according to Rob) no emotions at all.

But if that were true, how had one of them become friends with Zoe? Was she that inattentive to the niceties of emotion? Was that why she'd been attracted to Travers?

(Which wasn't really fair on Megan's part. Travers had emotions—a lot of them—but he usually tamped them down. Although he wasn't doing that much this week.)

She made herself take several deep breaths. She drove past several darkened buildings—most of them closed down casinos being readied for demolition. Zoe had mentioned that this area was the next one up for renovation, and Megan could see why.

This far out on the old highway to Boulder City, ghosts of the past remained. Old eateries, warehouses, and empty lots where important places once stood brought back a time when this was one of the main drags of the Vegas area.

Now it felt creepy and deserted, the kind of place she wouldn't go alone in her own town of L.A., let alone here.

But she couldn't abandon the mission; she was the distraction. Although she wasn't sure how just walking into a casino, even one run by faeries, would make a big enough distraction so that the men could steal the spinning wheel.

They all assured her it would work.

So she was going to try it, even though she was more nervous than she had ever been in her life.

She pulled into the parking lot of the casino. The Es on the CRAPS, SLOTS AND BEER sign were starting to go out. The neon crackled and faded in and out, sending weird red light across this part of the parking lot.

For the life of her, she couldn't see any other sign—not even one that used to say the name of the casino. She had hoped to prove Zoe wrong about that, but there was nothing.

Beer cans and old cigarette wrappers littered

the parking lot. The front page of the *Las Vegas Sun* blew across the concrete, even though she didn't feel much of a wind.

The air smelled faintly of smoke and stale beer. If it was this bad out here, how bad would it be inside?

She hurried across the cracked sidewalk and pulled open the double glass doors—no name on those either. The place was just as dark inside as it was out. In fact, the level of light seemed about the same, red and blue and yellow neon coming from slot machines so old they looked like they belonged in a 1950s movie.

The air smelled so strongly of cigarette smoke, she had a hunch it would take fifteen showers over five days to get the stench off her skin just from this momentary contact. Everyone inside the casino—all of whom looked "mortal" to her— was smoking, from the elderly man who sat at the corner slot machine to the woman beside him who had an oxygen tank on wheels and breathing tubes in her nose.

Megan resisted the urge to cough. So far, no one had noticed her. She had thought she'd be rushed by faeries. But she hadn't seen a one.

Was that a bad sign?

She wished she had someone to ask.

The low ceilings held the smoke down and made the ka-ching! ka-ching! of the coins falling into the metal trays seem even louder. The slot machines here were truly one-armed bandits, with the lever that the gambler had to pull. A few of the gamblers looked like they'd been attached to the machines in 1966 and were being kept alive by the same electricity that kept the machines going.

Megan kept walking. Her breath was coming in short gasps, but she couldn't tell if that was from the smoke or from her nervousness. She was glad that faeries didn't have empaths—someone like her would be able to sense her fear from miles away.

She passed craps tables that were mostly empty except for a croupier and two other employees all watching one or two players. In a room to the side, ten people played poker, and judging by the stack of chips that each had in front of them, the game had been going on forever, with no end in sight.

Megan swallowed, feeling nerves churn her stomach. She followed her wounded nose to the buffet, where a beef roast looked like it had been glued to the tray five weeks before. Next to it, a congealed white gravy mound pretended to be some kind of chicken, and beside that, pork so dried that it could have served as shoe leather rounded out the "meat" portion of the serving area.

Nonetheless, she took a table as instructed. A greasy menu stuck into one of those metal holders informed her that the buffet was $3.95 and all U-Can-Eat (which, judging by the food, would be exactly none). But she was supposed to buy something and pick at it while she waited to attract someone's attention.

Two little old ladies with hair as blue as the air sat two tables down, waving cigarettes as they spoke to each other. A few more tables away, an elderly man ate scrambled eggs covered in ketchup. The only person near Megan's age was an obese young man who hunched over a cup of coffee as if he didn't have a dime to his name.

She got up, grabbed a chipped white plate off the stack, and proceeded to fill it up with beet salad, tuna casserole, and old-fashioned macaroni and cheese, the only things on the buffet that looked halfway agreeable.

The dessert section had Jell-O filled with lime slices, which she believed was indestructible, and chocolate pudding, which she would have thought was indestructible until she saw the thick skins on the surface.

Still, she took one Jell-O and one pudding, poured a cup of coffee from the pot, and headed back to her table. A keno runner (invisible, apparently) had left a keno card next to her napkin, but other than that, Megan had seen no sign of any other employee, whom Zoe had assured her were all faeries.

Was Zoe wrong? Someone had mentioned that things changed hourly in Faerie. Maybe they didn't own this place anymore.

Megan slipped into her chair, looked at the unappetizing food, and hoped Rob was all right.

She hadn't been told exactly what his part of the plan was—in case she was "compromised" (whatever that meant [and she certainly didn't want to speculate])—so she had no idea what he was doing.

Except going for the wheel.

With the help of her accountant brother and the big, sensitive man known as Little John.

36

The fact that the main entrance to Faerie was near the Mirage seemed appropriate to Rob. Faeries probably liked the irony: they had to create a mirage to hide the entrance.

What surprised him was how close the entrance was to that fake volcano that pretended to spew lava every half hour. The entrance was right near the volcano's base, which took some work getting to because the Mirage's security was pretty tight.

Travers was surprised that the entrance had been moved. Apparently, the night before, the entrance had been several yards away in a concrete block of the sidewalk.

But the faeries were well-known for moving the entrance to their little hideaway, and since they had figured out that Zoe had been in Faerie uninvited, they had probably changed all the entrances.

This one was still surprisingly close to where it had been before.

John had wanted to use an invisibility spell to get

them near the volcano's base, but Rob wouldn't let him. Mage magic was like a beacon to the faeries, and using it this close could alert them to something going on.

So Rob and his team did it the old-fashioned way: they snuck behind tourists and guards, and crawled part of the distance on their bellies.

It felt like the good old days.

Rob loved that.

John lifted part of the fake lava rock to reveal a hole the size of the door to Rob's office. The entrance to Faerie beckoned.

"If you're going to back out," Rob whispered to the other two, "the time is now."

John grinned at him, revealing startling white teeth. Rob wasn't sure he'd ever get used to his friend looking like a troll on stilts. "I'm in."

"I'm an old hand at this," Travers said, and Rob would have believed him, if it weren't for the tremor in his voice.

"All right," Rob said. "John first, Travers second, and I'll bring up the rear."

John slipped into the door feet first and waved as he disappeared. Travers took a deep breath, like a man about to dive into an ocean, and then slide in behind John.

Rob made sure no one was watching, grabbed the edge of the fake lava rock, and pulled it closed as he went through the door. There was a small slide that just ended.

He found himself in midair, free-falling in the darkness.

He couldn't hear anything except his own breathing.

Somehow, this no longer seemed like a good idea.

He resisted the urge to make a fist and cast some light. He let himself fall through air that got progressively cooler. It smelled of earth and damp—oddly enough, given this was the desert—and mold, and he worried suddenly that he wasn't falling down, that he was falling into some other part of Faerie, some part nowhere Las Vegas.

Then he heard voices, all of them speaking faerie, and the cling-cling of slot machines, and a strange glow appeared at his feet. It took him a moment to realize the glow was neon.

The air got drier and stank of cigarettes.

Then he fell into the light, landing on a silver net and tumbling off in the middle of a casino floor.

John and Travers already stood to one side, looking very nervous. They were both too tall to be in Faerie—by nearly two feet—and Travers was blond.

A faerie woman put her hands on Travers's chest. "Nice to see you again, big boy."

John's already upswept eyebrows went up further. Rob picked himself off the floor, amazed he hadn't had the wind knocked of him or felt bruised from the fall.

"Playing with the mortals for a second night in a row?" she asked Travers.

He gave her a nervous smile and said, "Is it that obvious?"

She rubbed his hair. "I like you blond. I don't think I'd recognize you with dark hair."

Then she grinned at John.

He gave her a startled look back.

"I don't think we've been introduced," she said in a seductive tone.

"And I don't see any point, since you've already claimed my friend there," John said, sounding as nervous as Travers.

Rob stood and brushed himself off. No one seemed to notice him. Of course, he was the only one of the three short enough to fit into Faerie. He looked like countless other faerie men standing around the machines.

And that was the problem. There were countless faeries all over this section of the makeshift casino.

Shouldn't they have been gone by now? Megan had gone to the faerie casino on Boulder Highway, hadn't she?

He would have sworn that her presence would have attracted them.

If he was wrong, then this plan wasn't going to work.

If he was wrong, they had just placed themselves in serious danger.

If he was wrong, everything was going to fail.

37

The hotel suite looked like something out of an X-Men movie. Kyle sat in a big leather chair—the kind that Professor X would use, only cooler—and Zoe sat a few feet away. She had ordered complete quiet, mostly so that the Fates, who were on the other side of the room, wouldn't distract everyone with their talking.

Zoe had cleared most of the furniture out of this bedroom in the suite, except for the chair (which she had conjured out of somewhere), the table in front of the Fates, and the big screen TV, which showed a faint picture of the casino that Aunt Meg had gone into.

Zoe couldn't use mage magic inside the casino—that would point out the plan to the faeries—but she had installed real surveillance, like in the movies, on the outside. What they all saw was a real picture of the place from a little digital computer camera and a strategically placed computer not too far away.

Wireless. Like magic, Zoe said.

Kyle's stomach was doing somersaults. Dad didn't want him involved in this, but Zoe and the Fates promised he'd be all right.

He knew he would be, but everything rested on him—or at least, Aunt Megan's safety did. He had to be calm and receptive to her thoughts even though he wouldn't get the simple, every-day ones. Only the panicked scared ones, and only if she had any of those at all.

His mouth was dry. He hadn't been this nervous ever. At least, that he could remember.

Fang waddled into the room and jumped on Kyle's lap, startling him. Kyle petted the heavy dog, glad for the company.

The Fates weren't paying any attention to him. They were studying the Faerie map, which was spread out on the table before them. If there was some kind of problem with the wheel—and they didn't expect it—they were to let Zoe know, not that anyone could do anything about it, at least that Kyle knew about. Because there wasn't a backup for this part of the plan, unless Robin Hood had only told Zoe and her thoughts were blocking whatever it was, which Kyle hoped was the case, because he was really, really nervous . . .

"Kyle," Zoe said softly, "I'm not an empath, and you're making *me* nervous."

"Sorry," he said, and hugged Fang. Fang uttered a little squeak—a very undoglike noise—and struggled to get free. Kyle let the dog go.

He'd never been the center of a magical adventure before.

And he wasn't really the center now. He was

more like the fail-safe backup. In some ways, Aunt Megan was the center.

She had sure looked nervous on the camera as she walked into that ratty casino. But she didn't have to do anything except sit there and look pretty, at least that's what Rob had said, and he'd meant it too. He thought the faeries would surround her like moths around really bright light.

So far, Kyle couldn't tell if it was working. But he'd be able to tell if it went wrong. They'd tested it, and Aunt Megan had a pretty good mental shout, especially after Zoe enhanced his abilities to pick up over a distance.

Kyle swallowed against his dry throat. He'd have to trust everyone and hope this worked.

Because really, this whole thing was his fault. If he hadn't insisted that Dad drive the Fates to Vegas, if he hadn't introduced them to Aunt Megan, if he hadn't goaded Robin Hood, then no one would be in Faerie right now.

But he had, and they were, and he was waiting.

He hated the waiting most of all.

38

Megan poked at the Jell-O, trying to get to the lime slices inside. The Jell-O jiggled, but its surface seemed impenetrable. She sighed, and glanced around.

The blue-haired old ladies were still waving their cigarettes, the obese young man was at the buffet proper, filling his plate with the so-called food, and another elderly man was peering into the service area, as if he were wondering whether or not he could sit down without a hostess escorting him.

But no faeries. Was the thing about faeries being drawn to empaths a myth, the kind *not* based in fact?

She didn't even look at the roast beef, which she had gingerly taken a piece from, nor did she try to figure out whether or not the mashed potatoes were edible.

She did wonder whether the faeries' lack of time sense applied to how long food had been sitting under heating lamps, and then she shivered, trying to resist the urge to warn that poor young man away from his meal.

A door from the kitchen opened, and a small woman wearing spiked heels and a full-skirted cocktail dress backed her way out. As she turned, it became clear why she had had to back out. She had a large tray braced against her stomach. Part of the tray was held in place by a strap around her neck.

She pasted a smile on her face and said, "Cigars? Cigarettes? Cigarillos?"

Megan gawked. A cigarette girl? She'd never seen one outside of the movies. She actually thought they were a Hollywood construct.

"Cigars?" the woman asked. "Cigarettes? Cigarillos?"

Her voice had a warmth to it that Megan hadn't heard before. It almost shimmered with magic. Her hair was black and cut close, hiding her ears, but her features were delicate, like Zoe said faerie features were.

"Cigars?" The word just drifted off toward the end, and it wasn't followed by cigarettes or cigarillos. Instead, the woman turned toward Megan and raised one painted eyebrow.

Megan froze in her chair, afraid to move, afraid she might do something that would break the moment.

The woman started toward her. The tray really did have cigar packages, cigarette packs, and long boxes of cigarillos, as well as candy cigarettes and a small box filled with change.

Were they even charging twenty-first century prices for the cigarettes?

Then the woman unhooked the strap from around her neck. The strap slid to one side, and the tray fell to the floor, spilling cigarettes and cigarillos all over the threadbare carpet.

The blue-haired old ladies looked—not to see if the cigarette girl was all right—but to see if anyone would notice if they stole cigarettes.

The cigarette girl headed toward Megan, eyes glittering. The girl's expression looked like something out of a zombie movie, which made Megan shudder.

The girl reached her side and touched Megan's arm, ever so gingerly.

"Are you . . . ?" she asked, but didn't finish the sentence.

Megan had been instructed not to volunteer anything, no matter how much she wanted to.

"The emotion radiates off you," the girl said, her voice filled with awe. "You're not real, right?"

"I'm real," Megan said.

The girl plucked at Megan's shirt. Megan suddenly wished she had worn a suit or several leather jackets piled one on top of the other.

No one had told her this would involve touching. Or plucking. Or that glassy-eyed stare.

"Wow," the girl said, ever so softly. "Wow."

The kitchen door banged open, and a willowy man with a goatee and the same black hair as the girl peered out. "Brooke? Is something wrong? I heard the tray . . ."

And then he came out, a frown on his upswept features.

"What's this?" he asked as he approached Megan.

The little old ladies had given up on discretion. They were grabbing cigarette packs and shoving them in purses the size of the Hindenburg.

The two faeries didn't seem to care.

"I thought you people were legends," he said softly. "I never thought I'd see one of you in real life."

This was real life? Megan preferred her own, even with the psychology practice that she was shutting down. Given her choice, she'd be back in her office at this moment, facing very wealthy, very screwed up, irate parents who had huge trouble accepting responsibility for any one of their actions.

The new faerie plucked at the same sleeve the cigarette girl kept touching.

"Wow," he said with just the same measure of awe. "Wow."

"Chauncey!" a voice bellowed from the kitchen. "Hey, Chauncey, where in the six woods are you?"

The kitchen door opened a third time, and a squarely built man with similar upswept features and the same black hair came out. He was wearing a chef's apron that looked like it hadn't been cleaned since . . . well, since time began.

"Hey, Chaunce . . ."

Then the familiar glazing began, and this guy got a goofy smile. The smile freaked Megan out more than the rest of it did.

She wished she had thought through her side of the plan better. She should have gotten a table in the center of the room so that she had an open side, rather than a table against the wall with nowhere for these freaky faeries to go.

Others were coming in the main door, their eyes glazing as soon as they saw her. Or was it just because they were in her proximity?

She didn't know, didn't want to know. She did want to know if faeries could be held back with lime Jell-O. Or with congealed roast beef.

She hadn't taken enough burnt coffee, and it wasn't hot enough to do real damage.

Zoe wanted her to stay here until the mission was over?

That would take all of Megan's considerable strength. There were at least twenty faeries in her vicinity and more on the way.

The blue-haired old ladies were scurrying from the dining room. The obese kid set his food down and scurried after them. Only the elderly man continued to watch as if he had never seen anything like it before.

Well, Megan hadn't either, and she was part of it. And what was really creepy was that they all repeated the same words and then ended with "Wow," like she was the Queen of England or Brad Pitt or something.

Maybe, in Faerie World, she was the equivalent of Brad Pitt. Or the Queen. If she had a choice, she'd be the faerie equivalent of Julia Roberts.

Megan carefully set down her fork—she had been clutching it—and pushed her plates away. The faeries were pressing against her table, but no one had taken the seat opposite her.

It was almost as if they were afraid to.

More and more came through the doors. This place was getting packed.

With the low ceilings, lack of fans, and no windows, there couldn't be a lot of oxygen in this place.

Did faeries breathe air?

Megan suddenly found herself hoping they didn't.

Because if they did, they were going to use up all of hers.

She resisted the urge to look at her watch, but she sent a mental message, one she knew wouldn't get through.

Hurry, Rob. Please. Just hurry.

39

The faeries were leaving, marching away from their slot machines as if they'd received a message from an unseen god. Rob had never seen anything quite like it, and it unnerved him.

Even the faerie who had her arms around Travers excused herself.

"This's big," she said. "You guys coming?"

"In a minute," Travers said.

John crossed his arms, looking something like his old powerful self. The floor pulsed beneath Rob almost as if he were inside yet another machine.

All those warning movies he'd seen about the future—from *Metropolis* to *Matrix*—came to mind somehow. He never thought of Faerie as a place as soulless as the inside of a machine, but that's how it felt.

"Okay," Travers said as more and more faeries moved away from them, heading to the exit. "Creepy."

"No kidding," John said.

Rob stared at a nearby slot. Lives rotated on it, not cherries. But in the middle of the machine, he saw a faint map, and on it, a white glow.

Megan.

His heart went out to her. How was she holding up, suddenly the center of all this attention? He hoped she was doing all right.

The sooner he finished this, the sooner he would find out.

He glanced around the large—and now mostly empty—main room. "We need to do this thing," he said softly.

Travers nodded. "Follow me."

He led them through a maze of slot machines. Sometimes it seemed like Travers was walking them through a wall, only to have the wall dissolve into nothing as they approached. Travers walked through video poker games and baccarat tables and even a stage with a very confused stand-up comic still clutching a mike.

The comic, who was clearly human and who looked like he was dressed for vaudeville, saw them and said, "Where'd the audience go?"

"They'll be back," Rob said.

If the situation were different, he would have spelled the poor sap to the surface. But he didn't dare, at least not yet. Mage magic: he wasn't willing to risk it.

But he asked Travers to make a note of where this guy was so that they could rescue him if they got the chance.

"Softie," John whispered and then grinned.

Rob didn't smile back.

After a few minutes, they reached a fork in the

path that actually appeared in the fakey visuals. A sign post grew out of a bank of slot machines. The signs, like the ones in *M*A*S*H*, pointed every different direction. Some showed the way to a buffet, others to a bar, even more toward various parts of the gambling floor.

And one, pointing up, said simply THE CIRCLE.

Rob's breath caught. "This is it."

"Don't let that fool you," Travers said. "The arrows point the wrong way."

Rob nodded. That didn't surprise him. "But we want to go there, right? That's the Faerie Circle."

Travers looked at him sideways. "We want to go there, but I have no idea what it is."

"Faerie Circle," John repeated loudly—that old dodge—if they don't understand, shout. "You know, where the Great Rulers used to sit and rule Faerie. You know, the Seelie and the Unseelie Courts?"

"Noooo," Travers said.

"Where the Faerie Kings overthrew them and started the Great War that ended only when all the pixies died?"

"No-*o*-o," Travers repeated.

"History doesn't matter," Rob said. "Getting this done does. Let's go."

Travers headed down a flight of stairs, and suddenly Rob recognized where he was. It was the room of Zoe's memory—and it was a circle, a big round area filled with games (not at all like the ones she had seen) and dozens of small roulette wheels, and a large perimutual betting area—all set up to bet on future human events.

Rob didn't look at the odds: he didn't want to see any of it.

But he did turn toward the center of the circle, and there, just like he expected, was the giant spinning wheel, done up like a giant roulette wheel.

And there, next to it, but not at all like he expected, were three men, sitting in those three chairs he'd seen from the vision.

They were faerie, but they looked almost satanic as they sat in those big thrones next to the wheel, their hands gripping the armrests. They wore black clothes that accented their dark hair and dark eyes, and when they smiled, they did so in unison—shades of the Fates.

Rob shuddered.

"Welcome to Faerie, Sir Robin Hood," said the faerie farthest to the left.

"And his Merry Men," said the next, nodding at John and Travers.

"We're the Faerie Kings," said the third, "and we're here to prevent you from dismantling our home."

40

The dining room was getting unbearably warm. A drop of sweat ran down the side of Megan's face, stopping on her chin before leaping to freedom.

The cigarette girl reached out a hand and caught it, grossing Megan out.

How long had she been here? One day? Two? An entire century?

Even though she knew that wasn't the case. She'd probably been in her seat an hour, maybe less.

A sea of black heads filled the room, with more arriving all the time. If there was a fire, no one would get out, least of all Meg. She'd never been claustrophobic before, but she was now.

At least, the faeries didn't seem to sweat—or perhaps they didn't stink when they did. The place smelled faintly of cloves—or maybe that was all her nose could pick out after that liberal dosing of cigarette smoke.

What she wouldn't give for a glass of water. Or

a cool breeze. Or someone to talk to, someone who didn't end every sentence with "Wow."

If she hadn't heard how scary these people were, she wouldn't have believed it—scary smart, that is. Right now, they were scary zombie, which actually worked up close (it had never worked for her in the movies—but oh boy, had she been wrong).

Not looking at her watch was becoming a big issue. She kept her hands clenched in her lap, just so she wouldn't be tempted to look. She was afraid that then the faeries would catch on that she was a diversion and not the main event at all.

And then—suddenly—a bright blue light exploded in the room. Only the faeries didn't seem to notice. Megan blinked hard, seeing yellow and green reflections on her eyelids.

When the reflections cleared, a man sat in the chair across from her.

He looked vaguely familiar, and he certainly wasn't faerie. Even though he had dark hair, his face was too craggy, his ears too round. He reminded her somehow of a bull, but she wasn't sure why.

When he saw her looking at him, he grinned.

"You seem nervous," he said.

He had a bit of an accent, but it didn't sound familiar to her. The faeries near him glared at him, and a few made some kind of warding symbol with their fingers.

"Are you nervous?" he asked.

"Who are you?" she asked.

"Silly girl, haven't they taught you names have

power?" He smiled, and there was a smarmy charm in it. He had charisma, which made her shiver.

Some of the faeries turned toward him as if noticing him for the first time. He waved a hand, and the faeries looked back at Megan as if they had forgotten him.

"You know, they say you have magic, and perhaps you do, but what you really have is so much more interesting. An overflow of emotions. How very female." And then he laughed.

She didn't. He might have charisma, but that didn't mean she liked him.

"Of course, you don't have enough magic to get yourself out of this pretty little mess." He tilted his square head. Definitely a bull. All she needed now was a china shop because she felt like he was heading for destruction.

"I'm fine," she said.

"Suuuuure you are. That's why you wanted 'this' to be over soon. Don't think someone didn't notice your little message." His grin widened. "I do so love coming to the rescue of beautiful women. Their gratitude always astonishes me."

She wished she really did have magic now. She'd turn him into a real bull and paint this entire room red. See how he'd like that.

"Ah," he said, "did I anger you?"

"I'm fine," she said, and that was when she realized she got no emotional hit off of him either. She hadn't expected any off the faeries—she'd been warned about that—but this guy was as cold as the creatures around her.

He smiled, but this time, it didn't reach his eyes. "You and I have unfinished business."

"I've never met you," she said.

"It doesn't matter. My daughters have. And you've ruined them."

Megan felt a chill run down her back. "Ze—?"

He put a finger over her lips. His fingertip smelled of wine. "No names, little girl. Are you ready to leave?"

She shook her head.

"Good." He removed his finger from her lips.

"I said no," she snapped.

"And I'm ignoring you. But there seems to be a reason you're here, so we'll just add a little confusion into the mix, shall we?" He clapped his hands, and a woman appeared on a chair next to her.

Megan looked. It wasn't just any woman. It was a woman who looked just like her, right down to the extra forty pounds, the too-pale skin, and the mole at the edge of her collarbone.

"What're you doing?" Megan asked.

"Creating a diversion," he said.

The faeries looked at her, then at the unmoving woman, and it seemed to be waking from their trance.

"Oh, what a titanic nuisance," he said. "Let's douse her in emotion, shall we? I think all the emotion from the last five minutes in Chicago will do nicely."

He clapped his hands again, and a sheath fell over the other woman. Then Megan felt like she was hit with a tidal wave—anger, fear, lust, hatred, love, more love—and she couldn't separate it out, it was too overwhelming, she would drown in it . . .

The square little man grabbed her hand, pulled her to him, and grinned.

"Time to pay the piper, sweetheart," he said, and together, they disappeared.

41

"Something's wrong," Kyle said.

Zoe turned to him, her face filled with concern. Behind her, on the screen, thousands of faeries, more than Kyle had imagined possible, crowded against the entrance of the casino.

The Fates were identifying some of them by name, calling them long-lost or tricksters in disguise.

"What do you mean, something's wrong?" Zoe asked.

Kyle shook his head. His stomach wasn't just queasy, it was rolling. He'd gotten a real sense of disgust, followed by a sense of panic, and then anger, and then complete overwhelmedness (if that was a word).

All this was coming from Aunt Megan. He knew it, even though there weren't any words. He had expected words, but for some reason, she was just sending emotion.

"Aunt Megan, she's overwhelmed." His voice was shaking.

"Of course she is, Kyle. Look at that building." Zoe's lips were set in a straight line. "I'm not sure how much of that *I* could take, and I'm not new to my powers."

"She's not either," Kyle said, feeling the need to defend his aunt. "She's just new to identifying them."

Zoe nodded, but a frown still creased her forehead. "Should we go get her?"

Kyle tried to send a message to her, but he didn't get a response. Not that he could have. He had no idea if she could just send back at will. They hadn't tested that part.

"I don't know," he said.

"Are you still getting her emotions?" Zoe asked.

The Fates had turned in their chairs too. They had their hands folded in identical ways, and were staring at him. His cheeks grew warm.

"No," he whispered.

"Then maybe it was a momentary thing?" Zoe asked.

"I don't know," he said.

"If we break this up too soon, we put the men in danger," Zoe said.

"I *know,*" Kyle said.

"So, you'll have to tell me—"

"I'm ten," he snapped. "I'm ten, you're the grown-up, my aunt is overwhelmed, and I'm scared. You decide."

Zoe stepped back as if he had hit her.

"He has a point," Clotho said.

"You should never put children in charge of things," Lachesis said.

"It's not fair," Atropos said.

"Besides, it makes for very messy business," Clotho said.

"As the Interim Fates have shown," Lachesis said.

"Enough!" Zoe snapped. "You were supposed to be quiet."

She put her hands to her head and looked at that mess still surrounding the casino. Kyle closed his eyes, feeling for Aunt Meg with his brain, but he couldn't find her.

That was okay. Everybody said that might happen. This was a scary thing, and the faerie casino might make a sending inside impossible. Besides, he might call too much attention to her if he wasn't careful.

His eyes filled with tears.

"We give it just a few more minutes," Zoe said. "If you get another feeling or if you hear from her, you tell me. Otherwise, we go after her at my mark. Okay?"

He blinked his eyes open. The tears stuck to his lashes. He felt like a dork, a really scared dork.

"Okay," he said.

"Do you think that's too much?" Zoe asked.

"You're asking the child again," Atropos said.

"He has to tell me if he has another sense of Megan," Zoe said.

Kyle shook his head. He had no sense of her at all, and that really bugged him.

It was almost like she was gone.

42

They weren't supposed to be here.

The all-powerful Faerie Kings should have been heading toward that casino on Boulder Highway, if they were even in Vegas, off to see the empath, like the rest of their tribe.

Instead, they were sitting on thrones, looking every bit as regal as kings should.

And those thrones ringed the spinning wheel. There was no way Rob could just lift it loose, and these guys out-magicked him a thousand to one.

There was no way he and John and Travers could take on the Faerie Kings and win.

But this was like the old days. They didn't have to take on the kings and win.

They just had to divert the kings and steal their attention for a moment, so that someone could grab that wheel.

"You know me," Rob said. He had to come up with a plan, and he had to do it fast.

The third Faerie King smiled at him. "We've been

waiting for you, Sir Robin of Hood. We've heard that you are our destiny."

Great. He didn't want to hear his prophecy, but he got to hear theirs.

"So we've been following your career," said the first Faerie King. "Quite stellar."

"Thanks," Rob said. "I think."

Travers was shooting him a panicked look. Rob couldn't do much with Travers, but he and John had been fighting side by side for centuries.

Rob flashed John a look. John raised his weird eyebrows—code for whatever you want to do, boss.

"How *are* the Fates, anyway?" the second Faerie King asked.

"Just fine," Rob said, wondering why they asked.

"Because they're supposed to be here too," said the third Faerie King.

"Really?" Rob asked, moving forward just a little. "Says who?"

"We don't have an oracle," the first Faerie King said.

"But we do have access to this lovely wheel," the second Faerie King said—and he spun it as he said that, sending lights everywhere in the faerie circle.

Which was just the diversion that Rob wanted. He conjured three swords, one for him, one for John, and one for Travers, and tossed the other two men theirs.

Then he leapt, Errol Flynn style, onto the platform holding the wheel, grabbed the first

Faerie King, and yanked him out of the throne, placing the sword at his neck.

He doubted he could kill a faerie, but he sure as heck was going to try.

43

To Megan's surprise, she wasn't frightened of the most powerful man in the magical world. He had her in some kind of spell and had moved her from the casino (for which she felt a little too much relief, considering how much danger it probably put Rob in) to somewhere else.

It felt like they were suspended in time. And then they landed. They didn't end up in some giant Greek coliseum or even in the smelly library, but in her office. It was after hours, and the place had a dry, unused smell, even though she'd only been gone for a day or two.

Lights were on that should have been off, and the door to her therapy room was open. Zeus strode across the carpeted floor like he owned the place.

She certainly didn't want him in that room—it was a safe room, a place where her clients felt comfortable to say anything they wanted, and even though she was closing it down, she didn't want him violating it.

"Daddy, jeez!"

"Oh, *man!*"

"This just blows."

Megan felt stunned. She recognized those voices. The Interim Fates. Why were they here and not in their library, attempting to govern the world?

She peered in the doorway. There they were, all three girls sitting on her extra-long couch. Brittany clutched a Raggedy Anne doll that Megan used for the younger patients. Crystal was examining a naked Barbie. And Tiffany had both hands clenched into fists. She was glaring—at Megan.

"It's about time," Brittany said.

"We've been waiting, like, for*ever,*" Crystal said.

"You promised you could help us," Tiffany snapped, "and then you bring *him.*"

Well, this situation was out of control. These girls were furious and terrified, and Zeus wasn't exactly calm. He stood just inside the door, his hands at his sides, watching his daughters as if he'd never seen them before.

Megan stepped inside the room. They all had more magic than she did—that was the risk—but this was her place, the place where she confronted people who always had more something than she did—whether it was real power or real money or real chutzpah.

Actually, she usually had the most of that, and she was going to use it now.

"I didn't bring him," Megan said. "He brought me."

"Grrrr-ate," Brittany said.

"You're right," Crystal said to Tiffany. "This blows."

"You were supposed to be here," Tiffany said, ignoring the others.

"Well, no," Megan said. "I'm supposed to be babysitting my nephew."

"In a casino?" Even Zeus sounded shocked, although why should he? This was a man who had more love affairs than anyone else in any mythology, a man who carelessly abandoned children after, of course, fathering more of them than any other so-called god she could think of. Why would he care if a child was in a casino?

She didn't answer him. She wasn't going to let him distract her from the girls who had come to her for help.

(Not that she was really in a position to give it, given that she had just been kidnapped herself. But no matter, Zeus had brought her here for a reason, and she would figure out what that reason was.)

"I was in Las Vegas," Megan said to the girls.

"Isn't this Las Vegas?" Brittany said.

"It's Las something-or-other," Crystal said.

"It's Los Angeles," Megan said gently.

"You guys screwed up again!" Tiffany snapped. "You said you could handle this one. You said it was a simple spell. I trusted you."

The infighting was coming from the fear and the stress. The levels in the room had risen to unbearable. Megan walked in farther and went to her chair. She realized now that she had protected it, made it slightly walled, so that she could feel emotions when she sat in it, but they didn't become part of her.

Sitting in the chair felt like coming home.

"What spell did you cast?" she asked the first two Interim Fates gently.

"I did it." Brittany's voice was filled with tears.

"She said to come to you so you could help us," Crystal said.

And this was where Megan helped people. So that made sense. These poor girls. They were so out of their element.

"And it didn't work!" Tiffany snapped.

"Actually, it did," Megan said, keeping her voice level. It was Zeus, still standing by the door, who made her nervous. "I'm here now."

"And you're going to help me," Zeus said. "These girls have to get back to work. It took me forever to find them."

Megan raised her head and looked at him. She couldn't think of him as the head of the Powers That Be. She couldn't think of him as the man with the power to destroy true love forever.

She had to think of him as an abusive, out-of-control father who had no idea what he was doing to his daughters.

"Thank you for bringing me to them," she said. "You can wait outside."

Zeus drew himself to his full height—or maybe more than his full height—and yelled, "I DO NOT WAIT OUTSIDE. WE SHALL RESOLVE THIS HERE."

That wasn't really a yell. It was more like a decree from on high. The girls cowered on the couch. But Megan didn't move. She could feel the impotent anger behind Zeus's shout.

"'We' won't do anything if you raise your voice at me again. Either speak to me civilly," Megan said, "or leave."

The girls gaped at her. Zeus stared at her, clearly stunned.

"I could blind you," he said in a civil tone.

"Yet, if you do, I'll continue right along, doing what I do." Megan hoped her own bravado didn't show. She told herself that her calm counselor demeanor had gotten her through worse, although she wasn't sure if that was true.

"Then I'll turn you into a wolf," he said.

Megan rolled her eyes. "Are you so old and out of ideas that you're repeating yourself? First, you act as if I'm Lycurgus, and then you treat me like Lycaon. For the record, I would never serve you human flesh for dinner."

The girls' eyes were wide. Zeus's were wider.

Megan smiled serenely. "I had a classical education. If you want to threaten me, come up with something new."

Zeus opened his mouth, but nothing came out. She had unnerved him after all.

"All right then," she said. "You brought me here. You must know that this situation is out of control and that I can help you."

"I want you to take back everything you said to my girls." Finally, Zeus found his voice.

"And lie to them? I would never do that. Nor would I manipulate them or use them to my own ends. Like you have. Which, I must say, is disgraceful in a father."

The girls ducked. Zeus's cheeks reddened, and Megan did wonder if she was going to end up as a statue or a bear or pushing a rock uphill for all of eternity.

But he didn't do anything, at least not yet.

"Here are my rules," Megan said. "I assume you want this dispute with your daughters settled—"

"They ran away," he said, sounding like a child.

"We escaped," Brittany said.

"We're no good at Fating," Crystal said.

"We're never going back," Tiffany said.

"—and," Megan said to Zeus as if she hadn't been interrupted, "I will help you resolve this if and only if you do not interrupt me again, yell at me again, or threaten me again. You will take the spell off your daughters so that they can speak like individuals—"

"If I do that, they won't be Interim Fates," Zeus said.

"That's an interruption," Megan said. "It's your last warning."

"Or what, puny Empath?"

"Or I will throw you out of here," Megan said, not sure how she'd accomplish that. "And you'll lose any chance you might have to work with your daughters."

He closed his mouth. He glared. Lightning bolts actually appeared in his eyes, but didn't shoot out of them (even though the girls did duck again).

Then the bolts faded, and he nodded, once, as if it hurt.

Megan took a deep breath. "You will take the spell off your daughters, who will then be able to speak like normal people. Each girl will get the floor to express her grievances. No one may interrupt her. You *must* listen, no eye-rolling, no faces, and no lightning bolts. Can you follow these rules?"

Zeus's lower lip came out. He looked petulant. "I guess."

"Yes or no," Megan said. "You cannot act like a child here, I won't allow it. You're an adult, and have been—well, a lot longer than the rest of us here. You will act like it. Can you follow these rules?"

Zeus's lip went back in. His eyes narrowed. "Yeah."

"All right then," Megan said, her stomach in knots. She made herself look at the girls. "Who wants to go first?"

44

The second Faerie King leapt up from his chair, holding a foil.

He pointed the tip at Rob and said with a grin, *"En garde!"*

Robin's sword should have been able to snap a foil, but he had a hunch it wasn't going to work that way. So he used the first Faerie King like a shield and responded to the second Faerie King's *en garde* with a thrust of his own.

Suddenly he was in an old-fashioned sword fight, the kind that he had privately missed for centuries. The third Faerie King leapt off the platform and engaged John. Travers stood back, looking at his blade as if it could bite him.

"Remember Marian?" Rob yelled at John.

"What?" John yelled back.

The first Faerie King struggled, but Rob had him around the throat. This wasn't going to last long, especially if the guy used magic on him.

"Remember the rescue?" Rob slapped his blade

at the foil. They clanged, but the foil didn't collapse. "The first one?"

"What?" John yelled back.

"He said remember the first rescue of Marian," Travers yelled.

John's Faerie King had him backed against the platform.

"Are you nuts?" John asked.

"No, dammit," Rob yelled. His breath was coming in large gasps. "I'm trying to tell you something."

About how he had created a diversion while John and the Merry Men rescued Marian from the clutches of the sheriff—the first time. Other times, the situation had been reversed.

That woman had had a gift for getting herself captured.

John flipped the third Faerie King around and slapped him on the back with the flat of his blade. The Faerie King gasped as if he had lost air.

"Oh," John said. "Right."

The second Faerie King thrust at Rob. Rob parried and turned at the same time, so that the point of the foil nearly stabbed the first Faerie King.

"Do that!" Rob said.

"There's only two of us," John said as the third Faerie King turned around again, his blade now a broadsword. Travers still hadn't done anything. "Make that one and a half."

The first Faerie King was still struggling. Sweat was running down Robin's face. He was lucky that the second king was more interested in traditional fencing than in an actual sword fight.

"So?" Robin said. "Just do it."

"Now he's quoting Nike slogans at me," John muttered, but he shoved the third Faerie King at the second, and both faeries went tumbling. "Get up here, Travers!"

Travers didn't have to be told twice. He jumped on the platform.

The first Faerie King shook loose of Robin. The other two started to get up.

"And throw me your blade!" Robin yelled at Travers.

"Okay." Travers looked terrified. His throw was awful, but Robin managed to catch it.

Now he stood in the center of the Faerie Circle, two swords in hand, one Faerie King facing him and two more about to join the fray. He needed more help. He needed extra power. He needed—

He looked at the wheel. Travers had said it could boost his magic. It was worth a try.

John was behind the wheel trying to pry it loose. Travers was standing next to him, looking as helpless as a regular mortal.

Robin pointed his blade at the thing and summoned power to him.

A beam of light crackled against the black casino ceiling, then floated down, hit the sword, jumped to the other sword, and sent power through him like an out-of-control electrical current.

His teeth chattered, his head rattled, and he couldn't see a damn thing. He smelled smoke and heard a ka-pow before something blasted him across the room.

When he opened his eyes, he was at the far end
of the Faerie Circle, the swords glued to his hands.
He couldn't see the wheel anymore, but all three
Faerie Kings were advancing on him—

And he wasn't even sure he could stand up.

45

The light was a great distraction, but John wasn't about to touch that spinning wheel when power was flowing off it like a river. Still, he got behind the thing, figured out how to lift it, and beckoned Travers.

Travers came around, his skin so white he looked translucent. "Shouldn't we help Rob?"

"Rob's been in worse situations," John said, not sure if that was true. "We're carrying this puppy outta here."

"Carrying?" Travers asked.

"Shut up and help," John said.

Something ka-boomed, and the entire Faerie Circle went dark for an instant. John lifted the wheel—it was lighter than he imagined—and glanced up.

"Is that out of the hole it was in?"

"Yeah," Travers said.

"Well, get us out of here."

Travers flung his arms around the wheel and John, and suddenly they were floating upward.

John did not want to be floating. He wanted to disappear and appear, but that wasn't possible from Faerie, so he preferred to be zooming. He added some of his own power—or maybe some of the wheel's power—and headed toward the surface.

They shot through the ground like a rocket, coming up through a sewer grate on Las Vegas Boulevard, startling dozens of drivers and causing a near pileup.

John saw no reason to stop zooming, so he headed immediately to the hotel. Travers was protesting, but John couldn't hear him.

Or maybe John didn't want to hear him.

They zoomed through the front doors—Travers remembered to open them somehow—and up the stairs and through (whoops! No one opened that) the door of the suite and into the room with the kid, the Fates, and Zoe Sinclair.

Everyone turned to greet them.

John landed beside the kid's chair and bowed, then handed the giant (but light) spinning wheel to the Fates.

And as he stood, he realized they looked disappointed.

46

Rob wasn't sure how long he was going to hold out. Two swords—stuck to his hands no less—against three Faerie Kings were not good odds, no matter how much the stupid wheel had enhanced his powers.

All three kings had foils. They were using them the way the Fates talked—the first Faerie King thrust first, followed by the second, followed by the third. Which made fighting them easier than it should have been, but Robin expected a group of faeries to run into this part of the casino at any moment.

So far they hadn't.

So far, Megan had held them off.

He hoped she was all right.

Yeouch!

The first Faerie King had made contact. Rob looked down at his arm, saw a scratch with blood starting to leak out of it, and every single fairy tale he'd ever read came back to him. Something

in the blade would weaken him, take his magic—
hurt him somehow.

The kings had stopped too, staring at the blood
as if they were surprised.

Then the second Faerie King stepped forward,
thrusting with his blade, and Robin parried with
his left hand. He should have parried with his
right because the third Faerie King came from
the far left side and was about to hit Rob's skin
when—

Rob blanked out.

Actually, he suddenly went to a completely
white environment and then landed, as if he'd
been dropped from a great height, on the floor
of the suite.

The landing knocked the air out of him, but he
probably would have lost the air anyway. The Fates
stood above him, looking taller than he remembered. Taller, and prettier, and *bigger* somehow.

The spinning wheel, now set properly on its
legs, stood behind them, and even farther
behind them, a television screen showed hundreds (thousands?) of faeries pressing against
each other in the casino parking lot.

Poor Megan.

Rob tried to sit up, but couldn't. The dang
swords were still fused to his hands, and they
flopped around like solid shirt sleeves.

"Can someone help me?"

The kid reached down, saw the swords, and
looked at the Fates. Clotho smiled, Lachesis
pointed, and Atropos touched the top of his hand.

The swords fell away.

"Got your magic back, I see." Rob looked at his hands. No damage, no danger. So far.

"Thank you," Clotho said, much more primly than he would have expected.

"They're annoyed at us," John said.

"Why?" Rob stood up. He was dizzy. Travers stood near an empty chair. Had Zoe gone for Megan? Rob hoped so. He would ask in a moment.

"Apparently, we were supposed to bring the Faerie Kings along with the wheel," John said.

"Why?" Rob asked, putting a hand to his forehead. All that had taken a lot more energy than he expected.

"Something about destiny," Travers said.

Rob looked at him, forced himself to focus, and asked, "Did Zoe go for Meg?"

"Yep," Travers glanced at the screen. There seemed to be even more faeries than there had been before. "And I hope she gets back soon. It's looking bad there."

Worse than Rob had expected. He wondered if he should go help. He rubbed his forehead. He hadn't been this tired from magic use in—he had no idea how long. He probably should call Felix, his falcon, and use the strength of his familiar to make himself feel better before he went for Megan, but he wasn't sure he had that kind of time.

"You okay?" Kyle asked him. The boy was still sitting in that chair he'd insisted on. He looked a little peaked too.

"Yeah," Rob said.

And then Zoe popped into the room. Her hair

was mussed, and her shirt had a rip on one sleeve.

"What happened?" Travers asked.

But Zoe didn't look at him. Her gaze met Rob's, and it was filled with panic.

"Megan," she said, "is gone."

Rob felt like he'd been punched in the stomach. He'd been afraid of this from the moment he'd met her. Losing her was worse than never meeting her at all.

"Gone?" he repeated. Then he looked at the screen. The faeries still crowded the door of the casino as if they were trying to get in. "But what's that?"

"That's a mannequin, a diversion. It's chock full of emotion, and looks just like Megan. I can't imagine who would have the power to do that, but whoever it was got in and out without anyone noticing." Zoe tugged on that ripped shirt, ripping it further. She grabbed the tear and absently repaired it with a tiny magic.

"Let me see," Lachesis said, and waved an arm at the screen.

The view changed from the parking lot to the interior of the casino. In a dark and ratty buffet, a woman sat at a table, looking cool and collected. Hundreds of faeries pushed toward her, creating little eddies in the sea of bodies.

Megan would never have been that calm in that place. She would have tried hard, but she wouldn't have succeeded.

The Fates crowded against the screen, peering at it.

"I thought you were supposed to track her," Travers said to Kyle.

"I don't track, Dad. She was supposed to contact me if she got in trouble." And then he gasped on the last word.

Rob whirled. The boy was pale.

"She did contact you," Rob said.

The boy shook his head. "But there was a weird feeling, like scaredness or something, and then everything went okay."

"Before she disappeared," Zoe said.

Kyle sniffled. "I didn't mean to lose her. I was really trying . . ."

It was John who put a comforting hand on Kyle's shoulder. "Of course you were, kid. They asked the impossible of you. We'll find her."

"We can trace her," Atropos said.

"But we're not going to like what we find," Clotho added.

Rob's stomach flipped. His headache had gotten worse. "Why not?"

"Because," Lachesis said, her green gaze meeting his. "She was taken by Zeus."

Rob didn't wait for the others. He zapped himself to the casino, not caring if his magic broadcast to every faerie in receiving range. Besides, every faerie in receiving range was here, trying to get near the tower of emotion that Zeus had left in place of Megan.

Rob landed on the table in front of her, startling several faeries, one of whom shoved him and told him it wasn't his turn. That was when he remembered that he still looked like them. He was tempted to undo Zoe's spell, but he didn't have time.

He had to find Megan. He frowned at the mannekin in front of him.

The likeness wasn't very good. The face was waxy, and the eyes were empty. They blinked much too slowly, which was the only sign of life, such as it were. Her breasts were too big (what a Zeusian touch!), her shoulders too narrow, and her spine too straight. Megan hadn't sat up straight since Rob had met her.

And even he could sense the emotion coming off this thing. It wasn't one type of emotion either. The thing was broadcasting emotions like some kind of signal, probably to draw faeries.

He used a magic he hadn't tried in ages. He touched the thing's shoulder, startled that it was as hard as steel. The skin was cold too, although the faeries hadn't noticed.

Under his breath, he recited a spell that would take him to the creature's maker, and it was not until he was hurtling down a magical line that he realized he might have used the wrong spell.

If Zeus hadn't created this thing, just borrowed it or "improved" it, then Rob was going the wrong way.

And wasting even more time.

Of course, he wasn't sure what he'd do when he found Megan.

How did one simple mage take on the greatest of the Powers That Be?

47

"... and you know, like, he kept saying how smart I am, how I'm, like, the most brilliant daughter he's ever had, which isn't true because I met Athena, like, more than once and she doesn't even have a mother, you know? She sprang from his mind, although she says forehead because, you know, coming from *his* mind is really icky ..."

Tiffany stood in the middle of the floor, tugging on her cornrows as she spoke. She looked at Megan, but every now and then her dark gaze would flick to her father's face.

Zeus still leaned against the door, his arms crossed and his eyes hooded. He hadn't moved since the girls started their tirades, and at one point, Megan worried that he had left a fake body there and checked out.

But he hadn't. She sensed his anger and confusion and complete shock whenever she searched for his emotions.

No one had ever confronted the old man like

this, particularly not his daughters—not any daughter from the ones Megan had heard of, like Artemis and the Muses, to ones she hadn't heard of (at least before today), like the Interim Fates.

Zeus was handling this rebellion better than Megan had hoped. And his daughters—all three of them present here—were being as open as any client she'd ever had, letting him know his successes and his failures, although Tiffany was mostly reporting on the failures.

Tiffany was the angriest of the Interim Fates, mostly because she was the responsible one who had done most of the work.

". . . so he says it's not gonna be hard, you just gotta do what I say, little girl, and then he won't say—"

A large flash of light interrupted her and made her step backward. Megan's heart slammed against her chest, but she wouldn't let herself move.

Had Zeus attacked?

Then the light faded, and Rob stood where it had been. His left arm was bleeding (but it was just a scratch), his hair was mussed up, and he still looked like one of the faeries, only sexier.

"Oh, Megan," he said with obvious relief and headed toward her.

And because she was a professional, she had to hold out her hand and stop him.

"You can't be here," she said.

"What?" He looked around, saw Zeus leaning against the wall, the girls—two on the sofa and Tiffany standing just behind him—and Megan in her chair. "Look, we'll do what it takes to get you out of here—"

"You can't stay, Rob."

The girls looked stunned. Zeus raised his head, his eyes narrowing. He was going to unleash that pent-up anger on Rob.

"What?" Rob said again.

"I'm conducting a therapy session. This is private. You have to leave."

"But I came to rescue you," he said.

"And I'm just fine." She hated her own tone, but she had to use it. She had to get him out of here before he ruined the progress everyone was making. "Can you wait outside until the session is over?"

"Outside?" He looked around.

"In the waiting room?"

"Wait?" He repeated.

Megan nodded. "Only family members can be here right now."

He frowned. "You don't need rescuing?"

"This is my office," she said. "I never need rescuing here."

"Oh." He ran a hand through his magically darkened hair, then looked at Zeus, who elaborately stepped away from the door. "You're sure?"

That last was addressed to Megan.

"I'm sure," she said.

Rob nodded, then walked like a man who'd been banished from his own house. He opened the door and stepped into the waiting room, closing the door quietly behind him.

Tiffany looked at Megan. "Can I go on now?"

"Is everyone all right?" Megan asked.

The girls nodded. Zeus sighed, but, to his credit, didn't speak. He nodded too.

"All right then," Megan said. "Continue."

Tiffany did.

Megan tried to concentrate, but all she could think about was how strong Rob had seemed, ready to take on even the Powers That Be to save her. She allowed herself one small, private little smile before forcing herself to listen to Tiffany.

". . . and he never, ever says anything nice to my mother. He's like a big bully who doesn't care who he hurts . . ."

It was going to be a long night.

48

Rob closed the door behind him. The waiting room was empty but comfortable with two sofas, soft lighting, and shaded windows. Comfortable and confusing.

He stopped, rubbed his hand through his hair (which didn't feel like his hair), and then frowned.

He'd come to rescue a damsel in distress, only to discover that she wasn't in distress, and she wanted him to leave.

To leave?

What did she think, that therapy could make Zeus change his ways?

And what was Zeus doing? Playing along?

Rob was. He didn't want to argue with her—she certainly seemed like she had everything under control—but he wasn't sure how she had done that.

He shook his head and looked at the couches, not wanting to sit down. At any moment, she would scream for help, and he would have to go running.

Or not.

Then a thunderclap sounded beside him, and John appeared. John still looked too thin and too tall, his features pulled into a replica of faerie features.

"Where is she?" he demanded. "Is she all right?"

"She's in there." Rob pointed at the door.

"Do you need help breaking it down? Is it magicked?" John asked.

Rob shook his head. "She's conducting a family therapy session in there."

John frowned just like Rob had, then blinked, and stared at the door as if it held the answers. "Huh?"

"She has Zeus in there, and his daughters, and she's making them talk to each other."

John's mouth opened, and then he let out a loud, shocked laugh. "That woman has balls!"

"That's one way to put it," Rob said.

"So why aren't you there?"

"She kicked me out," he said. "Said I don't belong."

John's grin widened. "I told you she was special."

"Yeah," Rob said, still feeling shocked. "I guess that's one way to put it."

"Listen," John said. "Travers and Zoe are staying with Kyle, but the others are coming, and you'll never believe—"

More flashes of light, and the Fates appeared. They were wearing armor designed in the Trojan style, with metal skirts, high-laced boots, and breastplates that accented the breasts. Their hair was pulled back, and they seemed more alive than they had since the day began.

Rob was about to tell them what was going on

when even more lights flashed, and the Faerie Kings appeared behind them.

Rob grabbed John and moved him out of the way.

"What are you doing here?" Rob snapped at the Faerie Kings.

"We brought them," Clotho said.

"We've just finalized an alliance," Lachesis said.

"If that's what you want to call it," Atropos said, and all three Fates took the hands of the Faerie Kings.

"If you'd've let me finish," John said, "I'd've told you that the whole wheel thing was some kind of stupid courting ritual."

"It was destiny," Clotho said.

"'The wheel shall bind the Circles of Faerie with the Fates of the world,'" Lachesis said.

"Only these guys expected us to come after it," Atropos said and grinned at the third king.

"And then when we got it back, we expected them to come," Clotho said, smiling at the first king.

"And it wasn't until young Kyle said we were all being stupid that we realized he was right," Lachesis said, already smiling at her king. "So we went to Faerie, finished our alliance, and here we are, to rescue Megan."

"She doesn't want to be rescued," Rob said.

"Nonsense," Clotho said. "Every woman wants to be rescued." And this time, the first Faerie King grinned at her.

"Not in today's world," Rob said.

"You still have a few modern things to learn,"

John added, then ducked when he apparently remembered that they had their powers now.

But the Fates seemed pretty happy, and so did the Faerie Kings. Which explained why none of them had fought Rob very hard and why it had been relatively simple to get that dang wheel.

"What we need to figure out," Lachesis said, "is if we should go through a formal ceremony."

"We like the Heart of Elvis Chapel," Atropos said.

"It's not owned by Faerie, which makes it independent," Clotho said.

"But we're not sure any of us qualify for marriage licenses," Lachesis said.

"Or if we even need one, considering," Atropos added.

The Faerie Kings wrapped their arms around the Fates and murmured something. Rob shot a confused look at John.

"I thought you said alliance," Rob said.

"Well, they are uniting our world and Faerie," John said.

"But faeries don't feel emotion," Rob said.

"Technically not true," said the first Faerie King. He had a deep voice that shook the room.

"We feel many things, but our people just don't accept those feelings as real," said the second king, whose voice was even deeper.

"So we believe that we must lead by example," said the third king, and then all three kissed the Fates.

"Yech," Robin said and turned away. "That's like watching your parents make out."

John had turned away too. "This has been one

strange day. And now you're saying that in there Megan's taking on Zeus?"

Rob's stomach clenched. And he had left her alone in there. Zeus hadn't magicked her, had he?

At that moment, the door opened, and Zeus strode out, followed by the Interim Fates, whose faces were tear-streaked. Zeus didn't look much better.

He saw the Fates kissing the Faerie Kings and let out a gusty sigh.

"You failed," Clotho said.

"You should never fight Fate," Lachesis said.

"Because you'll always lose," Atropos added.

"You don't have to gloat," Zeus said. "I've had a hard day."

"What's going on, Dad?" Brittany whispered, tugging his sleeve.

"Not only have my daughters rebelled"—and he sounded a little proud about that—"but my prophecy has just come true. The ascendancy of the Powers That Be has declined because of True Love."

He spat on the carpet.

"We'll treat you fairly," Clotho said.

"Which is more than we can say for you," Lachesis said.

Zeus glared at them. "I've got more important things to worry about," he said and disappeared.

Rob let out a breath he hadn't even realized he was holding.

"Where'd he go?" John asked the girls.

"To talk to all 500 of his other daughters to see if they're as angry as we are," Crystal said.

"Most of them are angrier," Tiffany said, and then she leaned back through the door. "Next week?"

She must have gotten a response because she nodded at her sisters, and then all three of them disappeared.

Megan hadn't come out of the room, and Rob wasn't going to let her banish him any longer. He didn't care what she said.

He was going in.

And nothing she could say would stop him.

49

Megan sat in her chair, feeling more drained than she'd ever felt in her life. At least they hadn't killed each other. At least Zeus had listened.

He'd actually looked crushed.

Apparently, he had always thought he was a good parent.

What a surprise to discover he was one of the worst in recorded time.

She ran a hand over her face. Voices echoed from the waiting room, but she couldn't place them. A little sleep would be nice. A little sleep and some reevaluation—

A hand touched her arm. She lifted her head. Rob crouched before her. He looked shaken.

"Are you all right?"

She nodded. She couldn't tell him much about the therapy session. Confidentiality and all.

"I don't know if you realize that you've just changed the entire magical system in this world. You've only known about it for twenty-four hours, and you've united the Faeries and Mages, dethroned Zeus, and helped the Fates take their jobs back, saving true love."

Megan smiled. "I didn't do that."

"You did." Rob took her hand in his. "You took on Zeus. You weren't afraid of him at all."

"I think he was ready to change," Megan said. "He's the one who brought me here. You can't help people who don't want to be helped."

"Megan," Rob said gently, "I'm trying to tell you that you're the most amazing woman I've ever met."

"Yeah, right," she said.

"You are," he said. "No one has ever taken on Zeus and won."

She raised her gaze to his. Then she frowned. It hadn't felt like she was taking on Zeus, although admittedly, she had yelled at him. He was just such a bully.

She wasn't very fond of bullies.

"And," Rob said with a soft smile, "no one's ever told me to stuff it when I came to rescue them."

"I was working," Megan said.

"I know." He went down on one knee, extended the other hand, and a box appeared in it.

Megan frowned.

Then he let go of her hand, touched his face, and cursed. "I look like—what would Kyle call it?—a dweeb."

He blinked, and all that magic that Zoe had done vanished, leaving him the Rob Megan had met in the middle of the Nevada desert one day and a million years ago.

She had driven into a magic bubble and was going to stay there for the rest of her life. She'd already made a follow-up appointment with Zeus and the Interim Fates, who had resigned their job.

Apparently, she wasn't closing down her practice after all. She was just switching it to a newer—and needier—clientele.

Then Rob took her hand again.

"Megan," he said, and he sounded serious.

"What?" she asked.

"I know we haven't known each other very long, but I also know you know how I feel and that I've never felt this way before—not for anyone."

She nodded, not quite sure where he was taking this.

"When I thought that Zeus had you and I was never going to see you again," Rob said, "I panicked like I never had before. I couldn't lose you, not after just finding you."

"You didn't lose me," Megan said.

He smiled. "I know. You were working."

Her face warmed. "I'm sorry. You know what I meant—"

"Yes," he said, "but what I mean is this."

He flipped open the box with his left thumb. Inside, a large, and somehow not gaudy, jewel-encrusted ring caught the light.

"Will you marry me?" he asked.

"Me?" she said, stunned. Why would someone like Robin Hood want her?

He smiled. "Do you see anyone else in the room?"

"Just you," she said, and her voice shook. The perfect man. That's what she thought when she first met him. He looked perfect.

"Just me," he said, "and just me would like to spend the rest of his long, unnatural life with you."

"But I won't live as long," she said. "You'll get a mortal again."

"You're going to live just as long," he said, "if not longer. Not that it matters. I want to spend my life—and yours—together. So let me repeat: will you marry me?"

She flung her arms around his neck, crushing the ring between them. A joy like none she'd ever felt filled her.

"Yes," she whispered. "Of course, yes. Yes."

And then he kissed her, and the kiss built like their first kiss had, and the passion rose, and it wasn't until John peeked his head in the door that Rob raised a hand, closing the door with a bit of magic.

Then he picked up Megan and carried her to the couch. In the past, she wouldn't have let anything like this happen in her safest room.

But this was the man she was going to marry, the best person she'd ever met, and besides, the couch was right here, long and soft and inviting, and he was right there.

She reached up and pulled him down beside her.

"Lock the door," she whispered.

"Already done," he said, and then he kissed her, and he kept kissing her, and she kissed him back, realizing, for the very first time, how lucky she was—how lucky the world was—that he and his modern band of Merry Men had helped her and her family save true love.

<u>BOOK YOUR PLACE ON OUR WEBSITE</u> AND MAKE THE <u>READING CONNECTION!</u>

We've created a customized website just for our very special readers, where you can get the inside scoop on everything that's going on with Zebra, Pinnacle and Kensington books.

When you come online, you'll have the exciting opportunity to:

- View covers of upcoming books
- Read sample chapters
- Learn about our future publishing schedule (listed by publication month *and author*)
- Find out when your favorite authors will be visiting a city near you
- Search for and order backlist books from our online catalog
- Check out author bios and background information
- Send e-mail to your favorite authors
- Meet the Kensington staff online
- Join us in weekly chats with authors, readers and other guests
- Get writing guidelines
- AND MUCH MORE!

**Visit our website at
http://www.kensingtonbooks.com**